About the Author

Scarlet lives in the South West of England with her adult son and two doggies, Teddiebear and Evie. Only discovering her talent for erotic writing in 2022, she decided to try her hand at an erotic romance novel. *The Red Wine Diaries – Volume 1,* is the result of her naughty endeavours!

The Red Wine Diaries – Volume 1

Scarlet B Moore

The Red Wine Diaries – Volume 1

Olympia Publishers
London

www.olympiapublishers.com
OLYMPIA PAPERBACK EDITION

Copyright © Scarlet B Moore 2024

The right of Scarlet B. Moore to be identified as author of
this work has been asserted in accordance with sections 77 and 78 of
the Copyright, Designs and Patents Act 1988.

All Rights Reserved

No reproduction, copy or transmission of this publication
may be made without written permission.
No paragraph of this publication may be reproduced,
copied or transmitted save with the written permission of the publisher,
or in accordance with the provisions
of the Copyright Act 1956 (as amended).

Any person who commits any unauthorised act in relation to
this publication may be liable to criminal
prosecution and civil claims for damage.

A CIP catalogue record for this title is
available from the British Library.

ISBN: 978-1-80439-684-1

This is a work of fiction.
Names, characters, places and incidents originate from the writer's
imagination. Any resemblance to actual persons, living or dead, is
purely coincidental.

First Published in 2024

**Olympia Publishers
Tallis House
2 Tallis Street
London
EC4Y 0AB**

Printed in Great Britain

Dedication

To the girl who no longer exists; the shy girl, the repressed girl, the girl with no voice, no fire, no desire – this one is for you! Rest now, my darling. Scarlet will take it from here!

Acknowledgements

Eternal thanks to:
My beautiful children, Ben and Jessie, for patiently putting up with my filth on a daily basis and for being so supportive and encouraging, even when you didn't approve. I love you to infinity & beyond;

My Mommy, Hazel, for giving me wings to fly, for always being my biggest fan & for enthusiastically reading everything I wrote - you dark old horse, Mother! I love you with all my heart;

My Twinnie, Kel, for all the nights spent up late with me online and for all the laughs, support and sister-love. I adore you endlessly;

Deb, my very dear friend across the pond, for painstakingly reading everything I wrote, providing feedback and being honest, for all the many chats of love and encouragement and for all the numerous times you lifted me when I was low, doubting myself and for bringing me down off of the proverbial precipice when I had a wobble. You are my earth-angel;

Myself, for having the courage to open up, dig deep and pour my heart and soul into creating this book full of devoted naughtiness;

A very special man, who shall remain nameless, for simply being your lovable, brave, humble, awe-inspiring, brilliantly talented, devastatingly handsome, cheekychappy self! Without you in this world, Scarlet would have no material to pen so thank you for being such a heavenly muse;

And lastly and most importantly, very special & grateful thanks to Adam Ant for the genius of his huge catalogue of songs, some of which played an inspirational part in the writing of The Red Wine Diaries, Volume 1!

I adore you all
– Scarlet –

Part 1 – In Her Wildest Dreams

Scarlet knocked.

The door opened and there he was. That devastatingly handsome rogue, the debonair Stewart Sloane, who had captured her fevered attention, stolen her sanity and blown her knickers off months before.

Fuck – He looked just as she'd imagined he would.

So very lickable!

So very fuckable!

When she'd received his invitation for drinks at his home, she knew it wouldn't be just 'drinks' or at least she'd 'hoped' it wouldn't. So she'd prepared herself and gone to great lengths to ensure she could please him in every wickedly filthy way possible as he was quite renowned for his fetishes and kink!

He invited her in, taking her coat and kissing her on the cheek very respectfully, 'Good evening, Miss Adams!'

In her head she was screaming, *Don't be so bloody respectful man – forcefully throw me against the wall and fuck me to within an inch of my life.*

She was so desperate for an alcoholic beverage and for him, that her tongue was almost hanging out. And her knickers were already damp! So when he offered her a glass of wine, she accepted hastily but gracefully and they sat down to commence their evening. One glass, two glasses, then a third – every sip warming her throat, her insides and her lady parts. As he was pouring her fourth, he said, 'If you'd like to slip into something more comfortable, please do!'

Having not been sure how to dress for this auspicious occasion, she'd donned a simple black cocktail dress and elegant heels. The heels had been abandoned after glass number two as wine went straight to her head and she wasn't about to thoroughly embarrass herself by teetering about and tumbling arse over tit. But the cocktail dress was, most frustratingly, still firmly zipped in place.

Cleverly though (as rather clever she was, especially when thinking up devilish plans for this naughty bugger), she'd pre-empted this scenario by bringing a change of clothes in an elegant tote bag, doubling as her handbag and he'd obviously noticed.

He continued with a slight smirk, 'You seem a little fidgety. If you're uncomfortable, feel free to use the bathroom to change – it's down the hall, second on the left.'

She wanted to shout back *Of course I'm uncomfortable you wicked tease – I'm still wearing this bloody dress when all I want to be wearing is YOU and all your scrumptious bodily fluids.*

But that may have ruined her very carefully devised plan so she bit her tongue and slinked off to the bathroom, taking her rather generously poured fourth glass of wine with her.

Ensconced in his luxurious bathroom, she retrieved the items of clothing from her bag and changed.

Now the dangerous part of the evening had arrived!

Instead of more comfortable clothing, she'd brought slinky, kinky night garments instead. The brazen hussy!

But if he reacted the way she predicted, it would all be so incredibly worth the initial shock and humiliation.

So off came her dress and undies and on went:

A black silk and lace negligee

Matching Brazilian Knickers (dry ones, if only for a few minutes)

Black suspenders

The sheerest black silk stockings

And the pointiest, highest and sexiest pair of black satin and lace detail heels

All finished off with sultry makeup and her favourite Dior perfume.

She was ready!

Now all she needed to do was exit the bathroom and walk towards him without face-planting his hallway floor in those heels!

Then – doubt set in.

What would he think? Would he take one look and run a mile because there's a crazed sex fiend in his house, stalking about in her underwear? Or would he like it?

She had to get a grip, and fast!

So she necked the glass of wine, gulping down the sweet, ruby nectar way too quickly, took a very long, deep breath and carefully turned the door handle, all the while hoping to goodness he wasn't stood on the other side of it.

She opened the door a crack – relief. He wasn't there!

She also noticed that the lights were off, candles had been lit and there was 40's jazz music coming from the living room. This gave her courage and hope as why would he do all this unless he'd had the same sordid ideas as her?

She finally managed to pry her hands off the door – her knuckles were white from where she'd been gripping it out of nauseating fear – and started her elegant, graceful walk towards his living room. It wasn't far but it felt like The Long Walk at Windsor Castle – never bloody ending!

She spotted him, hunched over his record player – he was playing vintage jazz vinyls on a rather lovely turntable.

She'd been practicing her walk, pose and stance specifically for this moment. She did NOT want to come across as timid and shy but bold, confident and incredibly sultry.

Her last few steps took her to the end of his sofa, directly opposite where he was bent over. Oh his arse – his sexy, taught, gorgeous arse – she wanted to march over and bite it but that wouldn't be very sophisticated, now would it?

She had to think quickly as he could turn around any minute.

Luckily, his home was carpeted so he hadn't heard her heels clippety-clopping on the floor and had no idea she was behind him. She knew she had to stop fannying about and get on with it so she gently approached his behind and just stood there, looking deliciously sexy and elegant.

He sensed her presence, as she saw him tense and his ears prick up. Her heartbeat and breath quickened and butterflies started flitting about inside her belly as he steadily straightened himself and very slowly turned around.

This was it – the crux of the evening!

Then his eyes fell upon her.

She gazed back hoping for some sort of visual reaction which, luckily, she got as the right corner of his mouth curved upwards, his eyes glinted and flashed and he licked his lips, ending up with his bottom lip tucked away under his teeth. The reaction she'd hoped for!

Then, he emitted a deep, husky growl '*Grrrrrrrr*' from within his throat and took the two steps that separated them.

Her knickers became damper!

He was close enough for her to feel his breath as it exhaled from his glorious mouth. His experienced hands slid up her arms towards her shoulders where they delicately grasped a handful of her long, satiny, raven hair, raising them up to his nose, inhaling deeply, breathing in her Dior essence.

Another growl!

Knickers getting even damper!

Words whisperingly escaped his mouth. 'I was kinda hoping you'd be brazen enough to dress like this for me, Scarlet. I approve!'

'I aim to please,' she retorted in a quivering voice.

He beamed that impish grin at her as both of his hands now softly cradled her face and he leaned in and kissed her. He kissed her deeply and she bit his lip.

He growled again!

Knickers are now wet!

'Do that again!' he commanded.

She put her arms up around his neck and leaned forward, kissing him. She was biting and sucking his lower lip which drove him wild. The kissing became more frenzied – no longer soft and gentle – they became ravenous.

Tongues lapping and swirling.

Heads dancing.

Hands pulling hair.

His hands then started their descent towards her voluptuous bottom, grabbing and kneading her cheeks.

Her arms around him, her hands trailing all over his masculine body – his arse, his back, his arms.

He grabbed another handful of her hair, yanking her head back to expose her neck and his warm tongue licked her from collarbone to chin, his sharp teeth biting her neck, followed by more dirty, noisy kissing.

They were feasting on each other, as if they hadn't eaten in months and were starving for each other's flesh. It was the most arousing make out session of her life! Nobody had EVER kissed her like this before and she was in a fevered delirium, her entire body trembling, beads of sweat popping out of her pores, warm, sultry trickles escaping her lady lips.

Knickers now soaked!

His hands lowered further, reaching under her buttocks to find her hidden depths and his nifty fingers danced on her lips, making her whimper softly into his open, hungry mouth.

She followed his lead, dropping her hands to his buttocks, grabbing wildly and pulling him into her. She felt his hardened, growing arousal and brought her hands around to the front of his cargo trousers, where she grabbed his cock through the tough material, rubbing the length of it with her palm.

Low, deep moans escaped him!

Her confidence at an all-time high, she unbuttoned his cargos, lowered his zip and reached in to extricate his hot, throbbing cock from its restraint.

She knew he wouldn't disappoint.

This untamed, beautiful male specimen was very generously hung and she thought about how it would feel when he finally thrusted himself deep inside her, stretching her walls to their limits and that thought was almost too much to bare!

She wanted him inside her now. NOW!

His hands had made their way around the front of her panties where he was now edging them to one side, his fingers making their entry between her lips, parting her folds and finding her maidenhead. He started to rub her!

His heavy, pulsating cock in her hand, she began to massage.

How much more could either of them take before they let loose with wild abandon, taking each other madly and without restraint? Not much!

She whispered firmly in his ear through quivering lips, 'Take me Stewart, take me now and do not be gentle!'

He didn't need telling twice!

No sooner had the word 'gentle' left her mouth, they were on the sofa, grabbing and tearing at each other's garments, underwear being tossed everywhere. A frenzied attack between two ravenous wild beasts!

Just a few seconds later, there was nothing between them other than skin; burning, slippery, wet skin.

He took her shaking legs, threw them over his shoulders, reached for his engorged cock and with one forceful, powerful thrust, he took her, just like she'd told him to.

Writhing, bucking, slipping, sliding, thrusting, moaning, groaning, growling – so ferocious, so untamed, so wild yet so very passionate, so very erotic, so very beautiful; unlike any other sexual experience in her fifty years on this earth. She'd never been this exposed to a man before, never given herself to any other man with such recklessness, never felt so free, so special, so exquisite and yet, here he was, making wild, passionate love to her as if she was the most stunning woman in the world, making her feel alive for the very first time. She felt that, at this very point in time, there was nobody else on earth except him and her. That's how powerful he was, that's how much of an effect he had on her. It was almost magical! Like a primal yet mystical force had possessed them both, creating the most surreal, time-halting moment and they both wanted it to last forever.

He'd leaned heavily forward by now, bending her clean in half as he wanted to end this supernatural act with their mouths joined. His thrusts got even deeper, harder, faster, the friction driving her, quite literally, mad with burning desire.

She could feel it coming, could feel the screams mounting in her throat and could hear his groans getting louder, deeper, more carnal as they both neared their dizzying peak.

Then with one final hip-cracking thrust, they both burst and exploded!

The most powerful orgasm of her life rocked her body – one that made her scream like a banshee and howl like a wild animal. She could feel the searing heat within as hot floods of what felt like volcanic lava gushed out, drowning his beautiful cock and his seed mixed with hers, creating steaming, burning, molten rivers that soaked everything in their path.

And hearing him howl – it was earth-shattering and soul penetrating. What an erotically melodic sound coming from an erotically melodic man!

He was still kissing her, still had her bent in half, in the tightest embrace. They were panting, kissing, gasping for air; hearts pounding, sexual organs pulsating and throbbing, bodies aching, skin burning.

He released her legs and they flopped down onto the sumptuous sofa cushions as he collapsed onto her!

They were spent, done in; a pile of wrecked bones panting in each other's ears!

Everything started to slow as they lay there, holding each other, his silvery head on her bosom while she gently scratched his back, softly kissing his forehead which made him smile and sigh.

She thought she'd known what to expect but she hadn't. She had not in her wildest dreams expected THAT! He had blown her mind into space, her womanhood into oblivion and her knickers into the kitchen.

She was complete now!

It didn't matter if it never happened again because he had completed her, he'd made her whole and she'd done the same for him.

He'd made her feel like the most beautifully exquisite woman on the planet and she'd taken all the sharp, broken shards of his heart and started glueing them back together. They'd found healing in each other's arms and in the throes of maniacal passion and, right now, they needed nothing else!

Part 2 – Her Dreams Get Wilder

She'd been wandering about in a fantastical daze since her delightful evening with that deliciously stunning creature. Stewart had put a pep back in her step and the light back in her eyes. He'd also put even more filthy thoughts in her head, leading to lip twitches and ovary cramps in rather inappropriate settings! Inhaling sharply whilst biting one's lip in an office meeting isn't a very good idea, now is it? And she was so frustrated again as she'd thought that that was that. They'd had their fill of one another, rocked each other's worlds and parted ways! He hadn't invited her to stay the night and she hadn't dared invite herself so she'd left after a rather yummy coffee, with the evidence of their raunchiness still trickling down her thighs.

But this morning, she'd received a text. She was at work when she saw his name pop up on her iPhone screen and the irritating thing was, she couldn't pick it up to read as her boss was in her office.

Damn!

Her stomach did summersaults, she blushed heavily and her heart fluttered – as well as other parts.

What could he want? He hadn't contacted her at all. Not one word since that salacious night!

Luckily though, it was Friday and a half day for her so she only had to wait a further fifteen minutes but they were the toughest fifteen minutes of her life!

All kinds of thoughts plagued her mind: *had she left something behind and he was letting her know? Was he just enquiring as to how she was? Or was it something more exciting?*

She couldn't think straight and watched the clock tick-tock away until it hit twelve p.m then she scarpered quicker than a bunny in the headlights!

Finally in her car, she opened the text: Hey you. How are you doing? Would you care to have dinner with me this evening, if you're free?

'Oh my giddy aunt Fanny – FUCK YESSS!' she shouted to herself, not quite believing her eyes or her luck. Dinner with HIM! She was so giddy with excitement that it made her feel a bit nauseous but she contained herself in her reply; Hello. I'm well thank you. And yourself? I am free this evening and would love to.

They messaged back and forth confirming the details and she drove the thirty minutes home on a rather floaty cloud.

*

She'd spent the afternoon preening herself: a lovely long, warm bath, soaking in oils and bubbles to make her skin luxuriously soft and delicately scented, a smoothing and nourishing hair mask, so her long, luscious locks would bounce and flow, wafting her Dior perfume his way and a face treatment to make her skin glow and radiate.

He'd chosen a lavish restaurant for this evening. She'd never heard of the place, so she'd googled it and it was very posh with opulent, velvet covered chairs, crystal chandeliers, soft lighting… Needless to say, she needed to look the part.

He was sending a car for her at six thirty p.m. and it was already five forty-five, so she needed to get her skates on.

She'd chosen a long, elegant, dark burgundy dress with cap sleeves, a deep cleavage and empire waist, high black velvet heels, a matching clutch bag and her favourite rose gold jewellery completed the look. She wore her hair down in long, sweeping, raven swirls that were set off by the dark burgundy of her dress. She took one final look in her mirror, smiled satisfactorily, sprayed another cloud of Dior over her hair and headed for the door.

*

It was 6:31 when the doorbell chimed. She was greeted by a very polite chauffeur who helped her into the black Audi. The drive to the restaurant took forty minutes and her butterflies were relentless. She was constantly clasping her tummy and swallowing hard, failing to clear the lump in her throat. And she was trembling!

Just as the Audi pulled up outside the restaurant, Stewart appeared. He was awaiting her arrival just inside the door, having been advised by the chauffeur of their eta en route. He looked simply divine, a stunning creature in a shiny slate blue suit with a long jacket. A deep burgundy velvet waistcoat set it off perfectly with no shirt underneath. His head was adorned with a deep red bandana and a grey peak cap topped it off. And he'd left his platinum ponytail loose at the back. He normally tucked it away when he went out but not today as he knew it would drive her quite mad! The bloody rascal!

He approached the car, opened her door and offered her his hand which she took gracefully and elegantly, swinging both legs around to exit the car like a proper lady. She was gripping his hand as she stood, taking the step up the curb. He shut the door behind her and tapped the car, signalling it to leave and there they stood, savouring this moment, both a feast for each other's eyes.

Oh, the sight! They just complimented each other. Even down to the colours - his waistcoat matched her dress!

She'd allowed herself a rather large glass of red wine before she'd left home – she had to in order to quiet her nerves but red wine always disintegrates her filter too so as she was taking in the breath-taking sight that was HIM, she unwittingly gushed out, 'You look delectable! Can I just eat you for dinner?'

No sooner had those words escaped her mouth, she realised her faux-pas and gasped shockingly, putting her elegantly clawed fingers over her mouth, 'Oops, I'm so sorry,' she uttered sheepishly from behind her hand, batting her eyelashes.

He leaned back, roaring with laughter. 'No, no, don't apologise. I could feast on you too, for you are quite ravishing!'

She sighed with relief as she took his arm and they walked giggling into the restaurant. They were ushered to their table, one he'd handpicked for its privacy and he chivalrously pulled out her chair, gently guiding it inwards beneath her. They were promptly furnished with menus, made their choices and settled down for a most appetising meal, complete with lashings of the most delicious wine, cheeky innuendos and rapturous laughter.

*

Their dinner date seemingly at its end, Scarlet politely excused herself as she was in desperate need of the ladies' room.

As she pushed back her chair to stand up, she teetered and wobbled on her stilettoed feet, almost tumbling to the floor in an inebriated heap of velvet and hair. She squealed and giggled, muttering one of her favourite words 'Whoopsies' and toddled off to the bathroom, trying desperately hard not to fall flat on her face with her curvaceous buttocks in the air.

Oh Lord, the humiliation!

She managed both the trip there and back and to pee IN the toilet and not all over the seat and floor.

Gosh, she was very VERY tipsy!

As she approached the table, Stewart stood up to greet her, slid his masculine arm around her waist, pulled her in and whispered in her ear 'Back to mine for dessert?'

She looked at him, eyes wide.

He was grinning with a very cheeky glint in his eyes and he flashed them at her.

He'd always had this very arousing way of quickly flashing his beautiful, sparkling eyes and it was enough to cause her panties to almost fall off all by themselves.

'Dessert?' she quizzed.

'Well, we didn't have dessert after our meal as I have something rather sticky and sweet awaiting us back at mine!'

'Sounds intriguing and very lovely,' she retorted. 'Lead the way, Maestro!'

Now because he knew without a doubt she'd not say 'No thanks, I'd rather go home,' he'd presumptively ordered the car whilst she was drunkenly tottering about in the ladies so it was there waiting for them as they exited the restaurant. She gave him a side glance and he winked at her. He could read her like a book, the naughty fiend!

Into the car they got and were whizzed off to his place. Upon their arrival, Stewart asked her to wait while he exited his side and made his way around to hers, letting her out himself. He offered her his hand again, saying 'My Lady.' Wow, what treatment she was getting tonight. She felt like a Princess. Chauffeur driven cars, opulent, crystalline restaurants, chivalry at its best, and then of course, the wining and dining.

Now, was the dessert at his the 'sixty-nining' part? She bloody hoped so! That was the one thing missing from their first evening, the one thing she felt slightly disappointed over, the fact that she hadn't had the chance to taste Stewart's delectable cock and she was quite desperate for the chance to glide her moist, warm tongue over his generous shaft, powerfully sucking him to the point of depletion.

Her knickers started getting damp again!

Up the steps to his town house they went with her prayerfully gripping his arm. Tripping would probably cause a limb fracture and there was no way she was gonna allow ANYTHING to ruin his wicked plans. And she knew they were wicked! There was no way on earth he'd actually stood in his kitchen, preparing dessert. He had sticky, sweet plans of a carnal nature because he was a damnable kinky rogue and she loved that about him.

Inside his lovely house once more, they kicked off their shoes and made their way into his kitchen where he proceeded to the fridge.

Her heart sank – *oh no, had she been totally wrong? Had he actually made dessert?*

With his back to her and the fridge door open, she could hear shuffling. She could also hear what sounded like a zipper! *What on earth was he doing?*

Then, he slowly turned around to face her saying, 'Something sticky and sweet to delight your taste buds, Madam!'

And there, in his hands, was a plate adorned with berries, a tub of clotted cream and a dish filled with maple syrup – all very cleverly arranged around his aroused, sturdy, throbbing cock!

He'd put his cock on a plate!

Scarlet just stood there, totally aghast, gawping at this hilariously erotic sight and she actually froze, not quite knowing what to do with herself. She felt a laugh bubbling up and even though she tried, she could not hold it back and she burst. She laughed so hard, tears streamed down her cheeks.

And Stewart? He was laughing too but with that tell-tale glint in his eyes!

She was holding her face with both hands, shocked and amazed at his brazenness. *My goodness, the dirty, filthy, wonderfully bold man!*

She walked towards him, still gawping at his cock on a platter of fruit, face still in her hands. She looked up and saw he was grinning slightly, biting his bottom lip. She didn't want to ruin this moment but she genuinely had no idea how to proceed. *Did he expect her to just dive in and munch away?* Luckily, instructions followed.

'Follow me!' He exclaimed as he walked away, carefully balancing his cock on the plate. She obliged rather hastily.

He lead her into his bedroom where he sat on the end of his sumptuous bed, legs akimbo, plate in one hand as he precisely dabbed cream on his already wet tip, followed by a strawberry half and a drizzle of maple syrup.

And now it was clear – she was to drop to her knees and eat yummy, scrummy goodness off of his parts while he sat there and watched.

Knickers were very, very damp as warm trickles started to meander from between her tingling lips.

She slinked over, carefully knelt before him, held back her hair with one hand and gently licked the melting cream, syrup and strawberry off of him.

He inhaled sharply!

She looked up at him, tantalisingly licking cream from her lips which made him grin!

For fucks sake – that bloody grin makes her lady lips seep!

He proceeded to pile on more, preparing himself for her each time and, as she continued, she got more confident, not being so gentle, not being so ladylike, not being so careful not to get sticky, delightfully sweet yumminess all over her face. Soon, she was smothered in it and she became ravenous.

No longer able to restrain herself and no longer able to only lick him on the plate, she grabbed it from his hands, slung it on the floor, grabbed his pulsating shaft and engulfed it in her hungry, salivating mouth.

Her knickers got soaked as she heard him moan!

Hearing him moan deeply because of her was so very erotic and it made her juices gush, making her even more hungry for him.

She let her silken tongue glide from the base of his bulbous shaft to the tip, releasing the suction and letting her tongue do all the work, gently flicking like molten lava about his generous head, stroking the length and breadth of him over and over again, making him gasp and he'd gathered her hair up into one hand, holding it back for her, bracing himself with the other.

She could feel his tension – his eagerness so she decided it was time; time to take him relentlessly, to take him to a place of pure ecstasy and she did - swiftly, without hesitation, no holding back!

Cupping his heavily laden balls in her hand, she used the other to massage the base of his shaft as her head started to rise and fall in his lap. Faster and faster she went, harder and harder, tighter and tighter!

She increased the pull and increased the pressure, all the while replenishing the moisture in her mouth to keep him slick.

Then music to her ears: his gasps turned to moans, his moans to growls, his growls to deep, guttural cries as he neared his dizzying peak.

He was thrusting forward, unable to hold back, no longer bracing himself but holding her head as they ramped up the speed, the most divine sounds emanating from his throat.

He suddenly cried out her name so loudly and blissfully, it echoed off the walls as Dante's Peak erupted – hot, gushing lava pulsating down her throat. His sparkling essence tasted sublime and she gorged herself on its salty yet sweet flavour.

The pulsating began to lessen, his vocal reactions reduced to whimpers, his breath coming short and quick, his brave heart beating out of the sacred walls of his tattooed chest as sweat dripped from every pore.

It was done – she'd fulfilled him! She'd taken him to the brink and brought him back again.

He'd fallen back onto the bed, depleted and done in, trying to catch his breath as she remained knelt between his legs, stickiness all over her face and hands and in her hair.

Fuck, that was so damn seductive, sensual and erotic!

He was laying there in a sweaty, breathless, sated heap because of her and it made her throb. She actually came too – she couldn't help it! She was completely drenched down there as the whole salacious escapade had made her gush uncontrollably.

He sat up slowly, still a bit breathless, reached out to her, pulled her towards him and kissed her then proceeded to lick all the leftovers from her face, all the while making delicious noises, 'Mmmm, you taste heavenly!'

'So do you!'

'That was fucking amazing – I was not expecting THAT! I'm very pleasantly surprised. You're a very sexy, beautiful, talented woman, Scarlet Adams, and now, it's my turn to completely wreck you, if I may?'

'Oh, you may – you absolutely 'may' and stop being so bloody polite about it! Just take me, wreck me, make me scream and burst to your hearts content. Whatever you want you can have, Stewart – I'm all yours!'

'Well, I've been properly instructed. Wait here and I'll be right back.'

With that, he left the room and her on the floor in a quivering, mumbling, sticky puddle.

Upon his return, he had a can of squirty cream which he placed on the nightstand next to his headboard.

He relieved himself of his creased, stained clothes and leaned forwards with his hands resting on his knees, saying 'Prepare yourself for the ride of your life, Madam. I promise you, when I'm done, you won't even remember your own name!'

And she melted…

Part 3 – The Night Continues

Scarlet was still on the floor in her delirious, sticky puddle when Stewart told her what to expect - he was gonna wreck her and relieve her of her faculties, including her memory. *But was she about to complain? Good lord no!* As far as she was concerned, he could do whatever he wanted and she'd told him so.

He was towering above her in his boxers, his hardened cock protruding blatantly. He offered his hand to help her up and she accepted it gracefully however, the standing up part wasn't graceful at all as she had to peel herself off the carpet and try to control her trembling legs. She failed miserably and teetered on her way up, causing him to giggle.

'Stop laughing!' she spouted.

'Sorry, you just look so cute and comical; staggering up, covered in cream with hair stuck to your face!'

He reached out and wiped her hair from her cheeks and walked her to the bathroom, suggesting she clean up a bit and she was grateful for that as dairy based products mixed with ejaculate and sweat wasn't the most pleasant of odours.

She removed her dress, had a quick shower, towelled herself off and rejoined him in his bedroom, wearing nothing but her rather damp knickers. The look on his face was a devilish picture and it made her recoil slightly as he honestly looked like he was about to pounce and rip her to pieces.

He approached her and kissed her saying, 'Before I make a total mess of you, would you like some wine?'

She nodded eagerly and he went off, bringing back two bottles and glasses. He poured generously for the both of them and sipped on his while she gulped hers, offering him her empty glass for a refill,

'Fill me up, please.'

'Oh I fully intend to!'

'I meant my glass!'

He laughed and obliged.

She took another long sip of the warming nectar and licked her lips 'Mmmmmm, yummy!'

He gently removed her glass from her hand, putting their glasses on the nightstand then led her to the bed.

While she'd been showering, he'd turned the bed down, pulling back the duvet and arranging the pillows for maximum comfort.

With her back towards the bed, he slid his gifted hands down her waist, over her hips and into the top of her Brazilians, sliding them down and off her feet. She looked down at the top of his head, wrapped in that gorgeous bandana and couldn't help but touch it gently.

As he stood up slowly, he eased her back onto the bed, helped her get comfy on the pillows then went to retrieve his cream and a straw that was cut in half.

'A straw? What do you need a straw for?'

'You'll see!'

She was quivering from head to toe, anticipating his lechery.

He climbed back onto the bed, knelt over her, parted her thighs, got himself positioned and proceeded to gently kiss her lips. Soft kisses and slight licks at first which made her catch her breath and sigh deeply but the gentleness soon turned more forceful as he parted her throbbing lips, flicking that talented tongue of his over her gleaming jewel and into her folds.

His hands were holding her hips at first but then he slid them under her buttocks, cupping her cheeks. He stopped, looked up at her, licked his lips, flickered his eyebrows and reached out for the cream which he generously squirted all over her aching honeypot then he dove straight in!

His fingers were holding her lips apart while he hungrily went to town within; licking, sucking, nibbling, lapping up the cream as he went – he was covered in it!

She was whimpering, trembling and responding with slight wet trickles as her hips began to buck.

Fuck, he was so very gifted! He was so experienced in these pleasures of the flesh and knew exactly what he was doing.

She was writhing uncontrollably now, grabbing at the sheets and breathlessly repeating his name as he pinned her pearl between his teeth and inserted his thumb deep inside her, each stroke making her buck, each flick of his tongue on her pearl causing the most divine sensations.

Then he reached for the straw, positioned it over her already swollen sugar plum and sucked, pulling her into the tiny opening.

She shrieked out loudly, 'Fuuuuck!'

He kept the pressure up, sucking, releasing, sucking, releasing, over and over again, sending her into an ecstatic state of madness. She almost begged him to stop as she couldn't cope but she didn't want him to stop either. She couldn't bare it any longer and she grabbed his head, knocked the straw away and pulled him further into her.

He realised she was peaking and ramped up the intensity, finishing her off with his tongue and fingers. She climaxed, howling uncontrollably, flooding his mouth and face with her sweet honeydew. Her walls were pulsating, her body convulsing as she cried out 'I want you inside me!'

He knelt up, slipped off his boxers, grabbed his beautiful cock and rammed it inside her, making her cry out again, his brutal entry causing a searing pleasurable pain to course up through her belly. Bloody hell, it felt like he'd pierced through her cervix and melted her ovaries with his hot, rock hard cock.

She'd been very pleasantly surprised at the virility and stamina of a man of his mature years. Not that she'd ever actually doubted him as he oozed testosterone out of his sexy pores, making you believe that he could hold his own for hours and hours, completely wiping you out before he'd even broken a sweat. And she was right! His thrusts were bone-jarringly powerful. So much so that she felt he'd dislocate her hip!

He had a savageness in his eyes that made him look almost angry and he was doing that thing with his mouth where he pouts as if he's concentrating on harnessing all that power – it was so damned erotic, arousing and fucking sexy and she couldn't take her eyes off of him.

She was shrieking on every crashing thrust and he must have realised that it was a bit too much too quickly, so he slowed down, lay atop her and started gently stroking and rocking whilst kissing her deeply. She bit his lip as she knew that drove him wild and would make him growl which she loved.

She had wrapped her arms around him and was clawing his back with her talons, making him arch backwards and, as he arched, she cried out and orgasmed explosively, spasming around his blazing cock which made him smile from ear to ear.

'Good,' he whispered.

The feel of her squeezing around him heightened his pleasure and he made even more sensual 'fuck me' faces and guttural sounds, arching again. This time, she grabbed his platinum ponytail, swiftly wrapped it around her hand and pulled his head back hard, licking and biting his neck, all the while trying to regulate her breathing after her powerful explosion. Keeping his hair tight in her hand, she pushed him further upwards with the other and licked his chest tattoo which she'd been dying to do. She then made her way down to his hard nipples and gently sucked them, pinching gently with her teeth and flicking with the warm, moist tip of her tongue.

All this made him growl – deep, husky, throaty, arousing growls. And that pleased her immensely for she loved hearing him growl because of her – she adored pleasing him sexually and she adored it because he was so sexually gifted and experienced and she wasn't. She'd figured that pleasing a man who'd had so much experience would be difficult but she was wrong!

Even though this was only their second time together, she already knew what he liked and she made it her mission to give it to him. She didn't want it to be all about her!

This beautiful man had battled many demons in his past, those demons still lingering and all she wanted to do was vanquish them for him and help him put some of the broken shards of his heart back together. She hadn't a clue if she was going to accomplish all of that but she was damned well gonna try.

With her making a very delicious meal of his chest, she made her way back up to his beautiful face and licked that too. She dragged her tongue along his chiselled jawline, up to his ears where she nibbled on his earlobes.

He let out a high-pitched whimper and bit his bottom lip, keeping it tucked under his front teeth as he continued to ply her with long, hot, gentle strokes.

She wrapped her legs around him and ground her hips up to meet him where they found a mutual rhythm.

This was fucking beautiful!

She'd sensed him nearing his peak a couple of times but, each time, he'd slowed down, withdrawing slightly so as to prolong their lovemaking but now, he was speeding up. They'd been going for a good while and she could sense his eagerness.

He pushed himself upright, put her feet behind his ears and started thrusting again, giving her the opportunity to use his shoulders as a lever and thrust up to meet him, matching his ferocity.

He leaned forward slightly and had his hands on her waist, pulling her towards him. Maybe he sensed her energy dying off as he had brought her to orgasm twice already because he twisted his head, lifted her foot and started kissing her ankle then switched to the other as he relented yet again, pulling back and gave her small, gentle strokes with just his tip as he kissed her ankles, switching from one to the other followed by a hip-shattering thrust, just one then back to slow and steady, followed by another hip wallop.

This went on for a short while until he could hold back no more. Then he went wild on her!

He dropped her legs, held one of her thighs up by his waist, braced himself on one arm and rode her like a savage beast – growling and breathing through gritted teeth.

It was maniacal!

She was almost screaming as he pounded her ferociously and she was now failing to keep up with him. He was like a man possessed! His speed quickened and revved until he howled – one final howl and he spilled his seed deep inside her. She could feel his cock throbbing within as she too orgasmed yet again, throbbing in tandem with him. His abs and chest were taught, his neck stretched upwards, his head falling back, the most divine noises emanating from his throat and out through his clenched jaw. Coupled with her cries and screams, it was a beautifully sensual sound!

He flopped down on top of her, panting as she engulfed him in her arms, breathless and weak.

He'd zapped her! Completely wrecked her as he said he would!

His head on her chest, she gently scratched his back, hoping to help calm his fevered state. She craned her neck in order to plant a long, loving kiss on his sweaty forehead and they lay there, panting in unison.

Their laboured breathing started to calm and he lifted his head to deeply kiss her. They kissed for a while, allowing their inflamed bodies to cool before he slid off and pulled her into a warm embrace where no words were necessary – the silence around them was what they both needed. It wasn't long before they both dozed off!

*

They'd only been snoozing for a few minutes when Stewart gently roused her. They were both very sticky, very thirsty and very, very knackered.

'Shall I fetch us a drink? What can I get you?'

'Something cold and fizzy if you have it please and some water.'

'I actually have flavoured sparkling water – will that do?'

'Yesssss – gosh yes. Pints of it please.'

He giggled and disappeared, returning with two bottles.

He handed her one, advising that they had one each and they both guzzled and glugged away. It was absolute perfection – cold, fizzy, sweet bubbles after a rampant bonk is always just the ticket.

After inhaling half of the one litre bottle, she realised she was actually sticking to the sheets so decided it was time for another shower. She didn't want to wash his sublime essence off of her but she was VERY sticky with dried up cream and cum everywhere so unless she wanted to smell like a dairy maid gutting a fish, she had no choice.

She tried to stand up – tried being the operative word as her bloody legs were having none of it. Her knees buckled and she plopped right back down on the mattress, laughing.

She composed herself and tried again – nope!

'For fucks sake, what have you done to my legs?'

'I told you I was gonna wreck you and I meant it!'

'You did indeed but now I can't stand up!'

He jumped up, went around the bed and helped her to her feet, keeping hold of her hands until she steadied herself.

'Now, let's see if you can walk, shall we?' he grinned at her.

'You're a cheeky bloody blighter.' And she clipped him one, right on his upper left arm.

'Ow, fuck me, woman, you've got a hard slap!'

'Awww, poor old sausage, I'm sorry, did that sting? Come here, I'll make it all better!' And she proceeded to lick his arm, tracing the tip of her tongue over his tattoos.

'Unless you want to end up needing a wheelchair, I suggest you stop that, young lady, cos I'm getting hard again!'

'Oh no you don't – you leave me and my lady parts ALONE, you brute,' and she shuffled off to the bathroom. She shuffled as she couldn't quite bend her knees and walk at the same time or she'd end up in a rather pungent heap on the carpet.

She showered yet again then returned to the bedroom in search of her knickers but couldn't find them.

She asked, 'Stewart, do you remember where you threw my knickers?'

When he'd relieved her of them, he'd tossed them rather eagerly over his right shoulder!

The search for her knickers under way, they looked everywhere but no, they had literally disappeared. She stood there, hands on her hips, looking very perplexed when he started howling with laughter and he kept howling, so much so she couldn't get a single word out of him for a few minutes.

'Will you tell me what's so bloody funny!'

He managed to compose himself then nodded upwards with his eyes raised. She looked up and there, swinging around on his ceiling fan, were her black, lace knickers. She looked back at him and they both burst out laughing together.

'That's hilarious,' she blurted out through cackles.

He grabbed a chair, climbed on top and retrieved them for her. When he got down, he said, 'Erm, I think you may need new ones, Scarlet. These look a little worse for wear.'

They did indeed – they were damp and had white marks in with dust from his fan clinging to them.

'Yuck! I see what you mean.'

'Yuck indeed, dirty girl!'

'Hey, it's all your fault for constantly making me cream in them. Always licking your lips, flashing your eyes and looking thoroughly fuckable! You should be honoured that my knickers are so mucky.'

With that, she flicked them firmly against the chair to get the dust off.

'Oi you, don't shake your dried up squirtings all over my room.'

She cackled again.

'I really don't think it'll make much difference – your bed is already covered in my wet squirtings.'

'You're so nasty!' He exclaimed then kissed her on her forehead saying, 'But I like it!'

'Are you gonna stay or shall I call you a cab?'

'Do you want me to stay?'

'I can't think of anything better than waking up next to you in the morning.'

'Well in that case, I'll stay but I have three conditions.'

'Oh, tell me?'

'One, you take a shower, two, you change those puerile sheets and, three, you refrain from touching my sore, raw, throbbing vagina!'

'Your wish is my command, Milady!'

He showered, swiftly remade the bed with fresh linens, they got into bed and very swiftly passed out in each other's arms.

*

It was nine a.m. when he awoke her.

'Good morning, sleepyhead.'

She blinked and opened her eyes to the most glorious sight – him, peering down at her with that beaming smile and those twinkling eyes of his.

'Mmmmm, good morning handsome.'

'I got us breakfast from the bakery. I wasn't sure what you liked so I got a selection: croissants, pain au chocolat, brioche and cinnamon buns. I also got you a large mocha as I do know that's your favourite coffee.'

'Oh, you absolute angel! Thank you – yum. I'm famished.'

She went to sit up and winced.

'Ouch.'

'What's wrong?' He looked concerned.

'I think, Mr Shaggamuffin, that you have quite literally broken my fanny!'

He roared with laughter.

'Well, if it makes you feel any better, I'm suffering too. My cock is chaffed. And NO, you're not allowed to kiss it better!'

'Hahaaaaaaaa.' She wailed.

He rummaged about in a paper bag, placed a variety of pastries on a plate and presented it to her with a hot, steaming cup of mocha.

As they were ravenously munching away, he said, 'How do you feel about, you know, kinky stuff?'

'Kinky stuff?'

'Well, light bondage, a bit of BDSM, that kinda thing?'

'I find the thought of it incredibly arousing! Why?'

'Well, I'm a bit of a master in that area and was thinking of introducing you to it – how do you fancy a naughty weekend at my place in Paris?'

Her lady lips quivered and tingled and she bit her bottom lip as she squeaked out her reply, 'I thought you'd never ask, you delightfully wicked man! When? The sooner the better please!'

His eyebrows went straight up as he wasn't quite expecting her to be so enthusiastic and his trademark lopsided grin emerged on his lickable face. 'Erm, are you quite sure? I don't want you doing anything you don't want to do just to please me, young lady!'

'Oh yes, I'm positively positive, old man!'

He laughed, 'Old man? You cheeky minx! OK then, two weeks from now, we'll take the Eurostar then a taxi from Gare Du Nord to my Paris home where I'll show you just how delightfully wicked I can be!''

The thought of being thoroughly manhandled by him made her parts twitch and trickle, making her already revoltingly stained Brazilians even worse.

These ones were going in the bin – they were past saving!

They finished breakfast, finalising the plans for their kinky weekend and he called her a cab.

She was actually very much looking forward to getting home, running a warm Epsom salt bath and soaking her sore muscles and raw lady parts in the comforting, soothing water.

They were both quite busy for the next two weeks so had agreed to not see each other again until their Paris weekend where, she was one hundred percent positive, he was going to completely annihilate her; thus she needed to be fully prepared, well rested and full of energy as she fully intended to annihilate him too!

Part 4 – Paris – Friday/Saturday

Her doorbell rang at seven p.m.

She opened her front door to a most delicious sight.

There he stood, sporting blue jeans, a blue sweater, grey loafers, a black beanie hat and that devilishly handsome grin of his.

'Good evening, Scarlet. Are you ready?'

'Good evening, darling man. Yes, more than ready!'

Stewart took her small suitcase and her hand and led her to the awaiting cab. He chivalrously opened her door and helped her into the taxi whilst the driver placed her luggage into the boot. Just before she swung her legs into the car, he said. 'You look very lovely this evening,' and he kissed her hand before shutting her door.

Jumping in on the other side, he signalled the cabbie to leave and they were off to London St Pancras station to catch the 20:01 Eurostar to Paris Gare Du Nord.

She was dressed comfortably. She'd made an effort of course but had just donned deep plum leggings, a black tunic sweater and over-the-knee black leather boots. Comfy but chic!

They arrived at the station a little after seven forty p.m. and made their way to the platform where the train was waiting. As he'd booked Premiere tickets, they were ushered aboard by a hostess and furnished with champagne. They sat at their table, chatting away, catching up on the last two weeks when he noticed she hadn't touched her glass of fizz,

'You're not drinking?'

'Erm, well, no. Forgive me but I don't actually like champagne!'

'Why didn't you say in the beginning?'

'I don't want to make a fuss. You've gone to all this trouble and I didn't want to spoil anything. It's fine. I'm OK, really!'

'Having what you like to drink isn't making a fuss and you're definitely not ruining anything, you plank! Red wine instead?'

'Yes please. I'd love some!'

'There ya go, that wasn't hard, was it? I'll be more upset knowing you're not enjoying yourself so don't hide anything from me. I've brought you here with me this weekend to share a special place and part of my life. I want you to relax and enjoy yourself. Anything you want, you can have. OK?'

'Anything?'

'Absolutely!'

She got up from her seat opposite him, leaned over and whispered, 'May I have you, with your cock out, in the 1st class toilet in five minutes please?' She then graciously sashayed off in the direction of the posh loos, giving him no time to answer at all.

He sat there slightly bewildered for a couple of minutes – *did she really just ask him to go fuck her in the toilet?*

When the initial shock had settled, he smiled to himself, got up and followed her.

He knocked on the door and as she opened it, he leant on both sides of the door lintel and said 'Why not!'

She grabbed him by the neck of his sweater, dragged him in, shut the door and ravenously kissed him.

'Fuck, I've missed you!'

'I've missed you too, but there's not much space in here!'

'There's plenty of room!' she retorted as she turned her back to him, pulled her leggings and panties down to her knees and bent over the wash basin.

She could see his excitement in the mirror as he unzipped his jeans, extricated his impatiently throbbing cock from its place of safety, parted her lips and slipped inside her with eager force. Not too rough though as he didn't want her screaming and howling, alerting security and having them forcibly removed from the train, being charged with Public Indecency so he kept it low key. Instead of thrusting into her, he went deep and ground into her instead.

They gazed at each other in the mirror while they grunted and ground their hips. He had both hands on her shoulders, pulling her back into him to keep his cock as deep as possible while he mercilessly pulverised her insides and grazed her G-Spot with rhythmic precision, causing her legs to twitch and shake beneath her. She normally hated not being in control of her bodily functions but with him, she didn't care.

Her desires were made even more erotic by the vision of him behind her, biting his bottom lip, grinding away, fully clothed with his zipper open. It made her throb – he looked so fucking sexy! She knew they had to keep it low key but she so badly wanted to whip round and lick him all over, sucking his cock until he wailed like a baby but she'd have to wait until later for that.

She felt him tense behind her and knew he was close to exploding and she also knew she was gonna rupture soon too.

His breath became laboured and he started that deep, guttural noise again – even if she hadn't been close to orgasm now, that would have done it. Hearing him make that noise made her squirt!

His grindings got more forceful and his noises more animalistic as his teeth gritted, his eyes closed and he abundantly came inside her. She met him with her own floods of sweet elixir, contracting around him and whimpering softly as he held her around her waist in his strong, masculine arms to stop her from collapsing onto the floor and he stayed that way until she returned to normal.

While holding onto his hands that were wrapped around her waist, she lay her head back onto his shoulder with a sigh and a smile, turned inwards and kissed his cheek.

'Thank you,' she exclaimed. 'I just couldn't wait to feel you inside me again.'

'I assure you, Madam, it was an absolute pleasure!' He grinned at her with a wink and a sparkle in the mirror. 'I must admit, I hadn't expected our next time to be in a public loo on a train but there's a first time for everything, I s'pose!'

'Well, isn't this weekend all about first times? As you introduce me to your kinky lifestyle, there are sure to be a good few 'first times' for me – and for you too as I have a few tricks of my own up my sleeve.'

'I didn't think you knew anything about kinky stuff?'

'Ah, well, I think that I know more than 'you' think I know! I don't confess to know much but I've done a bit of research these last two weeks.'

'Oooo, intriguing – now let's get you cleaned up before you ruin yet another pair of pretty knickers, shall we?'

He gently pushed her forward, grabbed what seemed like half a roll of loo paper and proceeded to clean her up, wiping away the evidence of their salacious public restroom antics. He redressed her, gave his cock a good old wipe too, popped it back into his boxers and zipped up his jeans! They both washed their hands before exiting the toilet separately so as to not arouse suspicion from other passengers or staff.

Back at their table, they realised just how long they'd been gone – forty-five minutes!

Blimey, really? Can't have been that long, it only felt like fifteen to twenty maximum. But clocks don't lie – not multiple ones anyway.

They knew if they were gonna enjoy their 1st Class dinner, they needed to order quickly or they'd never finish in time.

They placed their order, including a bottle of red for Scarlet as promised and they settled back to enjoy yummy food together.

By now, especially after their 'happy hip hijinks', they were both bloody starving!

*

Having arrived in Paris bang on eleven seventeen p.m., they'd whisked through the station, jumped in a cab and had arrived at Stewart's flat by 00:15, rather pickled. He'd polished off a bottle and a half of champagne and she'd guzzled almost two bottles of Rioja to herself.

Even though she'd stewed her brain with alcohol, she wasn't too pie-eyed to notice that all the windows in his bedroom were blacked out with a film coating and he had black curtains up too. His bed was decked out with black satin linens, the furniture was black and everything was highlighted with stunning Eighteenth Century style lamps which gave off a haunting glow – the room was beautifully eerie and it drew her in. It was almost like walking onto an old haunted mansion style movie set although this was very real and he'd put a lot of careful, clever thought into it! This was his Wolfs Den, his Foxes Lair where all the animalistic magic happened.

Her heart was skipping beats and butterflies were wreaking havoc in her tummy – she couldn't bloody wait but, unfortunately, she'd have to. They were both exhausted and rat-arsed and he'd told her in a slurred voice that there was no way he was gonna attempt any kink with her when he couldn't even walk in a straight line or speak coherently, so they'd agreed to shower and go to bed – to sleep!

Damn! DAMN! She wasn't happy!

She'd been looking forward to a right royal shafting for two weeks. Yes, they'd had a lovely time on the train but she was after those hip-crunching thrusts he stood and delivered so well.

She'd already showered and was in his dark, mysterious bedroom, already in bed. Stewart joined her wearing just his boxers and he snuggled up to her 'Mmmmm you're so warm.'

Arms and legs entwined, holding each other close, they fell very quickly to sleep.

*

Scarlet's eyes fluttered open!

The room was very dark with the heavily blacked out windows not letting any sunlight in at all.

She reached for her phone on the nightstand – nine thirty a.m.

With the gentle light from her screen, she could see Stewart snuggled up under the duvet, still sound asleep and he looked incredibly adorable. Serene! His black bandana was still in place but had started to slip backwards and she knew he'd be horrified if it came off. His hairline had receded somewhat a few years back and he hated being seen without a head covering and wasn't yet ready for her to see him without one either which she respected so she reached out and softly inched it forward, trying her hardest not to awake him from his sweet slumber.

Bandana secured, she got out of bed as quietly as possible and toddled off to the bathroom for a wee and morning ablutions then to the kitchen.

She wanted to awake him with a nice, hot, steaming cuppa – his absolute favourite.

She rummaged through the cupboards for tea bags and honey, boiled the kettle and retrieved the milk from the fridge. As the kettle was boiling, she looked for something for breakfast but there was no food in sight. The fridge contained milk, bottled water and a tube of what seemed to be lube – *really? REALLY?* She laughed to herself, wondering what lube was doing in the fridge!

Tea made with a spoonful of honey, off back to the bedroom she went. Switching on the glowing lamps, she set his mug down on his bedside table, sat softly on the edge of the bed, leaned over and kissed his forehead.

'Wakey wakey, handsome!'

He stirred, taking a gentle deep breath and opened his eyes slightly, smiling when he saw her radiant face.

'Good morning, beautiful.'

He reached up to check his bandana before moving, looking relieved it was still where it was supposed to be then sat up against the pillows.

Handing him his mug, she said, 'I made you a cuppa.'

'Oooo thank you. Can't remember the last time I got tea in bed!'

'The first time of many, I hope,' she replied.

He smiled as he slurped the golden liquid.

'That's quite perfect – you found the honey then?'

'I did indeed – honey, tea, milk, water and not much else. There's nothing for breakfast!'

'Ah, well that's because I always eat out. There's a lovely lil café just down the road where I go for breakfast so my housekeeper only shops for the basics for when I arrive!'

'And did your housekeeper shop for lube too?'

He whipped his head up to look at her, beaming cheekily and laughed.

'NO! I brought that with me and popped it in the fridge last night!'

'But why is lube in the fridge?'

'Ah, that's for me to know and for you to find out.'

'The mind boggles!'

'Oh, trust me, it'll be boggling an awful lot more later!' he retorted with an eye flash and glint.

He finished off his tea, thanking her again then went off to the bathroom saying, 'Get dressed and we'll go for breakfast!'

'Oh fab. I'm bloody starving.'

*

They were sat outside the quaint Parisian café, cups of steaming coffee in front of them. They'd both ordered Gruyère omelettes which arrived accompanied by fresh, crunchy baguettes and butter – heaven!

Having devoured every last morsel and with more coffee delivered, he said, 'We need to discuss something, luv.'

'OK. You look quite serious – is there something wrong?'

'No, don't be silly! Nothing wrong per say – you mentioned yesterday that you'd been researching for this weekend and that you had a few tricks up your sleeve.'

'Yes, I wanted to be prepared to please you too.'

'Well, that's not what this weekend is about. It's about me introducing you to my world of kink and fetishes. Introducing you to the idea of domination and submission in the bedroom and ONLY the bedroom. Introducing you to pleasurable pain. That's what I invited you for. I want to be your guide, I want to show you MY way. Don't get me wrong, I very much appreciate you trying to come prepared for me, wanting to please me. It's incredibly touching and just confirms what a big heart you have but I don't want you learning from the seedy internet as it's full of nonsense. I'm much better placed to teach you what I know AND the way I like things!'

'Ah, so you want to control me then?'

'No No! Not at all! A lady should never be controlled. Ever! Ladies should be respected and revered. My endgame is to dominate you with your permission – I want you to submit to me willingly because you trust me with your heart, your soul and your body. But to get there, I need to prove all those things to you by gently easing you into it. Nothing will happen that you don't want to happen. Everything we do will be agreed upon by us both and we'll have a safe word so if at any time you feel uncomfortable or it's just too much, you use the safe word and I stop! I'm not into the heavy stuff but I am into pushing your body to it's limits and seeing where it takes us! Are you OK with that?'

'Yes, I am. I already trust you but I know what you're talking about is a different kind of trust and I'm willing to explore that with you.'

'Good. GOOD'

'But, why can't I try things on you? I don't get that.'

'Because you haven't a clue what you're doing. You can't just read it on the internet, think it looks exciting and rush to have a go. It's not a fairground ride! It's someone's body, someone's feelings and emotions and you need to fully experience it BEFORE you can inflict it on another person. I'd love to get there one day and reverse rolls with you but only after you've learned – do you get where I'm coming from? Am I making sense?'

'Yes, perfect sense actually. I hadn't thought of it from that point of view before so I apologise.'

'No, don't do that. You've nothing to apologise for. You were trying to do something exciting for me. And you can do, with pleasure, but not that, yet! Of course, you're welcome to excite me in any other way you please.'

'*Hmmmmm*, OK so I can only please you with licks and nibbles but you get to please me with whips and shackles?'

'Does that help you get your head around it, luv?'

'Yeah, it does.'

'Well, OK then. There ya go. That's the way it is for now.'

'Well, it seems to me that I get the better end of the stick as you do all the hard work and I get to lay back and languish in your lechery.'

He laughed, 'Exactly! BUT only if you WANT to. You don't just have to take it because I want to give it. You can say NO whenever you want and it won't make me think less of you. In fact, I'll respect you more for being brave and telling me NO YOU FILTHY PERVERT, YOU'RE NOT DOIN THAT!'

She cackled, 'I'll never call you a filthy pervert!'

'Oh I wouldn't say that just yet. I'm a kinky fucker so you just might!'

Scarlet shivered as a thought crossed her mind.

Stewart asked her, 'What?'

'Well, I'm just imagining you tying me up and whacking me with a stick, it made me quiver!'

'A STICK? I won't be beating you, Scarlet, but I may whip you silly,' he retorted with a wicked look on his face.

'Will I be able to even move come Monday?'

'I highly doubt it but don't worry, Eurostar has disabled access!'

They both roared with laughter.

He got up to settle the bill, snapping at her when she dared offer to pay it herself. 'No! A lady never pays for anything when she's with me!'

She smiled at him, graciously accepting his terms.

*

Back at the flat, after having popped to the shops for further essentials, they sat on Stewart's bedroom balcony overlooking the street, the Eiffel Tower visible in the distance. He wanted to go over a few things before relieving her of her clothes, senses and speech.

'OK, so you remember everything I told you right? Anything you're not comfortable with – ANYTHING – you use the safe word!'

'Yup. What's the safe word?'

'That's for you to choose – whatever you want.'

'How about Kiss Me?'

'That's two words!'

'Yeah, but if I'm in need of using it, I'll probably need kissing too – require a bit of soothing from those gorgeously plump lips of yours!'

'Haha, point taken. That's perfect then!'

'There's only one problem though – if you've turned me into a mumbling, bumbling imbecile, as you've wholeheartedly threatened, how am I supposed to say the safe word, *hmmmm*?'

'Oh you'll find a way. I promise you!'

They discussed a few more bits and bobs and headed for the bedroom.

He'd been in there on his own for a while after they got back, letting her know she wasn't to go in until after their chat.

Upon entering, the bed was stripped of the duvet and, on the end of the bed, was a black box tied with a beautiful red ribbon with her name elegantly written in script on a card.

'Open it,' Stewart said, gesturing towards it.

Scarlets eyes widened and her tummy churned.

'What is it?'

'Just open it'

She obliged, pulling at the pretty ribbon and lifting the lid.

Her eyes widened even more as she glimpsed the contents and she beamed from ear to ear.

The box contained the most delicate and intricately designed wine-coloured lace underwear: a plunge bra with an attached bodice, a pair of high-waisted Brazilian knickers with attached suspenders, the silkiest stockings and a matching silk mask.

'Oh my, Stewart, these are beautiful! Thank you – I don't quite know what to say!' and she hugged him tightly.

'You're very welcome but they're not just for you, they're for me too. I've been fantasising about you wearing 'em for a week! Pop into the bathroom and put 'em on for me. I'll be waiting with baited breath!'

Another glinting eye flash ensued with a cheeky lip-lick and he left his tongue poking out the corner of his slightly opened mouth and it was a good job she was changing her knickers as the ones she was wearing just got soaked!

Fuck, he knew exactly how to get her going! And he always seemed to do it at certain times, knowing she'd get riotously horny and not be able to do anything about it. Bloody rotten bugger!

She did as request and slinked into the feather soft undergarments. She also lathered herself in Cocoa and Cinnamon shimmering, edible body oil and misted herself with Dior L'Or Essence de Parfum – his absolute favourite!

She exited the bathroom to find him standing at the end of the bed in nothing but a pair of black leather trousers and knee-high black leather boots.

FUCK!

Damnable rogue – he knew that would turn her to jelly straight away. She'd told him previously how bloody aroused she got at the sight of him in his very tight leathers and boots with his ample cock and bollocks all squished in with no room to spare and he'd positioned them perfectly today, the very naughty bulgy man!

His eyes lit up when he saw her,

'Well, Fuck Me! You look tantalisingly edible.'

'Erm, so do you, Mr Bulgy!' she replied, gawping at his protruding crotch.

He looked down 'You like that don't ya? Makes you wet!'

'Mmmmhmmm,' was all she could manage as she licked her lips, warm trickles releasing from the other ones that were fluttering away.

Extending his hand towards her, he beckoned to her 'Come over here to me, I want to inspect you!'

She sidled over to him and he drank her in with his sparkling eyes.

'Exquisitely ravishing.'

She blushed and fluttered her eyelashes, looking down sheepishly. He lifted her chin with one finger and kissed her softly then pulled her into him and kissed her again, deeper and harder this time, pressing his hardened cock into her groin.

She moaned gently, 'I want you!'

Sliding his talented fingers between her thighs, through the side of her knickers and into her folds, he felt the fluid evidence of her arousal, replying, 'Mmmm, evidently! But not yet.'

She groaned disapprovingly, pouting and he giggled as he poked the end of her nose.

'Now, onto the bed with you, lil lady!'

He walked around the side of the bed, summoning for her to climb up and get comfy on her back against the plush pillows.

'Spread out your arms for me!'

She obeyed willingly as he gently but firmly tied each of her wrists to the bedposts with black, silk ties.

He then went back to the end of the bed and bent down, retrieving a small, black, vintage valise which he plonked on the mattress. He clicked it open to reveal its sordid contents which weren't many. He'd told her they'd be starting off lightly, just the minimum of requirements! Reaching inside with a look of glee on his chiselled face, he withdrew a short whip, a long, black feather and some sort of battery powered device.

'What's that? 'she enquired.

'This? This is a clitoral air stimulator!'

She wriggled slightly. 'I've seen those. They sound marvelous.'

'Shhhhh, no more words now,' was his very soft response.

He then reached for her silk mask that matched her lacy ensemble and walked back around to her, reaching towards her head.

'Wait! Take a step back into the light please. My eyes need just one more vision of you bulging out of those leathers!'

He grinned, stepping backwards for her so she could savour his heavenly self for a few moments.

'My gosh, you are a breathtaking sight!'

'Thank you. Now, hush.' And with that, he placed the mask over her head, tying it at the back.

With one of her senses now withdrawn, she tensed slightly.

'Relax,' he whispered, stroking her arm, still kneeling beside her. 'You've nothing to fear. Just relax and trust me!'

She felt him start to kiss her shoulder and heard him inhale deeply as he buried his nose in her hair.

'You smell so elegant. You're wearing my favourite scent and it's making me throb.'

She squirmed!

He continued with gentle kisses down her left arm and over her wrist 'A keyboard of delicate perfume – heaven!' then onto her palm, finishing off with light sucks on each of her elegantly clawed fingertips.

The feathery kisses continued across her belly to her right arm where he repeated the process, covering her in what felt like fluttering fairy wings.

Every now and then, she'd feel the tip of his warm tongue as it darted out to find her fevered skin.

She was moaning softly, her body trembling as it responded to his gentle touch.

He made his way over each breast, squeezing it as he went, down over her belly, her hips, her mound, each thigh, each calf, ankle and foot until he'd literally covered every inch of her in loving kisses.

She felt him leave the bed then return, a soft feather touching her face. He flicked it over her forehead, down her cheek and her neck until it rested on her heaving breasts.

He reached up, sliding her bra straps over her shoulders and lowered each cup, revealing her hardened, pink nipples then glided the feather back and forth over each one, making them grow even harder.

She could hear him making low, grunting noises as his arousal grew at the sight of her responding to him.

She started tugging slightly on her restraints, wanting so badly to touch him but he'd tied her up good and tight. She wasn't getting free that easily!

She sensed him approach closer then inhaled sharply and deeply as he engulfed her left nipple in his moist mouth, his talented tongue flicking as he sucked gently. Whilst he made of light meal of her left breast, he lowered the feather down the right side of her waist, over her hip then in towards her mound where he flicked it enticingly between her thighs, causing her to buck and whinny like a mare. Making his way over to the right side of her quivering body, he sated his appetite on her right breast, still flicking the feather between her now damp thighs. Then he brought his teeth into play as he pincered one of her nipples, holding it just tight enough for it to be mildly painful and she gasped. His tongue flicked back and forth as his teeth pinched and released over and over.

She could feel herself building as he continued to pry soft, whimpering cries out of her with his teeth, his tongue and that bloody feather that was driving her wild. Her back arched, pushing her breast further into his mouth as she orgasmed, letting out satisfied moans and gushing into her Brazilians.

His mouth left her nipple as she heard him say 'Good! One down, many more to go!'

Oh fuck no. She couldn't cope with more of this. It was making her quite mad with passion but she knew this was what he wanted – he wanted to push her to her limits before giving in but how on earth he was holding himself back from ripping her knickers off and fucking her to within an inch of her life was beside her. What a very clever, gifted lover he was!

Right now, all she wanted was to feel him between her legs, pushing into her with that engorged cock of his.

'I want you, please!'

'No! Not yet! Patience, madam!'

She kicked her legs in protest which made him laugh.

'Ah, here comes lil Miss Grumpy. Lovely!'

That made her even grumpier. Him being happy that she was suffering – the sadistic devil!

He went away then returned, a buzzing noise in the air.

She felt him unclip her suspenders and slide her panties down over her legs and feet, parting her thighs on his way back up before she heard a squelching noise then he parted her lips and placed what must have been the clitoral stimulator within her folds.

It was a gentle sensation at first, lightly tingling. Then she heard clicks and the sensation got stronger and stronger until,

'FUUUUUUCK!'

Her hips bucked upwards as her throbbing pearl was sucked into a tiny vortex and she knew he'd be smiling!

As it was a suction device, he didn't have to hold it in place so she could buck and flail about to her hearts content and it wouldn't budge.

He grabbed her hips to steady her, stroking her gently and telling her to breathe as she was panting wildly.

'Control your breathing darlin. Deep, steady breaths!'

Him stroking her helped and she focused on his voice which was very soothing indeed. His dark, molten voice could literally soothe her soul!

'Now, I want you to twist your hips slightly to your right and place your left leg over your right side!'

She attempted this but her legs were twitching and shaking as the device sucked her poor clit into oblivion.

She heard him giggle again!

'Will you stop bloody laughing and help me, man!'

'I do love it when you get cross – it's very exciting.'

'You're a sadistic bugger.'

'Oh darlin, you haven't seen or felt the half of it yet.'

With that, he flipped her left leg over her right and got her into the position he wanted.

And there she was, lying in a twisted heap, having an epileptic fit while he watched and enjoyed himself!

She was enjoying it too – immensely so but she felt out of control which she hated.

But he had warned her so she couldn't really complain, now could she?

Then came the part she'd been dreading – the whip!

She felt the soft leather graze her left bum cheek as he gently guided it across her damp skin. Then a soft flick – that wasn't so bad. He can do that again.

Then another, a little harder. *Hmmm*, that was OK too. Quite exciting in fact.

Then they started getting harder as he whipped her with exerted control, grunting as he did it, obviously incredibly aroused. She was inhaling through her front teeth as each whip made her wince but it was pleasurable.

He kept up the momentum, whipping her with rhythmic force as the evil little machine between her legs kept on engulfing her clit with a suction so powerful.

He'd set it to a certain rhythm: one, two, three short sucks then a fourth long one and her body convulsed in tandem with its rhythm and intensity and she had absolutely no control over any part of herself.

The whips got harder, more frequent and more painful until one was just too much.

'Kiss Me'

Another hard whack!

'Kiss Me!'

Yet another!

'KISSSS MEEE!'

'No Scarlet. Not yet. Be patient!'

'THAT'S THE SAFE WORD, YOU TWAT!'

He stopped abruptly.

'Oh fuck me, I'm soooo sorry, luv! So so sorry.' He gushed as he crawled up and held her. She was crying silent tears under her mask which were trickling down her cheeks and he wiped them away, kissing her gently between further offers of sincere apology.

'Please forgive me!'

'Of course I forgive you but you're still a twat!' She managed to utter in a tearful, quivering voice.

'Yes. Yes I am. I'm a twat!'

But as the hungry little gremlin between her legs was still going full throttle, the only relief she got was one of not being walloped into next week and she peaked again while he was kissing her. She bucked, cried out, trembled and gushed!

His merciless machine was now a very drenched little gremlin!

The convulsions slowing, he switched it off and removed it to her utter delight – relief!

With her little pearl now feeling like the size of a gold nugget, she flopped back down onto her back, writhing and panting.

'Oh my gosh! I don't know whether I love you or hate you right now, you delightfully evil tyrant!'

'Haha, probably both!'

Having disposed of his device, he climbed back on top of her, stroking her hair and kissing her tenderly.

'Ready for more?'

'Please be advised, dear, sweet man, that my legs are free so any more brutality may result in me crushing your gonads up into your abdomen!'

He roared.

'Ah well, I won't mind. I like a good gonad crushing!'

'You're such a freak.' She laughed out, still panting somewhat. 'OK, if you insist on submitting me to more of your perverse actions, please do so but not with so much force!'

'No more force, I promise. That was the worst of it.'

'Oh goodie!'

He reached behind her back and unclipped her bra, took it off and threw it across the room, starting to make a meal of her breasts again - teeth, tongue, lips, suction; he had such a powerful mouth!

With one hand cupping her left breast, he slid the other between her legs.

'Wooooooooooaaaaah, kiss me, kiss me, kiss me!' she wailed as pain seared through her sore fanny.

'What? What's wrong?'

'My clitoris is what's wrong. Fuck me, it's way too tender for you to be twisting it like a radio dial!'

'Shit, sorry. I'll be very gentle with it.'

'Please do!'

She felt him lick her face, her chin, her neck as he slid his middle finger inside her, avoiding her gleaming jewel as promised. He was very gentle and it felt sublime as he slid it in and out, slowly.

Continuing the devouring of her upper torso, he started gently biting her shoulders and neck, working his way down to her breasts then up again. He nibbled her nipples, her chest, her neck, her jawline then kissed her deeply, jutting his tongue passionately into her wanton mouth and she sucked on it.

She LOVED his long tongue – it drove her crazy so she kept hold of it for as long as she could, gorging herself on it.

As the dirty kissing got even dirtier, he removed his middle finger then slid it back in, together with his forefinger, stretching her walls.

She moaned into his mouth then threw her head back.

He lapped at her neck as she writhed against his hand, squirming and rocking her hips. It felt simply amazing – he had the most talented fingers and the friction they caused was so pleasurable, her moans turned into groans, her hips rocking harder.

'Are you ready for me, Scarlet?'

'Yes. YES! But please release me so I can touch and see you!'

'I will, I promise but not just yet!'

That said, he backed up onto his knees and she heard his zip as he slowly lowered it.

She so badly wanted to watch his hard, throbbing cock thud out of his restrictive leathers with passionate force and watch him hold it as he thrust it inside her but she just had to imagine it which made her even more aroused.

Atop her again, he placed one hand behind her head, lifted her hips with the other then brutally entered her, causing her to scream and, from there on in, there was no gentleness to him.

He pummelled her!

He knew that's what she wanted – he knew she loved him pounding her into oblivion.

And he did – with thrust after bone-jarring thrust, he ruined her lady parts, bruising her inner thighs with his hips, the zip of his leathers scratching her abdomen.

She'd ALWAYS wanted him to fuck her with his leathers and boots on and now he was.

She was in ecstatic heaven!

They crunched, banged, moaned, groaned and gasped as they made a heady meal of each other.

Then he slowed, withdrew, raised himself up onto his knees, released her wrists and gently removed her mask.

Finally, she could see him!

And what a sight he was: kneeling between her wet, trembling thighs, all sweaty and panting, leathers open, heavy, glistening cock suspended in mid-air, looking at her with those 'fuck me' eyes and his sexy tattoos on full display.

'Fuck me into tomorrow – NOW!' she ordered.

With that, he dived onto her, savagely pierced her soul with his cock and rode her like the wild beast that he was.

There was no tender kissing, no sweet nothings, no reprieve – just wild, maniacal fucking.

She held onto him as tight as she could, digging her nails into his glistening skin and biting his shoulders between high-pitched outcries.

He reached beneath her and lifted her hips, getting himself as deep as he could, each thrust getting faster and wilder as his breathing became more laboured, his deep moans turning to guttural groans as he neared his peak!

And with one final, brutal crunch, they exploded together.

She screamed like a banshee and he roared like a savage animal as liquid TNT gushed and squirted, engulfing their sexual parts in searing floods.

He remained within her as she convulsed, squeezing his beautiful cock with her elegant walls and he groaned; groaned deeply and huskily as he too, trembled in her arms.

She held him close and tight as they quivered in luxurious sync; hearts beating as one, sexes pulsating in perfect harmony, wheezing breaths making the most beautiful of melodies – Annihilated!

They remained there, in a conjoined, sweaty, breathless heap for a very long time, drinking in the beauty of their animalistic act.

He seemed to be taking his time to come down off his precipice so she soothed him with soft back scratches and loving caresses, stroking his head and shushing in his ear.

A few minutes passed and he lifted his head to look at her, kissing her once again.

'Are you OK, darlin?'

'I'm fine – it's you that I'm concerned about!'

'Oh I'm all right. Just takes me a little longer to recover sometimes but I'm OK. I promise.' And he kissed her again, softly, tenderly, lovingly.

'You genuinely care for me, don't you, Scarlet?'

'Yes, I do. Very, very much so!'

'Likewise.'

More loving kisses and warm, cozy cuddles ensued until,

'Shall we go and shower?'

'Erm, yeah but I think I'm quite literally glued to the sheet so I believe you'll need to peel me off.'

He helped her extricate herself from her entanglement of legs, sheets and sticky juices and she sat on the edge of the bed, her head in perfect line of sight with his groin.

'Fuck, I want to eat your cock SO badly!'

'Oh no you don't, young lady, that's quite enough for one day, thank you very much.'

'Oh, you spoil sport. I'm quite famished you know, you wouldn't deny a lady a meaty snack now, would you?'

'YESSSSS, I fucking would! Now, up with you and into the shower.'

'All right, but at least let me strip you of your leathers and boots?'

He grinned, giggled and nodded approvingly saying, 'If you must but no cheeky licks while you're at it Missus!'

She proceeded to peel him out of his sticky entrapments but the temptation was just way too strong so she blatantly ignored his orders and licked his beautiful pink tip.

'You naughty, naughty girl!'

She looked up at him, grinning wildly, licking her lips and making yummy noises 'Mmm mmm mmm, I do luurve a bit of juicy sausage, especially when I'm starved!'

'You're a wicked, disobedient wench. I'll get you for that tomorrow! You think you're a mess now? Just you wait. You won't know what's hit ya!'

'Oh my, are you gonna slap me about with your meaty sausage? Yaaayy!' she mischievously retorted, clapping her hands with glee.

'For fucks sake, will you shut up, you mad woman and get in the bloody shower!'

She couldn't stop laughing which, in turn, made him laugh too – roaring away they were.

Once thoroughly and stunningly naked, he leaned down and peeled off her rather damp stockings then put his hands under her arms and lifted her up, holding her in place. He knew her legs wouldn't work properly or even at all and he was right as they buckled beneath her straight away and she fell forwards into him. Thankfully, he had braced himself so instead of falling backwards into the wall, he managed to catch her 'I've got you, I've got you!'

'You've broken me! My legs don't work and my fanny feels like it's been split in two!'

More laughter.

'I've got something for your poor fanny for after your shower.'

'Have you?'

'Yeah, it's in the fridge.'

'Oh, the lube!'

'Well, it's not exactly lube. It's a soothing balm with Aloe Vera and Calendula for sore lady parts. I predicted the mess you're in!'

'Awwwww, my very own personal gynaecologist.'

'You're hilarious!' He giggled at her.

He helped her waddle like a cowgirl into the shower, he washed her off, dried her and helped her back to the room where he sat her on a chair whilst he changed the sheets.

He then popped off to the kitchen and fetched the lube from the fridge, came back and helped her onto the bed.

'Right, lie down and open wide.'

'Why?'

'So I can soothe your throbbing bits.'

'You're gonna put it on for me?'

'Yeah, I did this to you so I'll fix it.'

She lay back, opened her legs and he squirted from the tube.

The cold jelly felt divine, instantly soothing the raw heat between her lips. He gently spread it about, paying extra careful attention to her clitoris then went to wash his hands and came back with a very pretty deep purple negligée and matching panties.

'Another gift for you!'

'Oh Stewart, you are so sweet. It's beautiful. Thank you.'

He slid the panties over her feet, up her thighs and over her hips then helped her sit up and slid the nightie over her head. He went on to arrange pillows carefully behind her for maximum comfort and disappeared again, returning with a bottle of wine, two glasses and another glass filled with fizzing liquid.

'What's that?'

'It's painkillers. You'll need 'em, luv.'

'You've thought of everything it would seem!'

'You can't just ruin a lady then leave her to pick up her own pieces. Aftercare is hugely important.'

'Come here!'

He did and she kissed his forehead.

'You're a very special man, you know and I'm a very lucky lady!'

'I'm the lucky one!'

'Now, drink your medicine and have some wine while I go and order dinner and shower. When I get back, we'll kick back, stuff our faces with pizza and brownies with ice cream and watch mindless telly, yes?'

'Oh yes. Sounds bloody perfect to me!'

'Oh, when you're ordering pizza, could you please order some—' She couldn't finish her question as he interrupted with,

'Coke Zero? Yes. Already on the list. I know you need your caffeinated fizz after a thorough rogering!'

'Hahaaaa, brilliant! Thank you'

'My pleasure, Madam.'

And off he popped to complete his ablutions.

She drank her medicines, retrieving her wine from her nightstand and lay back against the pillows to take the pressure off her throbbing nether regions. The pain and heat were definitely subsiding but the throbbing was still quite powerful.

As she languished in sated bliss, she pondered over the events of the day and how bloody lucky she was to have him.

She'd never thought it possible!

She'd wanted, craved him for so long and now, here she was in Paris with him treating her like a Queen.

And she pinched herself, wondering what tomorrow would bring!

Part 5 – Paris – Sunday

Scarlet awoke to the feeling of a hand on her face; a soft, soothing hand gently stroking her cheek.

As her eyes batted open, there he was. A beautiful sight for sore eyes, lovingly peering at her though darkened lenses, a warm smile on his stunning face.

'Good morning, young lady.'

'Good morning, old man.' She sleepily sighed back at him 'What time is it?'

'It's eleven fifteen. I let you sleep in as I figured you'd need it after last night's shenanigans.'

'You wrecked me!'

'I know and I'm not sorry,' he retorted with a giggle.

'Evil brute!'

He chuckled.

'Right, up you sit. I've brought you breakfast!'

'I think I may need help – I feel like I've been hit by a bus!'

He leaned over and helped her sit up. Again, arranging the pillows comfortably behind her then left the room.

When he came back, he was carrying a tray which he placed on her lap.

'Coffee, baguette, butter, jam and chocolate croissants for madam!'

'Oh my, bloody perfect. You clever man.'

'If you're gonna make it through this weekend, you're gonna need carbs luv, so eat up.'

'Oh I will. I could eat a horse.'

He kissed her forehead and told her his plans for the afternoon while she rather ravenously stuffed herself.

He was taking her to Versailles – a place she'd ALWAYS wanted to visit as she adored French history, especially the Louis XIV period. It fascinated her so she was very excited indeed.

Stewart helped her choose what to wear – an empire waisted, burgundy midi dress with an embroidered scroll design, black knee-high boots and a fitted 50's style black bolero. Chic and elegant!

She showered, dressed and fixed her make-up, piling her raven locks into a chignon on top of her head and finished it all off with long, gold and pearl chandelier earrings and, of course, a generous spritz of Dior.

She was just having a final check over in the mirror when he appeared behind her 'Well, fuck me! You look beautiful!'

'You're not so bad yourself,' she responded with a cheeky grin.

He was wearing black dress jeans, a black shirt open to his chest with a part of his tattoo visible. His burgundy velvet waistcoat was over the top and a black bandana and grey peak cap finished it off! Bloody hell, he looked the perfect sexy, roguish gentleman and she was salivating.

He must have noticed her dribbling as he quickly chimed up, slowly backing away from her. 'Now now, don't you go getting any filthy ideas, woman. We have a car waiting!'

She approached him step by step as he continued to back away, right up to the bedroom wall. She got right up close, licked his chest and grabbed his crotch.

He batted her hand away while laughing out 'Behave yourself!'

She was giggling and grabbing at him, his cock now protruding, making his jeans stick out.

'Now look what you've done, you naughty lady!'

'Awww, I'm so sorry. Would you like me to ease your discomfort, darling?'

'NO! GO AWAY!'

'Hey, listen, it's not my fault you're such a sexy fucking scoundrel!'

'Just control yourself, woman! Keep your hands and that dribbling mouth of yours to yourself…until later!'

'Well, OK. If I must.' She sighed. 'What about your soldier? He's still standing to attention!'

'Well exactly. I can't go out like this now, can I? So back off and leave me alone so I can calm down, you wicked temptress.'

She backed off, hands in the air, laughing her head off then spun about and fetched two clean pairs of knickers from her drawer.'

'What are they for?' he enquired.

'Ummm, the ones I'm wearing are a tad damp!'

'Oh for fucks sake, really?'

'You have that effect on me! I'm always dripping!'

He was grinning from ear to ear.

'But why two pairs?'

'One to change into now and another to change into later after you inevitably make me wet again!'

He roared with laughter, shaking his head.

She quickly changed her knickers and they headed downstairs where a car was waiting to whisk them off to Versailles.

*

She'd managed to curb her cravings en route to the palace although it took every ounce of control. All she wanted to do was unzip his jeans, extricate his delicious cock and devour it in the back of the car.

She was obsessed with his divine appendage which he knew and that is why every item of clothing he chose to wear hugged his hips, showcasing his generous groin in all its blazing glory. The devious rascal!

They'd spent the afternoon floating through the palace halls with her holding his arm the entire time. The difference between him in public and him in private was stark – a chivalrous gentleman in public and a savage beast in the bedroom!

They were both fluent in French so they were able to read all the historical articles on display and navigate their way with ease.

It was breathtaking, especially the gardens where they'd stopped to sit and take in the lavish resplendence of it all and where he'd stolen a sweet, warm, romantic kiss from her amidst the roses. It was dusk at the time and as they sat on a bench, new fountains sprung up, the water lit by the pretty lights that flickered on and it was then that he'd kissed her! The blissful man!

'Time to go, lil lady. We have a table booked for an early dinner. And I don't know about you, but I'm rather hungry!'

'Oh no, do we have to go? It's so lovely here!'

'They'll be closing soon anyway and you'll not want to miss this restaurant. It's not easy to get a table but I managed to swing it especially for you so we really do need to go.'

'Well, in that case, Allons-y, Monsieur!'

*

They arrived at the restaurant at six fifteen p.m. and were greeted by a Maître D in a tailcoat who ushered them to their table.

The interior was sumptuous and stunning!

Most of the tables were set back into half moon nooks with plush red velvet covered benches and black tablecloths that hung to the floor. The décor was red and black with softly lit golden wall sconces and golden candles on the tables.

Two chairs were on one side of the table but they chose to slide into the nook on the half circle bench and sit close together.

They were provided with a wine list, menus and a jug of iced water but Stewart quickly ordered the wine in beautifully spoken French which the waiter hastily delivered and poured. They toasted each other, clinked their glasses and took deep swallows of deliciousness.

Once they'd ordered their starters and main courses, they had a chat about their afternoon, reliving the excitement and beauty.

They got through the first bottle of wine very quickly so another was ordered as they were enjoying their first course.

They were chatting away when an older and rather stuffy looking couple approached their table.

'Stewart, so lovely to see you! How are you old fellow?'

Stewart stood up, shook the man's hand who then introduced him to his wife.

'Lovely to meet you, Mary. This is my lovely lady, Scarlet.'

Scarlet stood and shook both their hands, smiling kindly, 'It's a pleasure.'

The men exchanged pleasantries, pointing out how long it had been when the older man, Charles, piped up 'May we join you both? Seems silly to sit separately!'

Stewart looked at Scarlet who nodded politely. Neither of them wanted extra company. This was their special weekend but how could they politely say 'No. Fuck off'? They couldn't so they agreed, hiding their reluctance.

Charles and Mary sat down on the chairs, ordered their own drinks and food and the evening continued.

It actually wasn't that bad. There was good conviviality and a few jokes. It was pleasant enough but Scarlet, after one too many glasses of red, was itching to get her hands on Stewart and she'd sidled up closer and closer to him over time.

They'd finished their main courses but Charles and Mary were just starting theirs so it was going to be a while till they could politely excuse themselves so Scarlet, having no inhibitions or filter after buckets of wine, slid her hand under the table and started massaging Stewart's cock through his jeans which made him flinch.

He gave her a stern side glance, trying not to be obvious and attempted to push her hand away but she was having none of it, sat there grinning wickedly and she held her own, refusing to move her hand. She continued her light strokes under the tablecloth which was very long so it hid the movement of her arm.

His cock was hard and bulging and he looked a little flushed but he kept it together as he continued chatting with their guests.

Scarlet then decided to up the anti by quietly undoing his belt and very slowly unzipping his jeans, letting his pulsating shaft get some air and space.

There was never ever enough space for that monster in any of his trousers. It was always squished in with his bulgy bollocks with no room to breathe, the poor thing!

She gently retrieved it from his boxers and peeled back his skin, brushing his head with her thumb. Stewart inhaled sharply, flinching again and clenching his jaw.

Her lips started to tingle as she sat there, massaging his shaft up and down, over and over again, rubbing his head with her thumb and watching him desperately trying to control himself in this very public setting.

She could see he was bloody fuming with her but also enjoying every stroke, every rub and every filthy second of her manual invasion and she noticed him swallow hard, his Adam's Apple bobbing in his throat.

He was constantly licking and sucking his lips which wasn't unusual as it was a habit anyway but tonight, it was more excessive than usual.

He became fidgety and kept coughing to cover up his grunts as she rhythmically drew him closer to his peak.

To her, this was the most gloriously erotic sight – him sat there, all virile, gorgeous, delighted and cross, the muscles in his jaw visibly clenching, attempting to control himself while she wanked him under the table. It made her squirt into her knickers. *Good job she'd brought clean ones in her handbag!*

Her hand got slightly faster, its grip tighter as she felt him tense. She knew his release was close so she buried his head between his boxers and jeans so he wouldn't shoot his stickiness onto the restaurants plush, pristine carpet.

As he exploded, his hips surged forward. He couldn't help himself and he coughed loudly, his eyes watering.

'Are you quite all right, Stewart? Are you unwell old chap?' chimed in Charles.

'Oh no, no. I'm fine. Just a slight tickle in my throat.'

'I must say, you're looking rather peaky and flushed!' exclaimed Mary. 'Are you sure you're not coming down with something?'

Scarlet decided to be naughty and injected the words 'Oh, he's definitely "cumming" down with something!' Emphasising on the word "cumming" with a very cheeky grin on her face.

Charles and Mary frowned quizzically and Stewart coughed again, giving her another stern look.

As she knew he'd be a bit sticky, she decided to take it further.

She accidentally on purpose knocked her spoon off of the table and as she fished about under the tablecloth, she pushed it further away with her foot, giving her the excuse to get onto her knees to retrieve it. As she dove into the tablecloth layers on the hunt for her spoon, she purposefully made a b-line for Stewart's lap, grabbed his glistening cock, sucked it and licked it clean. He jumped, accidentally kneeing her in the chin and causing her to bang her head on the table 'Fuck!' she involuntarily let slip then followed it with drunken giggles.

'What are you doing under there, Scarlet?' Mary enquired as she lifted the tablecloth to have a look.

Luckily, she'd managed to drape the tablecloth over his lap so all Mary saw was her rummaging about for her spoon which she finally found, returning to her seat looking slightly dishevelled.

'You do know the waiter would have brought you another spoon?' said Mary.

'Oh, I know but I like to be helpful.' Scarlet shrugged back. 'Now, if you'll excuse me, I'll pay a visit to the ladies room!'

She tipsily made her way to the toilet, leaving Stewart slightly breathless and red in the face, with a crotch full of semen and she knew without a shadow of a doubt that he was gonna make her pay for it later! At least, she hoped he was – she wanted him to. That's why she'd done it. That and she just wanted to watch him squirm and be all sexy while he did it.

She hurriedly changed her soaking knickers, threw them in the bin and made her way back to the table where she found the three of them looking at dessert menus.

As she sat down, Stewart asked her what she'd like for dessert.

'Something "creamy"!' she replied, again with a naughty grin.

He GLARED at her, his eyes boring into her soul. He looked so cross and she loved it. It was very erotic!

They ordered dessert, Tiramisu for both herself and Stewart with coffees all around.

Their desserts delivered, Scarlet made a point of looking at Stewart every time she took a mouthful from her spoon, licking it clean with her tongue.

His face was quite a picture, a mixture of savage want, steady control and frustrated anger! It made Scarlet very aroused and amused at the same time.

Their dinner at an end and with Charles and Mary having taken their leave, Stewart called for his car to collect them.

They exited the restaurant and as they were awaiting their pick up, he powerfully grabbed her arm, pulled her to face him and said very forcefully through hissing teeth 'Madam, you have NO idea what you have done or what awaits you at home! I suggest you brace yourself because I'm seething and you, young lady, are in for one hell of a pounding! I promise you, by the time I'm done, you won't be able to walk, talk, sit down or think straight!'

'Oh goodie.' She gushed as she clapped with glee 'I can't wait!'

All she got was another glare but this time, there was a hint of a grin and a slight sparkle in his eyes. He knew she'd been goading him for a purpose, winding him up into a frenzy just so he'd be all cross and dominant. What she didn't realise, however, was just how dominant he could be and exactly what he had in store for her. That wicked grin and sparkle wasn't at her gleeful reaction, it was at her absolute ignorance of what was to come.

She was in for the shock of her life!

*

The car journey home was surprisingly cheerful with them laughing and joking. He'd kissed her a couple of times, quite tenderly and had her snuggled up under his arm the entire way.

But this was all part of his plan. He was lulling her into a false sense of security, wanting her to think his forceful declaration outside the restaurant had been nothing but his immediate reaction to her wilful, salacious behaviour. And it was working! She was none the wiser and little did she know that she was about to receive a sound pummelling.

He helped her out of the car, unlocked his front door and they made their way up the stairs, giggling and canoodling.

He unlocked the second door at the top of the stairs, stepped in and held the door open for her.

No sooner had he shut and locked it, he grabbed her from behind, both arms tightly about her waist, pinning her own arms to her side.

She gasped as he growled in her ear then he spun her about, bent over, threw her over his shoulder and carried her into the bedroom, throwing her down on the bed.

The look of shock on her face was priceless – hazel eyes all wide and glistening.

'Don't move!' He barked as he removed her boots.

He grabbed her ankles, dragged her to the foot of the bed, stood her up, yanked her bolero off then literally ripped her dress from the hem up to her chest.

'Hey, I like this dress!'

'Tough! I'll buy you a new one.'

He ripped the torn fabric from her shoulders and arms, snapped her bra off at the back, turned her about and threw her back on the bed.

'Stay there!' he commanded as he went to his dresser.

She was shaking and nervous but very excited and willing so did as she was told.

He returned with silk ties which he used to secure her wrists behind her back then reached up and released her hair from its elegant knot on top of her head. Reaching under her belly, he yanked her hips upwards and got her into a kneeling position with her shoulders down, head on the bed then fished beneath the mattress and pulled out his whip.

Then just stopped dead still!

Silence – apart from her quickened breathing and his low, guttural growls.

The silence was soon broken by his husky voice,

'I need your consent Madam. Do I have it?'

She turned her head as far as she could to look at him. 'I don't know what it is I'm consenting to but I trust you so, yes! You have my willing consent!'

He looked raw – a savageness in his eyes and on that chiselled face, his jaw clenching again.

He'd removed his waistcoat and shirt and was left in just his jeans. Fuck, he looked so damned sexy, masculine and animalistic! She didn't know why she wanted this but she did, very badly. She WANTED him to dominate her here, in this moment with all his virile power.

'Now, I need you to push yourself to the absolute limit tonight. I'm bloody FUMING and as horny as hell so only use the safe word when you're at your limit! OK?'

She nodded back at him, biting her lower lip.

'I'm ready!'

'Face forward, head on the bed!'

She obeyed.

Silence again followed by the feeling of cool leather on her back, softly trailing down her spine, over her restrained wrists and down to her buttocks.

Then a light whip on each cheek in quick succession.

Then again, a soft trail of leather down her spine, over to her waist this time followed by a light whip on her thigh, over to the other side, then the other thigh. All very sensual!

He repeated this, getting a little faster each time, each whip increasing in intensity and they now started to smart, her skin stinging!

He only whipped her on her buttocks and thighs, nowhere else. Never anywhere else!

He grunted, growled and hissed as he put more power into each stroke of the whip.

Noises began to escape her throat as the pain started to build on her delicate skin.

She knew she had to try to take as much as she could. After all, she did this to him. She wound him up like a tightly coiled spring and now she had to let him unwind, so she bravely bore it.

Until, he stopped, climbed onto the bed behind her and slipped two fingers between her tingling, aching lips and pushed them deep inside her, giving her a few strokes.

She let out a whimper.

He had very experienced fingers and knew exactly what to do with them and she pushed back against his hand which he removed immediately.

He got off the bed and whipped her again, always egging her on with teasing strokes of the leather strands on her spine, making her shiver.

Then the fingers again, in and out, stroking her into a maddening frenzy but as soon as she pushed back, he stopped and whipped her again.

It drove her positively wild; mad with want and need and she was able to handle the stinging pain from the whip as he cleverly built her restraint.

She was hot, panting, whimpering but not crying out.

She knew she had to handle more, wanted to handle more, for him!

He repeated his savage cycle a few more times, each lash increasingly harder than the last, her skin burning, her insides yearning for his fingers.

They entered her one last time, more forcefully, stretching her walls and creating friction.

A piercing cry escaped her quivering lips – it was a most blissful pain and she pushed back hard one more time but he quickly withdrew them and began lashing her again..

But this time, THIS TIME, it was too much. It now hurt!

Her skin was already inflamed and she'd taken as much as she could bear. She was crying, tears streaming down her rosy cheeks and she sobbed 'KISS ME, STEWART, KISS ME!'

She heard the whip hit the floor as he unlatched his belt, unzipped his jeans, climbed up behind her, pulled her Brazilians aside and brutally entered her, pummelling her with those powerful hips and that incredibly strong, virile cock; his skin slapping on her already red, inflamed cheeks, his hot shaft pulverising and decimating her insides.

She was gonna be very sore and red raw but she didn't care as THIS was what she'd been waiting for; his dominant thrusts, pounding her into a wild delirium!

He reached forwards and grabbed a handful of her hair, pulling it backwards, his other hand holding her tied wrists like reins as he rode her maniacally, his growling and groaning blending beautifully with her whimpers and cries.

His stamina was staggering as he kept going, keeping up the momentum, each thrust more forceful than the last. What an unrelenting, powerful machine of a man he was – how on earth was he still going? She hadn't realised just how tight she'd wound him!

She could feel herself building up to an earth-shattering explosion and hoped to goodness he was too. Her insides were like jelly and her ovaries were toast, her arms were aching and her arse was throbbing as his hips continued slapping her cheeks.

Then he quickened his speed.

She didn't think his pounds could get any harder but they did. She thought at one point he was gonna shoot her flying through the wall into next door!

Then with one final, bone-shattering blow, he howled.

This man literally howled like a Viking Berserker after conquering in battle. A sound she'd never heard before – it was fucking beautiful and it finished her off.

And she matched it with her own Valkyries war cry as hot, boiling floods squirted everywhere. The most powerful orgasm of her life, even more powerful than the one she'd had at his London home. Her walls convulsed around his throbbing, pulsating cock as they drowned each other in liquid bliss.

He was deep inside her, hunched over her back, panting, still pulsing within and she was a whimpering, quivering puddle beneath him!

He felt so heavy but somehow it was comforting as the pressure of his body took her thoughts away from the pain in her lower regions.

He started kissing her back and untied her wrists, her arms flopping like wet noodles onto the bed. Totally depleted, she collapsed beneath him, a flat, soggy pancake, covered in his sweet syrup and slightly burned at the edges and he crumbled on top of her and they lay there, gasping for air for what seemed like hours!

*

'Scarlet? Scarlet?'

She didn't respond as she was in a deep sleep.

Stewart peeled himself off of her and went to the bathroom to shower, running her a warm, Epsom salt and calendula bath as he abluted himself.

Returning to the bedroom after drying and adorning clean boxers, he took in the exquisite sight that was her, lying face down on the rumpled sheets, breathing deeply and slowly – she looked so serene and beautiful.

Then he noticed how red her buttocks and thighs were and his stomach churned, feeling guilty at the thought of what he'd done to her. But she'd taken it, handled it all like a trooper and he was so very proud of her.

He leaned over the bed and tried to rouse her, gently stroking her hair and whispering her name in her ear. She started to come to and opened her eyes.

'Hey, there she is! Time for a soothing bath I think, my lovely.'

'*Hmmmm*, that sounds nice,' she croaked back at him, her throat a little hoarse and her voice weak.

He helped her to a sitting position but she winced loudly.

'Fuck!' Tears welling up in her eyes.

He hugged her gently, profusely apologizing.

'I'm so sorry darling!'

She took his face in her hands, whispering, 'No Stewart, do not apologise. I wound you up deliberately and not only did I get what I deserved, I got what I wanted – your experienced dominance. And although it was sometimes tough to bare, I loved every minute of it so you, my gorgeous, darling man, have nothing to be sorry for!' And she kissed his beautiful lips warmly.

He gave her one of his gleaming smiles and tried helping her to her feet but it wasn't happening as she was too weak to stand but he had to get her off her poor bottom as the sheets, even though they were buttery soft, were rubbing against her raw skin.

So he scooped her up with surprising ease, one arm beneath her knees and the other behind her waist and carried her gallantly to the bathroom where he, again very surprisingly, lowered her carefully into the warm water.

'Ahhhhh, that's SO nice. Oh my gosh!'

'There are Epsom salts and calendula oil in the water. They'll soothe your raw skin and sore lady parts. Just soak for a while, OK?'

He kissed her forehead as he left her alone to wallow and float away on a delightfully relieving cloud.

Before he'd awoken her, he'd also lit candles and put on some beautiful music, *LoFi Hip Hop,* which was her favourite for relaxing!

She lowered herself down further, nestled her neck onto the soft bath pillow and closed her eyes, allowing the water and music to carry her away.

About fifteen minutes had passed when he came back with a steaming mug of very rich hot chocolate and a glass with fizzing pills in it.

'Painkillers and hot cocoa!'

'Ooooo heavenly. Thank you, my love.'

He sat on the edge of the bath. 'How are you feeling?'

'Erm, sore but content and thoroughly dominated.'

'You keep mentioning that word – what is it about domination that excites you so much?'

'It's not just any old domination, it's YOUR domination! You're such a masculine, virile, experienced man and I find it so very arousing and captivating. Yes, I want the sweet, slow, gentle lovemaking but I also want you to sort me out with those skilful hands, gifted mouth and powerful cock!'

His face lit up like a Christmas Tree.

'Well, you've certainly been sorted out, young lady!'

She just beamed at him as she necked the now fully effervesced medicines and started sipping on the unctuous dark brown liquid in the mug.

'Mmmm, what's that odd taste? It's very yummy but it's not just chocolate?'

'I added a decent heap of turmeric for your inflammation!'

'Well, aren't you full of surprises!'

'I know you're into natural remedies so I've done a little research of my own in your honour.'

'That's why I love you so. You're so thoughtful, caring and attentive!'

She noticed a strange look on his face.

'What?'

'You said you love me!'

'Ah! Yes, that's because I do, Stewart.'

'Wow! I'm incredibly touched but also terrified!'

'Why?'

'Just past experiences.'

'Darling man, you can trust me. I WILL NOT hurt you, ever! I want to help you vanquish all your demons and put the broken pieces of your heart back together, not break you further, if you'll let me. I love you yes, but I care about you very very deeply too and want to make you happy.'

His eyes were watery and she knew she'd touched a nerve. She reached out, took his hand in hers and kissed it, resting her soft cheek on the back of it, hoping he wouldn't snatch it away.

Her heart leaped when she felt him stroke her cheekbone with his thumb and she swallowed her tears. She looked up at him, both of them teary eyed and he leaned in to kiss her deeply, cradling her face.

It was a life-altering moment – the moment he realised he could completely trust her with his heart, mind, body and soul. He'd seen it in her eyes and felt it in her heartfelt words.

The kiss was so tender and loving, as he gave himself over to her. As he pulled away slightly, he responded, 'I know. I believe every word. But can you give me time? I find it hard to express love in words.'

'I know you do. Take all the time you need because, I promise you, I'm not going anywhere. I'm right here, by your side, for as long as you allow me to be.'

He kissed her again, wiped his eyes and disappeared, probably to compose his emotions.

She polished off her warm drink and lay back again, wanting to spend as much time in the bath as possible. Her skin already felt much better but her poor vagina was still throbbing. Blimey, his cock was so powerfully generous! She should nickname him 'Vlad the Impaler'.

As she soaked away, she put one foot on each side of the bath, allowing the water access to her parts and she stayed like that for a while.

He returned a little later, brandishing a very fluffy bath robe.

'Ooo, what a lovely sight!' he exclaimed, eyes wide with excitement at the vision of her spread-eagled in the bath. 'But I think it's time to get you out before you turn into a shrivelled prune.' He giggled at her. 'And it must be getting a bit cold by now too.'

'It's lost its warmth, yes.'

He took her mug and with his arms under her knees and waist again, strongly lifted her out of the bath, carefully setting her onto her feet. Her legs didn't give way but they were still quite weak and they shook beneath her.

He wrapped her in the cozy robe and guided her to the bedroom where he sat her on a chair and proceeded to dry the ends of her hair.

After standing her up and drying off her trembling body, he lay her down on the clean sheets that he'd put on while she was bathing, opened her legs and put more of the lube he kept in the fridge on her sore, swollen honeypot then turned her over onto her front.

She felt a warm sensation on her buttocks as he squeezed calendula and aloe vera cream that he'd heated in the microwave on her buttocks and thighs, smearing her with a thick layer, then slipped her into the softest black cotton pyjamas, all while she was still lying on her front.

'Now, just stay like that for a few minutes while I go and order some food. I know we had dinner but I'm bloody starving and you must be too.'

'Ravenous!' she exclaimed.

She lay there, allowing the cream to soak into her skin. It was amazing stuff as it was working already.

She must have dozed off because when he came back, he had two large takeaway pots of Chow Mein, a portion of sweet and sour chicken, a box of spring rolls and an ice-cold bottle of Coke Zero for her.

'Do you think you can sit now, luv?'

'I don't know until I try!'

She rolled over carefully and lay herself up against the pillows he'd previously arranged for her,

'Ooooo shit! That's sore!'

'Hang on,' he said, as he got a bolster cushion from the chair and placed it beneath her knees, relieving the pressure from her hips.

'Better?'

'Yes, much. Thank you, sweet man!'

'Right, let's eat!'

He handed her her noodles with some of the chicken, spring rolls and a fork. 'Tuck in.'

They both sat in the bed, eating, chatting, joking and laughing.

Once they'd polished off every last crumb, he tidied up the dishes, switched off the lights, climbed back into bed next to her, snuggled her up closely and popped the telly on.

And there they lay, watching a movie until they fell sound asleep in each other's loving arms.

Part 6 – Paris and London – Monday

It was Monday morning, the final day of their special weekend.

They'd awoken at eight forty-five a.m. but hadn't arisen straight away. Instead, they'd sleepily snuggled very closely for close to an hour; not talking, no spoken words, just silent closeness.

Stewart felt different somehow; softer! Softer in his manner, softer in his voice, softer in his eyes. She liked to think that this slight tender change was due to her loving declaration the previous evening.

Had she managed to slightly crack the fortress surrounding his heart? Chiselled a little bit of it away?

She didn't quite know but she was gonna hold onto this for dear life as it was heart-melting.

She didn't just want his strong, masculine body but his entire being – body, heart, mind and soul! All of it and everything that came with it. Even the negative, dark stuff that lurked beneath the surface and all of his mental demons! As long as he was willing to let her in, she was ready to delve deep and deal with whatever she encountered with compassion, understanding, patience and lots of unconditional love.

They'd packed their bags, breakfasted at his favourite café and headed for Gare Du Nord in time to catch the 12:13 Eurostar back to St. Pancras where they'd arrived at 13:30 GMT to find his car waiting.

He'd received a call from his PA whilst on the train, alerting him to a work issue and he'd had to arrange to go into his office to handle it which put him into a bit of a mood. He wasn't happy at all.

As they approached their awaiting transport, Scarlet had an idea. One that, she hoped, would cheer him up. 'Stewart, instead of taking me home, why don't you drop me to yours? I could wait for you there!'

'Gosh no. You'll be bored! I'll be a good few hours.'

'No, I won't. I've got some writing and admin to take care of which can be done on my iPad. I'll be just fine! Unless, you'd prefer it if I went home. Either is fine. I just have a feeling your afternoon at work is gonna stress you out even more than your phone call did and thought you'd like to go home to a smiling face.'

'That's very thoughtful of you! How do you know the call stressed me out?'

'You've been rather quiet and lost in thought, sucking your lips excessively and playing with your facial hair for hours!'

He grinned and nodded. 'How observant of you and how very thoughtful too. Yeah, why not!'

'Perfect,' she responded, as she planted a light kiss on his cheek.

The journey to his house was a quiet one and she could see his mind was elsewhere so she remained silent to allow him space to think.

On the way, they'd stopped at a local supermarket so she could pick up some supplies as he rarely had much of anything in his fridge or cupboards, except honey, tea bags and milk which was probably sour by now.

He'd dropped her at his house, giving her his keys and telling her to make herself at home, waited to make sure she got inside OK then sped away in his chauffeur driven Audi.

Inside was a bit stuffy so she opened a few windows throughout and made herself a cup of coffee whilst packing away the groceries she'd purchased.

She'd bought the makings for dinner too without him knowing as she planned to welcome him home to a yummy evening meal. The way to a man's heart is often through his stomach and he did love his pasta so she'd carefully chosen ingredients for Fettuccini Carbonara which she made rather well and which she also knew was one of his favourites.

She'd then made herself some sourdough toast with avocado, spinach and eggs and ensconced herself at his dining table to work for a couple of hours!

*

It was almost five p.m. when she'd finished and she'd received a text from Stewart advising he was going to be later than expected. She'd responded by asking him if all was going well and he'd informed her that things were a bit of a mess and that she'd been right about it being very stressful which made her glad she was there and she planned to make damn sure he had nothing to stress about once at home. Quite the opposite! As well as dinner, she had other plans. Rather naughty ones!

She headed for the kitchen and prepared all the ingredients for the carbonara then washed her raven locks in the shower before running herself a bath, opening a bottle of red wine and languishing in the steamy water she'd laced with beautifully smelling oils.

She wanted to look, feel and smell heavenly for him.

Once washed and dried, she slipped into a bath robe and blow-dried her hair into shiny swirls of delight then popped it up into a soft ponytail and applied a fresh face of makeup. Nothing dramatic, just soft, pretty and natural.

She poured herself another glass of wine and went for a rummage in his closet for a clean pair of tight, hip hugging leathers, a sleeveless T-shirt, his chunky belt, silky boxers and black boots, laying them out carefully on his bed.

Back in the dining room, she found a block of sticky notes and wrote a few instructions for him on a few of them.

She checked the time – six fifteen p.m. – time to get dressed.

She retrieved her deep red casual, floaty peg trousers from her suitcase along with a long sleeved, black V-neck tunic blouse, dressed and headed back to the kitchen to start cooking.

She'd also bought the makings for fresh, cheesy garlic bread so began with that; softening salted butter, mixing freshly pressed garlic, parsley and Parmesan, spreading it liberally onto crunchy baguette and popped it in the oven on a low heat.

She fried of the chopped bacon and spring onions (her own secret ingredient) and set it all to one side.

As she didn't know exactly when to expect him, she decided to text him for an ETA.

He responded with, I'm literally just leaving now. Gonna pick up a takeaway on the way home. What shall I get?

Nothing. Just come home 🐾

I'm STARVING, Scarlet. I need to eat.

Yep. I figured you would be, so I've already sorted dinner. Just please come straight home, Stewart 🐾

She always sent emojis - he didn't but it was a habit for her.

Oh really? What have you ordered?

Stop asking questions and get your sexy backside home 😉 How long will you be?

Well yes, Ma'am! About 30 mins depending on traffic. I'll text again when I'm 10 mins away.

OK. See you soon gorgeous 🔥

Time to get to work on her devious plan!

She went to her suitcase, dug out the burgundy underwear he'd gifted her in Paris which she'd hand washed and her Dior perfume and hid them away in his spare bathroom.

She then began the process of running him a lovely hot bubble bath in his en-suite, making it extra hot so even if it cooled, it would still be hot enough for him. She lit candles, got Alexa set up with soft jazz music, placed a bottle of wine and a glass on the table next to the tub and headed back to the kitchen where she retrieved the sticky notes and placed them where she wanted them.

Back in the kitchen, she boiled water for the pasta, separated eggs and grated more Parmesan all whilst knocking back more wine. She'd almost finished her first bottle so she opened another. *Oops!*

Time check – six forty-five p.m. *Fifteen mins to go, hopefully!*

Most of the cooking was done so she dimmed the lights, lit more candles, put soft jazz on in the dining room and set the table, ready for his arrival.

Her phone pinged – **10 mins**

She popped the fettuccini into the bubbling water. As it was fresh pasta, it would only take five minutes to cook.

Once it was ready, she strained it, setting it to one side then got the garlic bread out of the oven. Perfection and it smelled divine.

She got to work on assembling the carbonara ingredients in a pan, threw in the egg yolk, Parmesan and a spoonful of pasta water and mixed vigorously.

Then the doorbell! He'd given her his keys so couldn't let himself in.

She opened the door and knew right away that he was in a bad mood. He was trying to hide it but she knew!

He stepped over the threshold into a pair of tender, loving arms which she wrapped about his neck and kissed him, welcoming him home.

As he walked in, he stopped, sniffed the air and turned to look at her 'I can smell garlic – it's strong. What did you order?'

'Nothing. I cooked!'

'You COOKED?'

'Yes!'

His face was a picture of surprise.

'Now, sit down, darling man.'

She pulled out his chair for him, poured him a glass of wine and went to the kitchen where she dished out the pasta and garlic bread onto plates and carried them back to the dining room.

Placing his plate in front of him 'Fettuccini Carbonara and Cheesy Garlic Bread made for Milord with lots of loving pleasure!'

His face, again, was such a picture. One of shock, surprise and glee.

'Oh wow – my absolute favourite. I can't believe you went to all this trouble. I'm honestly a bit taken aback! Thank you darlin'.'

'It was no trouble at all. Let's eat.'

She sat down and they tucked in.

'Fuck me. FUCK ME! This is bloody amazing, Scarlet. You clever lady. So yummy.'

'Good. GOOD.'

They ate, talked, drank wine and laughed a little but there was still stress on his face and in his eyes but the rest of her plan would sort that out!

He polished off his food pretty quickly then sat back and patted his belly. 'I really enjoyed that darlin'. Thank you again. I'm stuffed!' then belched.

He apologised through a laugh then belched again which made them both laugh even more.

'Right, if you don't mind, I need a shower.'

'Hold your horses there, soldier. Just wait here.'

With that, she got up and went to his bathroom to check the water which was the perfect temperature, poured the wine she'd previously left in there for him and got the music started.

Upon returning to the dining room, she advised, 'OK, so if you'd like to go to your bedroom you'll find instructions. Don't ask me any questions.'

He stared at her. 'What are you up to?'

'Didn't I say don't ask questions?'

She bent forward, kissed his forehead and whispered softly, 'Off you pop now, there's a good boy.'

He smiled quizzically and did as he was told.

Upon arriving at his bedroom door, he read a note that said GO STRAIGHT TO THE BATHROOM.

He did.

In the bathroom, he found another note stuck to the bath that read SOAK IN ME and another stuck to the glass that read DRINK ME SLOWLY.

He undressed, sunk himself down into the popping bubbles, grabbed his glass and laid back.

He soaked for about twenty minutes and got through two more glasses of wine, washed himself, got out, dried off and put on his bath robe.

Back in his room, he noticed his leathers on the bed with a note stuck to them: WEAR ME. The same note was stuck to every other item there too plus one more underneath it all that said, HEAD TO LIVING ROOM ONCE DRESSED.

He frowned, wondering why he was expected to wear leathers, a belt and boots at home but decided Scarlet must have her reasons so put them all on obediently.

He started to smile as something crossed his mind - She'd told him previously of her deep-seated desire to service him with her mouth while he was fully dressed in his leather gear so maybe that was her plan tonight and that thought made him feel very warm inside and slightly aroused.

He finished dressing, complete with black bandana then made his way to the living room, as commanded.

His stomach was churning delightfully. He had a slight idea of what was going on but not the full extent of it. *What was she up to, the lil minx?*

He entered the living room where he was greeted with the most exquisite vision: Scarlet, sat on the arm of the sofa, wearing the lacy undies he'd bought her, hair down and cascading in soft, sumptuous curls about her shoulders, her skin radiating in the glowing candlelight, his favourite Dior perfume wafting about her, carried his way as she purposefully flicked her hair.

He just stood there, stunned into silence.

She stood up and gracefully approached him, taking his hand and gently guided him to stand in front of the sofa where she cradled his face in her aromatic hands and kissed him, biting and sucking his lower lip, making a heady meal of his luscious tongue, causing him to moan into her mouth!

'Tonight is for you, my darling. I don't want you to do ANYTHING. Not a thing. Well, maybe just one but you'll probably do that naturally anyway.'

He went to respond but she stopped him by placing her forefinger on his plump lips. 'Shhhh. Don't say a word.'

She lowered herself to her knees at his feet and looked him up and down, taking in the breathtaking, resplendent sight that stood before her: an Adonis, tightly wrapped in leather, arm tattoos fully on show, his silver ponytail hanging over one shoulder, gracing his chest – My word. He was simply heavenly and she was going to worship him with her mouth tonight, on her knees in loving exaltation. He was an exquisite specimen of a man, with an equally exquisite specimen of a cock and she considered it her honour, her duty, to relieve him of all his worries and stresses, taking him to a divine place of pure bliss.

As she looked up at him, he met her gaze with his. He could see the love on her face and in her eyes and it gave him not just a sense of peace but a glowing feeling deep within his soul - a fervent feeling! He sensed her exaltation deep down in his bones and he wondered what he'd done to deserve such high admiration from this beauty at his feet.

He stroked her cheek and curled a strand of her hair around his finger, smiling softly.

His face was aglow from candlelight and he looked so beautiful.

She broke their gaze as she focused her attention on what was directly in front of her – his very generous groin.

His cock had grown and was protruding through the leather, threatening to break through at any moment so she slowly unclipped his belt and popped the three buttons of his leathers and as she did, they almost burst open.

As she raised his T-shirt, she placed gentle kisses on his lower belly, darting her tongue in and out as she ran it up and down his fuzzy pleasure trail.

Her elegant claws grazed the skin on his chest as she found his hardened nipples which she rubbed and squeezed as she continued to cover his pillowy belly in featherlight kisses.

She started nibbling around his waist and back down to the top of his pubic area, teasing him.

He was inhaling and exhaling slowly through his teeth; a most heavenly chorus and his hands were on her head, stroking her hair.

She wanted to play this out longer but both of them were desperate for her to move on. Move on to the task at hand.

She scratched her nails down his chest and over his belly to the band of his boxers, pulling it out and downwards to release his delectable cock and scrumptious bollocks which powerfully sprung free.

She took his damp cock in one hand and lifted his balls to her mouth with the other, trapping one of them within and sucked it. He made a sudden, low grunting noise, making her trickle into her knickers, her lips tingling. As she sucked, she played with it with her tongue, flicking it back and forth repeatedly which drove him wild then she released him and repeated her moist, warm pleasure on his other one, his moans and groans increasing in volume, all the while massaging his throbbing shaft and rubbing his wet tip with her thumb which she knew drove him quite mad with fevered passion.

Then the part they both craved, the part she desired so deeply – to trap his resplendent, pulsating cock within her mouth and suck him so hard, so forcefully that she drew out all his stress and his demons, taking it all within herself and inhaling his soul, merging it with hers.

She wanted him to submit to her, to give himself over to her completely, withholding nothing. Her sole desire was to leave him relaxed and at peace, a spent, whimpering puddle in her arms.

And that's exactly what she did.

She released his tight bollock and went to town on his pink, dribbling head, licking and sucking it with fervour, letting her esurient tongue lap, flick and trail from his tip to the base of his shaft and back again; the top, the sides, underneath – she smothered him in her warm saliva as he huskily groaned and gasped.

She could sense his eagerness. She knew he wanted her to engulf him NOW.

Under normal circumstances, she'd make him wait. Make him want it so badly, he'd beg but she didn't want that tonight. No! Tonight was about giving him what HE wanted, when HE wanted it.

So she took him – took him completely, without restrain and used her powerful suction to its full extent. Her mouth engulfed him, ALL of him.

In preparation for this exact moment, she'd worked on her gag reflex. She'd practiced with bananas! She didn't want to be seductively and lovingly sucking him and gagging while she did it so she'd had to practice in order to get it just right.

And it had worked.

His shaft was long, bulbous and very generous. This man had a 'show and grow' cock – generous when flaccid and even more generous when hard. It just GREW.

She gorged herself on it, delighting herself with the taste of his little salty pre-cum dribbles, lapping them with her tongue as they arrived then sucking him again.

She'd stop every now and then to lick his shaft and his head, attempting to delay the inevitable flood of his warm ejaculation in her mouth as she didn't want it to be over too quickly but he'd had one hell of a shitty day and she didn't want to wind him up too far either so she decided to just go for it!

Placing her hand at the bottom of his shaft and squeezing it as tight as she could, she started massaging up and down as she did the same with her mouth, gently scraping with her teeth to increase his pleasure as she now knew that a little pain was a huge excitement for him.

But now she also wanted him to fulfil one of her fantasies – for him to undulate those sexy, powerful hips as she sucked him dry.

She released him, looked up into his twinkling, glistening, giddy eyes and softly said, 'Undulate darling!'

He smiled back at her, raspy noises escaping his throat and nodded.

As she returned him to within her mouth and started to take him home, he started to 'undulate', just as she'd fantasised, gently thrusting forward into her mouth whilst holding her head, grunting and groaning while he did it. She was allowing him to now set the pace, allowing him to decide when he was to burst deep into her throat.

She looked up at him, wanting to gaze into his deep pools of blue water while he came and see the pleasurable release on his stunning face.

He started quickening the pace and the force, now holding her head firmly as he thrust himself deeply into her ravenous mouth.

He'd tightly wrapped bunches of her hair around both his hands and was pulling it as he pushed towards her which she loved. It heightened her own pleasure.

And this WAS her pleasure.

Her giving to him with nothing in return was so erotic for her, knowing that her actions were giving him such sweet release.

She opened her throat as he thrust deep into her mouth and she increased her suction and pull, his raspy noises turning to growls as his climax approached.

She released the grip of her hand and grabbed a hold of his hips as his engine revved, still looking up at him and he down at her, watching his cock slip in and out of her wet lips, her eyes longingly and lovingly worshipping him.

She felt him tense and knew this was it so she held his hips tighter as he forced himself into her throat one last time.

He craned his neck and released his melodic warriors cry heavenwards as he powerfully flooded her gullet with his sweet, hot, deliciousness then looked back down at her again so she could watch the divine happening on his face and, as he did, she too burst, gushing into her pretty knickers, her aching insides convulsing violently.

His seed spilled into her throat, sliding down as she repeatedly swallowed and kept sucking, draining him of everything he was willingly giving to her.

She didn't gag, she didn't wretch – she took it elegantly which was what she had badly desired and craved for so long.

She watched the strains and burdens of the day disappear from his face as she devoured them all on his behalf.

This, for her, was a cathartic moment and she felt so very blessed which was rather strange considering what they were doing was so carnal but she felt it all the same.

His powerful ejaculation over, she kept him within the warm confines of her mouth, gently sucking as his hardness relented.

She was still convulsing, her knickers soaked and sticky with her own honeyed release as his legs gave way, his knees buckled and he literally collapsed into the puddle she'd anticipated, ending up on the floor in her arms, quivering and whimpering like a puppy.

And she held him, held him as tight and as close as she possibly could, planting loving kisses on his head as he panted and gasped in her clutches.

And she started to silently weep, burning tears streaming down her flushed cheeks, dripping onto his bandana as she rocked gently, holding him tight with his precious head tucked under her chin and proclaimed in a slightly cracked voice 'I love you, Stewart!

He didn't respond, he couldn't. He was just too breathless to speak, too weak to acknowledge it but she didn't need any acknowledgment, she just wanted him to hear it in this moment!

They remained there, on the floor in an entanglement of sticky love until he'd regained his senses and breath and then she ushered him up onto the sofa where she joined him, cuddling his beautiful being up in her arms again and there they remained, an embodiment of bliss for a good hour or so.

*

Stewart had dozed off with his silvery white head on her chest and Scarlet had just lain there, holding him close, listening to his soft breath.

She adored listening to him breathing deeply and peacefully – it made her heart very warm and happy, as when he was asleep, his demons couldn't torment him.

He roused slightly, blinking his eyes open.

She looked down at him 'Hey, you!'

He gazed back at her 'Hey' with a gentle smile.

He looked so very relaxed which was a pleasure to see.

He asked her, 'What's the time?'

'It's ten forty-five, my darling!'

'Do you have work tomorrow?'

'Nope. Not until Thursday.'

'Good. That means you can stay then.'

'*Hmmm* – are you sure it's not too much for you? You like your alone time and, apart from a few hours today, we've been together twenty-four seven since Friday. I don't want to overwhelm you.'

'You're not overwhelming me. If you were, I wouldn't be suggesting you stay. I enjoy your company and I find you a very comforting presence; a beautifully elegant peaceful presence! There's something almost mystical and rather bewitching about you that just calms my mind, stills my soul and entrances me, so please stay with me until Wednesday evening?'

She'd never been so beautifully complimented before and what he'd just divulged made her soul melt. This was what she'd been hoping for, to be a gentle, calming force in his hectic life, somewhere he could lay his head and be at total peace with himself and the noisy, chaotic world around him.

'Of course I'll stay with you! Even if I was gonna decline which I wasn't, you'd have won me over with that little confession. You've made me feel quite special and I thank you,' she very softly said, as she kissed the top of his head.

He looked back up at her again with a sweet smile 'It's all true and you deserve to be made to feel special because you are special. Very special!' Then added, 'Is there any food left? I'm bloody starving!'

'There is indeed. I always make too much food. Shall I go and warm some up for you?'

'Yes, please but can you bring it to the bedroom? I really need to get into bed. You've made me feel quite weak. I've no idea where that came from tonight but it was magical and I felt loved and cared for – worshipped even which is a weird thing to say but you made me feel like some sort of deity!'

As she was entwining his platinum strands around her delicate fingers she whispered back in a bit of a daze, 'You are to me, Stewart!'

'But I'm not – I'm just an ordinary bloke.'

'Not to me you're not. To me, you're a remarkably brave warrior with a beautiful soul, an amazing mind and a precious heart who's overcome many a tough obstacle. To me, you're a hero and, just as you say I deserve to feel special, you deserve to feel honoured and adored! And I do adore you, immensely.'

He sighed deeply, his head still on her chest, her fingers still twirling in his hair.

Then he shifted his gorgeous backside and sat up on the edge of the sofa.

'Listen, I haven't done anything to deserve all this praise.'

'No, you've done nothing specific – you've just been yourself! And just being who you are authentically, the 'true' you deserves praise as it ain't easy being you! I'm in awe of you for everything you've overcome and how you're still standing today; healthy, proud and successful! There's just one thing you've yet to conquer which is your heart and that's where I come in with all of my devoted love, respect and adulation. I want to help your heart heal from all the brokenness of the past because you deserve to be happy, loved, adored and cherished.'

He made what she could only describe as a WOW face.

'Now, shift your delicious self so I can get up and get you some food!'

He shimmied backwards, allowing her room to get up and she went off to prepare him a plate of yumminess, leaving him tongue-tied on the sofa.

She made her way to the bedroom, arms full of nourishment for her hero and found him ensconced in his bed, sat up against the pillows.

'Here you go, my love.'

She grabbed a pillow and placed it on his lap, popping the plate on top of it and placed the hot cup of steaming tea she'd made him on his nightstand.

'Ooo, tea! I need that.'

'I thought you might!'

He sat and munched away, slurping his tea satisfactorily at intervals and polished off his late-night snack and tea at an alarming rate.

'Blimey, you *were* a hungry boy!' she proclaimed, relieving him of his plate and setting it on his dresser.

'I was indeed – you drained me! And now, I feel like I could sleep for a week.'

'So, sleep!'

'Are you sure you don't mind? Have you got anything else up your sleeve?'

'Gosh no, I think that's quite enough for tonight. I'll just go and change into my jammies. Be right back.'

He grabbed her arm. 'No, NO jammies. I want you naked next to me. Just skin on skin,' he almost whispered, as he flung back the covers, revealing his own stark nakedness.

She giggled and her eyes widened. 'Mmmm, what a resplendent sight! If that's what you want, that's what you'll get!'

She stood up, walked around the bed and stripped off her undies then climbed into bed next to him, snuggling herself as close to him as she could.

He engulfed her in his beautiful arms as she nuzzled into his chest and kissed the top of her head.

'Thank you!' She heard him say.

She looked up at him 'What for?'

'For tonight. For everything. For being so selfless and loving.'

'You, my darling, are so very welcome,' she replied as she gently kissed his chest. 'Now, go to sleep. Sweet dreams, sweetheart.'

No sooner had she said that, she heard him breathing deeply and looked up at him. He was gone! Sound asleep already, as peaceful as could be and she smiled to herself, feeling so very grateful and so very much in love with this precious soul, sweetly slumbering beneath her head.

She sighed with complete contentment as she too, drifted off into a very satisfied sleep.

Part 7 – London, Tuesday

They awoke in the morning at the same time but hadn't wanted to get up. All they wanted to do was snuggle and remain close for as long as possible.

After about an hour of dreamy, cosy cuddling, Scarlet broke the silence with, 'I think I'll shorten your name to Stew!'

'Don't you bloody dare!'

'Why not? It's rather fitting I think.'

'Why's that then?'

'Well, stew is a thick soup, rather like what you squirt down my throat!'

'Uugghh, don't be filthy! That's just nasty. Nooo! Yuck Scarlet!'

'Hahahahaaaaaaa.'

'You're NOT funny. You're just nasty! Fuck me, behave yourself, woman!'

'Why are you laughing if I'm so nasty?'

'Because you're laughing and because you find yourself so funny. Always tittering at yourself which is hilarious to watch! Just behave – you are NOT calling me Stew, especially after that repulsive reference. It's nauseating. NO!'

'Hahahahaaaaaa.'

'STOP LAUGHIN'!'

'NO! SHANT!' She cackled at him, now crying with the excessive laughter.

'You do know you're quite mad right?'

'Yep! But you love it! Admit it!'

'Oh, I do.'

'Evidently! Are you ticklish too?' she enquired as she grabbed at his waist.

He batted away her hand, giggling. 'Now now, don't start! I hate being tickled. Leave me alone!'

She refused to give in as she straddled his hips, sat on him and started tickling his waist which made him jerk about, wailing 'STOP. FUCK OFF YOU MAD FEMALE' laughing uncontrollably.

She was giggling excitedly as she continued her frenzied attack, his laughter now quite maniacal.

She tickled away as he jerked about the bed, trying desperately to get her off of him, tears of laughter now streaming down both their faces.

He finally managed to grab her wrists and restrain her.

She stopped, breathless and laughing.

'ENOUGH, WOMAN!'

'Oh, I do so love making you squirm!'

'You're a cruel, sadistic lady!'

'Yeah, but you love that too!'

He shook his head in dismay.

'Now, if you can pull yourself together, I have a bit of a confession and an idea!'

'Oh, do tell!'

'Well, I kinda like having you around. It was so nice coming home to you! I'm not used to having anyone at home as you know and I never thought I'd want it again after so long by myself but with you, it's different somehow! I don't know how to explain it really except to say that it's comforting and warm and makes me feel cosy! So, I'd like to know how you feel about being here a bit more often? Not all the time but more often!'

This SHOCKED her. She was definitely not expecting it at all and it took her a while to let it sink in. She was almost struck dumb.

'Wow. I NEVER thought I'd hear those words come out of your mouth! You've taken me quite by surprise darlin'! But we've not known each other long. I mean, our first proper date was only just over two weeks ago! Are you SURE this isn't too much, too soon?'

'Maybe but neither of us are getting any younger and with me being almost two decades your senior, I don't have time to mess about. And more importantly, when you have a deep connection with someone special, I don't think deliberately waiting an 'appropriate' amount of time is necessary. When you know, you know,' he retorted with a shrug.

'Oh, I completely agree.'

'Good! Take as much time as you need to think about it and let me know!'

'There's nothing to think about – YES! I'D LOVE to be here as much as you want me to be.'

He smiled, relief in his eyes. He sat up and hugged her tightly 'Good. Best answer!'

They hugged tenderly for a while as they both allowed reality to sink in.

Pulling back he added 'I guess then we need to discuss logistics. You'll need to bring a few things over; clothes, necessities etc. which means I'll need to get a new chest of drawers to accommodate you so why don't we get dressed, go out for breakfast and then go furniture shopping?'

'I'm sure you don't need new furniture, Stewart. I'll not need that much space. You've got loads of drawers in here already!'

'Yeah, but they're all full,' he replied with a chuckle. 'We'll go to the place I always go where I can get one that matches the rest of my bedroom furniture!'

'If that's what you want to do, then we'll do it.'

'It is what I want. I want you to feel at home while you're here and not be living out of a suitcase.'

'That's incredibly sweet of you, my lovely. Thank you,' and she kissed the palm of his hand as his fingers stroked her cheek.

'Right then, let's get a move on.'

They got up, washed and dressed, messing about and laughing while they did it then headed off for breakfast.

*

They arrived at his favourite furniture shop that specialised in vintage pieces after having a very yummy breakfast at a quaint little café by The Thames where they'd discussed a few details regarding their recent and rather big decision.

The owner, Frank, recognised him immediately and walked over to shake Stewart's hand.

'Good morning, Stewart, so nice to see you again!'

They exchanged pleasantries and introductions with Stewart explaining what he was after and Frank walked them over to a couple of pieces he had in mind.

Although he specialised in vintage pieces and antiques, he also made bespoke pieces too which could either be delivered assembled for an extra fee or flat packed to be assembled in situ.

Stewart made his choice and Frank enquired, 'Would you like it delivered assembled?'

'Yes please, Frank.'

Scarlet chimed in, 'No, we can do it ourselves. What fun!'

Stewart gave her a surprised look. 'Fun? Assembling drawers isn't FUN, it's a pain in the arse!'

'Yes, but we can make an afternoon of it and 'make' it fun.'

'Erm, I don't think so. That sounds like a nightmare to me.'

She leaned in close and whispered in his ear, 'Just think; screws, plugs, getting things to fit tightly in little holes!'

His face was a perfect picture which she wanted to bottle and preserve in aspic.

He looked away and said to Frank, 'We'll have it delivered assembled please.'

Scarlet called him a spoil sport, raised her eyes and tutted at him as he paid for his purchase, fixing a delivery date and time.

As they left the shop, he muttered in her ear, 'There are much better ways of fitting things tightly into little holes, Scarlet. And just so you know, I intend to show you exactly what I mean this evening!' Followed by a cheeky eye glint, wink and grin.

He then grabbed her hand and they walked back up the street to get a taxi back home.

*

They'd spent the afternoon relaxing at Stewart's place; watching TV, talking, laughing, snuggling, snogging – LOTS of snogging and groping!

It was the perfect afternoon; they got to learn more details about each other's lives and personalities; likes, wants, desires, future plans etc. all from the comfort of his sumptuous sofa.

It was six p.m. when Stewart announced he was hungry so Scarlet offered to cook.

'No. I don't want you doing anything like that today. We're both so relaxed so I'll just order in. What do you fancy?'

'I don't mind cooking, I find it quite rewarding. Especially when you make yummy noises!'

'Yeah but then there's clean up so I'd rather just order in and keep it all simple!'

'OK, my lovely! As you wish. I could really murder an Indian Korma!'

'YESSSS! A curry! Bloody good idea! I have a menu in the kitchen.'

He went to fetch it and handed it to her.

'What would you like?'

'Chicken Korma with coconut pilau rice and Peshwari Naan please.'

'Oooo, yum. I'll have the same.'

He phoned in their order and it was delivered an hour later, the aromatic smells from the packaging making both their tummies growl. They plonked themselves at the dining table, opened a bottle of red and tucked in, savouring every bite.

After they'd polished off every last morsel, Stewart suggested they shower then watch a movie which they did, snuggling down, replete with scrumptious food, feet up, smothered in a fluffy blanket.

*

With the movie finished, Stewart whispered in Scarlet's ear, 'Let's go to bed, Madam! I have delicious plans for you!'

Scarlet sighed deeply. 'Mmmmm, yes please.'

He stood up and offered her his hand, helping her up from the sofa and led her to the bedroom where he dimmed the lights and turned the covers down.

'This evening is all about you; about me giving back to you. It's my turn to do all the work while you lay back and enjoy it.'

She could only offer him a sweet smile as the anticipation was already making her tremble.

He ALWAYS made her tremble. Just the thought of him touching her erotically set her off as he was just so bloody arousing to look at. It didn't matter what he was wearing; even though she adored him in his leathers, it didn't matter. He could wear a bin bag and still be fucking sexy! But it wasn't just his body or looks, it was his experience and knowledge of a woman's body and mind - the way he skilfully used his hands, fingers and mouth, his commanding stature, his soul-penetrating eyes; his mind was just as erotic to her as his beautifully stunning body and he constantly set her soul, heart, mind and body ablaze.

He began to undress her; off came her sweater and jogging bottoms, her bra and then he slipped off her knickers, guiding her to the bed and laying her down.

'Just stay there. I'll be right back.'

He dimmed the lights, leaving an ethereal glow in the room and disappeared off to the bathroom.

When he came back, he was naked, sporting just his trademark bandana, his platinum ponytail trailing down his back and it made her gasp suddenly which made him smile from ear to ear.

He was standing in front of her, devouring her with his devilish eyes. He was about to take her!

He had his hot, pulsating cock in his virile hand, coating it with warming lube to ease its entry into her tightness and it was the most erotically arousing fucking vision her eyes have ever had the pleasure of witnessing; HIM – stunningly naked, beautifully tattooed, ruggedly chiselled, commandingly masculine, mighty sword in hand, ready to savagely plunge and all she could think was *Please… Please do not move! Just stay right there and allow me to drink in this breathtaking, captivating moment, indelibly imprinting it into the memory of my fevered mind!*

She knew she couldn't ask him to just stay there while she perversely watched him rub himself, so she didn't say a word but drank in as much as she could before he slowly crept up from the bottom of the bed towards where she lay, ready and waiting with fluttering anticipation.

As he approached her feet, he parted her legs and kept creeping upwards until he was hovering over her, his face right above hers, his eyes boring into her as if he was looking deep into her very soul and she felt it; she felt a tug in her core, pulling her soul towards his, making her catch her breath and gasp, again and he smiled as if he knew exactly what his eyes had done to her.

He lowered himself down onto his left elbow and reached backwards with his other hand, letting his fingers search for her entrance which they found, rather masterfully.

While still peering into her eyes, he slipped one finger inside her, gently caressing within then slowly withdrew it and slipped it back inside with another, stretching her.

With his fingers bent upwards, he grazed her G-Spot just once and she bucked upwards, letting out a piercing whimper.

'There it is,' he said with a slight cheeky grin, his fingers still inside her.

She managed a breathy 'There's what?' Looking at him quizzically.

'Your G-Spot,' he replied, as he flickered his eyebrows up and down whilst biting his bottom lip.

Then the rascal did it again, his eyes twinkling at her, still biting his lip through that same cheeky grin.

Again, she bucked and whimpered and he kept going, grazing her with skill, massaging her with just the right amount of pressure to drive her insane. She began to buck gently in tandem with his massages, her breath getting quicker, her body beginning to shake, as he started rubbing her throbbing pearl with his thumb, causing her legs to begin twitching and she felt like she was going, quite literally, mad and felt like she couldn't cope.

She cried out his name 'STEWART, PLEASE STOP!'

'STOP? Haha, No Scarlet, just let go!'

'Stop, STOP – I can't cope.'

'Yes you can, just relax and LET GO darlin'! This'll help.'

He edged himself over and engulfed her mouth with his, kissing her deeply, that long, silky tongue of his swirling with hers. She flung her arms around his back and held onto him as he continued to invade her with his skilful digits.

He'd slid his left hand beneath her head and was kneading her scalp through her raven locks, continuously kissing her with fervour and she relaxed into him, beginning to finally let go as he'd told her to. She whimpered and moaned into his luxurious mouth as he took her higher and higher and, as she completely let go, the overwhelming ache within her loins reached its crescendo and she orgasmed powerfully, Stewart still massaging her as she writhed under his hand and his mouth, releasing an ethereal cry which he muffled.

As she began to come down, he stopped kissing her and told her 'See, I said that would help.'

She smiled sweetly with quivering lips which he licked, gently then replied, 'My word, that was incredible!'

'I ain't finished with you yet, young lady!'

He moved atop her, still bracing on his left elbow, reached down, gripped his divine, slippery appendage in his hand and took her instantly, driving himself deep. His thrusts were gentle yet precise, slow yet forceful as he built a steady rhythm which she met with equal eagerness.

He was inside her, slowly massaging her G-Spot again, this time with his resplendently meaty cock; slow, precise strokes gently teased her into a frenzy and her head tilted backwards as he quickened, faster and harder strokes now pummelling her pesky G-Spot.

The sweet, pleasurable pain was almost too much to bear as she arched her back, craned her neck, dug her nails into his glistening flesh and whelped out his name, popping like a shaken champagne bottle – AGAIN!

Warm streams engulfed his beautiful cock, seeping out and trickling over her buttocks onto the sheet beneath them.

She fell back into the pillows as he came down to a soft, steady rhythm.

Left spent and panting, she whispered in his ear, 'Don't you ever EVER stop fucking me, you beautiful, heavenly creature!'

He whispered back, 'NEVER!'

He hadn't climaxed yet so he kept his rhythm slow and gentle as he allowed her to come down from the precipice he'd taken her to.

Once her breathing normalised and she'd stopped convulsing, he withdrew and flipped her over, moving the pillows in order to lay her flat on her belly. He gently spread her legs slightly and eased his dripping cock back inside her, causing her to gasp and sigh. It was a tight fit due to her position and the sensations were heightened one hundred-fold as he slowly but forcefully slid in and out of her with expert precision; leaning on his arms, both hands flat on the bed beside her, gently kissing and biting her back as he continued to stroke her cock-hugging walls with his generous breadth and length.

It was exquisite for them both!

It was slow, purposeful and extremely erotic with both of them making the most melodic, sensual noises; his deep and husky, hers high pitched and breathy.

She ground her buttocks back to meet him as he relentlessly took her, once again, towards Nirvana and she never wanted it to stop. She could, quite literally, do this with him all day long.

The deep grinding, the husky growling and heady whimpering went on for ages as they were both relishing in this moment, neither of them in any hurry to orgasm.

He was making love to her; no kink, no fancy positions, no commands, no rough stuff – just close, meaningful, powerful love making and it was blowing her mind and making her feel very emotional.

He had smothered her neck and back with kisses, grazing her delicate skin with the silver bristles on his chin which made her quiver as he remained inside her for what seemed like hours.

Then two words in her ear broke her seductive daze as he softly announced, 'It's time!'

With that, he raised himself up, lifted her hips skywards and pulled her back onto her knees, closing them tight together as he placed his own on the outside. He wanted to keep her as tight as possible as he plunged himself into her with warrior force.

And wow was he forceful! Where did he get his powerful strength from?

She raised herself up onto her hands and thrusted backwards to meet him, their hips jarring, their sweat mingling, their outcries in perfect tune with one another. So beautiful!

They could sense each other's pinnacles approaching as they rutted in perfect sync; thrusts getting harder, rhythms getting faster, noises getting louder until the heavens opened and they both erupted.

He held onto her so tightly as he shot his hot seed deep within her, her walls spasming around his perfect shaft, squeezing it with each powerful contraction, her juices flooding him with honeyed warmth.

His neck craned backwards before his head flopped forwards and she collapsed beneath him, as flat as a pancake on the bed, trembling, whimpering and convulsing as he too flopped down on top of her, his head on her back, still inside her as her walls had him in a vice grip.

The convulsions eventually relented, allowing her to release him.

Both panting and gasping, they lay there atop the soaked sheets, savouring this moment.

As her breathing started to normalise she heard him whisper in her ear, 'I think I love you too!'

She raised her right arm backwards over her shoulder, placed her hand on the back of his head and burst into tears.

The whole experience had been a deeply emotional one and that had finished her off completely. Hearing him say that filled her with such raw emotion that she couldn't help but cry tears of relief and happiness. Yes, he'd only said he THOUGHT he loved her too but, bloody hell, that was a massive step and for him to declare it in words was, well, it was miraculous!

He slid off of her, lay by her side, turned her towards him and engulfed her in his strong arms, shushing in her ear, stroking her hair and whispering, 'Don't cry luv, don't cry!'

She sobbed into his chest, trying desperately to control it but she couldn't. The emotion was way too strong so he just held her while she shook uncontrollably in his arms and continued to stroke her hair until her tears and sobs subsided naturally.

When she'd regained a bit of her dignity, she gazed up at him and apologized, 'I'm sorry.'

'What for?'

'For blubbering like a baby.'

'Don't be silly, I knew you'd get emotional when I said those words! I mean, I wasn't expecting THAT but I guess it hit an emotionally tender spot so no apologies needed!' And he leaned forward and kissed her little red nose.

'Shall I go grab you some tissues?'

She giggled and nodded. 'Yes please.'

He got himself up and wondered off to the bathroom in all his naked glory and came back with a box of tissues which he placed by her side. 'I'm gonna go run you a bath.' He kissed her cheek and disappeared again.

While he was gone, she sat herself up, wiped her eyes and blew her snotty nose! He reappeared a few minutes later and offered her his hand which she took, getting out of bed and following his lead into the bathroom.

The bath was full of bubbles and the room was filled with the most delightful of perfumes. He'd used bubble bath, Epsom salts and bath oils – he knew exactly how she liked her baths, bless his precious heart.

'Right, in you hop, lil lady. Have a lovely soak and I'll go grab us a snack and some tea which I'll make extra sweet!'

He put on his bath robe and went off to the kitchen.

She got herself into the bathtub and sunk down into the welcoming water, shimmying her buttocks down as far as possible so she could dunk her head and wet her hair. She didn't care if she got soapy bubbles in it, she just wanted to feel the warm, soothing comfort around her throbbing head.

She stayed beneath the surface for a few seconds then came back up and leaned backwards onto the bath pillow. *BLISS!* She closed her puffy eyes and just wallowed!

He returned a little while later carrying a tray complete with two cups of hot, sweet tea and a plate full of toast and butter, offering her the plate and handing her her mug.

She drank deeply. 'Mmmmm, heaven! Thank you!'

After scoffing down three pieces of crunchy toast and finishing her tea, she exclaimed, 'Well, this was a first—'

'What was?'

'It's the first time you haven't actually wrecked me!'

He laughed. 'I can't do that every time or you'll not be able to function like a normal human being. I'm not always a kinky perv, you know!'

'Oh I'm not complaining one bit – it was truly magical.'

'Why, thank you Ma'am.'

They beamed at each other.

'Why did you wet your hair?'

'Cos my head is pounding and I wanted the water to soothe it.'

'Did it work?'

'Erm, no! It's still throbbing.'

'OK, hang on. I'll be right back,' and he wondered off yet again, returning rather quickly with a glass of fizzing painkillers.

'Your medicine, Milday.'

'Oh I love these things, they work so quickly!'

'They do, they're brilliant. Now, drink up and then we'll get you out and I'll have a shower!'

She necked the sparkling mixture and stepped out of the bath into a warm, fluffy towel that he was holding up for her and he dried her off.

'Your hair needs drying too, I'll get the hairdryer out. Follow me.'

They returned to the bedroom where he handed her a hairdryer. 'Want me to dry it for you?'

'No, no. I can do it. You go ablute yourself.'

He gave her a wink and trotted off.

She roughly dried her hair then popped it up into a messy bun and proceeded to strip the bottom sheet off the bed. She rummaged in a cupboard and found a clean one, popped it on, rearranging the pillows and blankets then slid into the silky sheets, completely nude again.

Upon his gloriously naked return, he went to retrieve a fresh pair of boxers.

'Stewart, put them away and get your stunning self into bed just as you are!'

He nodded, grinning, put them away and joined her in bed where they cuddled up as they always did, all clean and smelling as fresh as daisies.

She asked him, 'Do you have to go into your office in the morning?'

'Nope. I cleared my schedule so I could spend time with you. I'll go in Thursday morning.'

'So that means neither of us have to wake up early, meaning we don't need to go to sleep yet, right?'

'We don't. What's on your mind?'

'Can you please do what you did before my bath again? I could honestly make love with you all night!'

'Madam, your wish is my command,' he retorted with glistening eyes.

He rolled her onto her back and began to make love to her all over again, taking her to the stars where they basked in the glow of the full moon!

Part 8 – She's So Brazen... but Devoted!

It had been ten days since they'd seen each other. They'd both been tremendously busy; her at work and him with his business.

Stewart had dropped her home last Wednesday evening. He'd insisted on accompanying her to make sure she reached home safely. Always the perfect, protective gentleman.

They'd discussed her moving some stuff over to his on the following Friday evening during the journey and had parted ways at her front door with a long, lingering kiss and warm cuddle.

*

His car had arrived at hers bang on six p.m. as always and Stewart had gone along too so as to help with the carrying of Scarlet's items and they'd arrived back at his by seven thirty.

After lugging in a couple of suitcases, Stewart had showed her the new chest of drawers that had been delivered two days previously. He had also made space for her in the bathroom cabinet and had cleared the drawers in her nightstand.

After helping her pack her things away, they'd ordered pizza and were now happily ensconced at his dining table, drinking red wine and catching up over the last ten days apart.

Stewart then changed the subject with a question: 'Did you remember to bring jeans, a sturdy jacket and your black leather boots with you?'

'Of course I did but I'm intrigued as to why I need specific items. Do tell!'

'Well, how do you fancy a trip out on my bike tomorrow?'

She gasped, wide-eyed. 'Really? REALLY? Yaaay – yes please,' she gleefully responded, clapping and bouncing on her chair. He laughed as he always did at her excited outbursts which were almost childlike and rather adorable.

Then a naughty yet surprised look appeared on her face 'Ohhhhhhh, that means you'll be wearing your leathers right?'

'Oh for fucks sake, here we go! What is it with you and my leathers?'

'Cos they're tight and hug you in all your bulgy, bulky places and it makes me horny and wet!'

He shook his head, laughing then a look of realisation struck his face.

'You've got to promise me one thing though and I'm serious Scarlet… NO reaching round from the back and grabbing my cock while I'm driving!'

She burst out laughing.

'I know what you're like when I'm in me leathers and that will be dangerously distracting… Promise me!'

She pulled herself together and placed her hand on her heart 'I promise darlin', I promise to not grab your cock while you're driving. But when you're not driving, well, I can't promise a thing!' she added with a shrug and a wink.

'Oh fuck me… I can expect scarlet coloured, filthy chaos tomorrow then, can I?'

'You decked out head to toe in black leather, straddled on a big, burley Harley with me having to keep my hands in only 'appropriate' places while you're driving… yep, you bet your gorgeous arse you can!'

He shook his head again, chuckling then responded, 'Well, I'd better get a decent nights kip then. I fear I'm gonna need bucket loads of patience and energy to handle you tomorrow which means no naughtiness tonight, young lady. Just a quiet snuggle on the sofa with a movie, then off to bed to SLEEP!'

'I'd normally be giving you grief right about now but I'm actually exhausted. It's been a brutally busy week at work so I'll not challenge you!'

'Blimey, you're not gonna argue? That's a first—'

She giggled and they cleaned up, watched their movie then went to bed; with Scarlet actually behaving herself for once.

*

They both slept like babies and awoke to sunlight streaming across his bed. They'd slept through his alarm and it was nine thirty a.m.

They had a quick morning cuddle before Stewart exclaimed, 'Right, I'll go and make breakfast. You take your time!'

He popped off, leaving her languishing under his soft, pillowy duvet.

She got up, used the bathroom, popped her curls up and slipped into her fluffy bath robe. It was a chilly morning.

As she arrived in the kitchen, Stewart asked her, 'How do you like your eggs?'

'Fertilised!'

He looked at her quizzically 'Fertilised?'

'Yeah, preferably rather brusquely whilst up against a wall!'

He burst out laughing then stopped very quickly, a serious look on his face.

'I see.'

With that, he turned off the stove, put down the spatula, grabbed her forcefully, dragged her to the dining room and threw her up against the wall with her hands pinned above her head.

'You're gonna need some fertiliser then!'

He then lunged into her, proceeding to lick and bite her neck while he raised her left leg, reached under her thigh, gripped his beautiful cock and rammed it inside her in his usual forceful way, making her inhale suddenly and sharply, keeping her wrists pinned above her head in a vice grip as he began thrusting into her maniacally, his other hand strongly kneading her buttocks.

As each thrust caused the most blissful ache deep inside her, she cried out; with him grunting and groaning as he nailed her to the wall.

But as this was their first time in almost two weeks, he didn't last long so after a few minutes of frantic thrashing, he climaxed and spilled into her, growling in her ear and following it with a high-pitched moan.

'Fuck, I've missed you,' she declared, breathlessly.

He didn't respond; he was still panting and swallowing hard. He released her wrists, let go of her leg and held onto her as she caressed his back. He then cleared his throat, looked at her and said, 'I've missed you too, darlin'!' kissing her lips softly.

'But you didn't cum.'

'No, I didn't. It was all a bit quick!'

'Oh I'm sorry. How selfish of me!'

'Not selfish at all, my darling! It's perfectly OK, this one was for you.'

She kissed the end of his nose, readjusted her bath robe which was all skew-whiff and wandered off to clean herself up, smacking Stewarts scrummy arse as she skipped off with his seed trickling down her thighs.

Upon her return, he once again asked her, 'How do you like your eggs? AND unless you wanna be stuck here, pinned up against a wall all day long, I'd be careful how you respond!'

'Erm, *hmmm*,' she grinned back. 'Sunny side up please!'

'That's better!'

He cooked her eggs as she'd asked and presented them to her on a bed of sourdough toast, with avocado, rocket, spinach and a sprinkle of feta cheese which was her favourite breakfast of all and what she ate daily.

He cooked his own and joined her at the table. 'Right, let's eat, dress and get a move on. We've got a lovely day ahead of us, full of delights.'

'Ooooo yay!'

They ate their healthy breakfast then went to wash and dress.

She'd chosen black jeans for today, with a black tunic sweater, black thigh-high leather boots and her absolute favourite plum coloured suede bikers jacket! He'd told her to bring a 'sturdy' jacket but hadn't specified why and it was the sturdiest one she owned. It had just been a coincidence that it was a biker's jacket!

As ladies always take longer to get ready, he was already waiting for her in the kitchen and, when she entered, his face lit up. 'Ahhh, perfect. You look just perfect Scarlet and rather gorgeous! That jacket it stunning! And those boots – very impressive!'

'Thank you, my love – you look exquisite as usual and, if I may say so, rather edible. I'm salivating!'

'Behave!'

'I'll try.'

He was wearing tight, hip-hugging black leather trousers with a grey sweater tucked into them, black biker boots, a black leather biker's jacket and a black bandana and Scarlet was fighting to control herself. He'd also left his ponytail out and that thing literally excited her to the point of distraction. She adored it.

'But if you want me to have pristine control, my lovely, you need to tuck that ponytail AWAY cos with that delightful thing whipping about my face on the back of your bike, I'm liable to lose it.'

He roared with laughter and quickly tucked it up into his bandana. 'Better Scarlet?'

'Much better... until later, you know, for that scarlet coloured, filthy chaos you're expecting!'

'Oh no, you're gonna pull it off one of these days?'

'Your ponytail or your cock?' she enquired with her eyebrows raised.

'Probably both; what with your hard pulling and powerful suction, I fear I might be left a hairless eunuch!'

She cackled loudly, tears streaming down her cheeks while he too laughed out loud.

Once she'd regained her composure, she added, 'My poor darling, would you like me to be more gentle in future? Can't your addled, ageing old body cope?'

'Oi, cheeky. Less of the old and addled! And no, I like your rough side. It's kinda nice and very kinky!' he retorted with a glint and half smile.

'Oh goodie,' and she kissed his cheek.

She grabbed her crossbody bag as he got his keys and they left.

It was only a short walk to the garage where he kept his Harley. He unlocked the door and raised it up, revealing the stunning machine within.

It was a Harley Davidson Sportster 883 in black and gold – a real beauty.

'Wow, Stewart. It's absolutely beautiful!'

'It's gorgeous, ain't it?' he retorted, lovingly stroking his big boy's toy.

'Oh yeah, impressively so!'

'Thank you. It's my prized possession'

He opened a box at the top end of the garage and removed two helmets, a gold one for her and a black one for him.

She'd left her hair down for this occasion to allow the helmet to fit and he helped her put it on then he straddled his bike and began to put his on too after which he started up, backed it off of its kickstand and out of the garage door before reengaging the kickstand and switching off the engine, dismounting to close and lock the door. He got back on and sat waiting for Scarlet to join him but she was just staring!

What a sight! Scarlet had frozen, tingling below and gawping at this incredibly jaw-dropping vision. His leathers were all bunched up around his heavy, ample bollocks and all she wanted to do was walk up and grab 'em. Fuck, he was just so bloody virile and was arousing her. She felt very warm inside with butterflies flitting about in her tummy and her knickers.

She heard him shout, 'On you hop then.'

She was still frozen, silent, gawping.

'Will you stop ogling my groin, woman, and get on the bloody bike!'

She snapped back to reality and obliged, getting on the back with her arms around him.

She HAD to remember her promise and NOT grab at his divine package whilst he was driving which was gonna prove a rather tough feat as she was already so horny but she was determined to behave herself. Well, at least while he was driving anyway.

He switched on the engine which roared and twisted the throttle making it roar even louder.

She was so very excited to be included in this, one of his deepest passions: motorbikes!

Her boss was a member of a bikers' group and they regularly met at The Hangman's Noose, a pub just up the road from where Scarlet worked. He'd invited her along a few times and that's where she'd met Stewart as he'd been invited by a biker mate of his on a handful of occasions too. That's where they'd become acquainted, where she'd seen him in his leathers and become hooked and where he'd invited her to his place for their first salacious evening that was supposed to be just drinks! And now, here he was, making her a part of his biking life. She was honoured; horny and honoured.

Stewart jolted the Harley off of its kickstand once more, shouting back at her, 'Hold on tight darlin' and off they roared!

*

They'd been driving for about thirty minutes when Stewart pulled up outside a very upmarket cafe and asked her to wait.

He went inside and returned with a very posh picnic basket, a rather large one. He strapped it to the back of the Harley and they continued on their merry way.

A further hour passed by and they were now in the countryside with views of fields, hills and wildlife surrounding them. The weather was crisp and chilly but the sun was shining – a beautiful autumn day in the stunning English countryside!

She noticed Stewart lowering gears and realised they were slowing down. He then made a left turn into a small track lined with trees, resplendent with jewel-coloured leaves. As they slowly crept along, the trees cleared and they came upon a small lake which had a few oak trees on its banks. One was particularly striking and was set back a bit from the bank with a huge overhang that you could sit beneath and Stewart made a b-line for it.

Once by the tree, Stewart switched off the engine and dismounted, holding out his hand for her. She got off and he unclipped her helmet, removing it for her then took off his own.

'You handled that amazingly well! I'm impressed. Have you been on a bike before, luv?'

'No. Never,' she retorted.

'Well, for your first time, that was pretty good going. You held on a bit tight at first but after that, you carried yourself well. I thought you'd be all tense and scared to be honest.'

'I wasn't scared because I trust you implicitly. I wasn't worried in the slightest.'

'Awww, that's good to hear. I'm glad you trust me. And I'm incredibly proud of you too – you didn't reach for my soldier once!'

'Hahahaaa, no I didn't. I promised you I wouldn't!'

He kissed her cheek then untied the picnic basket and led her under the tree.

He opened the basket and took out a lovely blanket which he spread on the ground, ushering her to get comfy as he settled himself on his knees.

'Right, we have water, two bottles of red wine, cheese, fruit, crusty bread, dark chocolate brownies and champagne truffles!'

'Mmmmmmmmm yum yum yum. Sounds fabulous!'

'We'll start with some wine, shall we?'

'Yes, please. I never say no to a glass of red.'

He opened the bottle, smiling and generously poured for them both, then sat next to her, leaning back against the tree.

'What a beautiful spot this is! I love it here. When I'm stressed out or been busy and need to chill, this is where I come to unwind! It's so peaceful and calming. One of my favourite places and I've never shared it with anyone, only you!'

'I'm glad you have. It's my kind of place too. I love being outside in nature, especially in autumn which is my favourite season. The crisp air, the crunchy leaves falling in pretty colours, the haunting glow in the sky… it calms my soul!'

'Yesssss. Exactly. It's soul calming. I knew you'd love it! We have lots in common it would seem and I think that's why we click.'

'We more than click though! We connect deeply.'

'That's what I meant!'

He reached out his left arm and pulled her towards him, urging her to settle back against the tree in the crook of his arm and they sat there, drinking wine and chatting for an hour, connecting even deeper.

They were so comfortable together; no awkward silences, no trying hard to find something to say, and when there was nothing left to say, they just sat together, staring out over the water, enjoying each other's peaceful company.

It was so very blissful until Scarlet had one too many sips of wine and all the control she'd been fighting to keep left her.

The light in the sky was dimming as early dusk approached and she could no longer resist the pull of his magnetism. She turned towards him and licked his jawline which was so chiselled, he could have been a statue, a masterpiece, then softly asked him, 'Are you ready for my scarlet coloured, filthy chaos, Mr Sloane?'

'Always,' he replied, as he put his head back against the trunk of the tree and let her devour his neck. She licked, nibbled and kissed his flawless skin over and over as his arousal became starkly evident, threatening to burst out of his leathers.

She popped down her cup and started to rub him, making him breathe harder before sitting up and removing his jacket. There was no risk of him getting cold; she'd keep him very warm.

Unclipping his belt and unzipping his leathers, she untucked his sweater and trailed her long, sharp, glittering fingernails up his belly to his chest where she played with his nipples. She straddled him, raised his sweater further and started sucking on them, teasing them with her tongue and pinching them between her teeth, as he inhaled sharply then sighed.

His hands were in her hair and all over her back as she raised her pretty head and kissed him, their tongues dancing and swirling. She managed to grab a hold of his own tongue and she sucked on it, ravenously; one of her favourite things to do then reached behind his divine head and pulled his ponytail out from his bandana, letting it hang down his stoic back. She wrapped it around her palm, pulled his head back, trying not to bang it on the tree trunk, and licked his neck from his collar bone to his chin; another of her favourite things to do.

It's one of the things she'd fantasised about before ever getting her hands on him. There were a few things she'd fantasised about; mainly biting his bottom lip, sucking on his long, moist tongue, pulling his platinum ponytail hard whilst licking his flawless neck and engulfing his tasty, meaty, bulgy cock in her mouth, making a heady delicious meal of it and his bollocks while he made growling, groaning melodies with his husky, masculine tones.

In fact, she'd imagined it all so vividly and gotten so turned on by her nocturnal musings that she'd had to buy herself a couple of adult toys so she could get some relief! And she'd had to use them daily, sometimes a few times daily as she was constantly fantasising about him and in a constant state of arousal, always soiling her knickers. She'd even gotten aroused at bloody work; she'd been in her office, thinking about him and had squirted into her undies there too.

But now, she had HIM and although she didn't require toys when she was with him, she did when she was home. She didn't even need to fantasise any more; all she had to do was just think of him briefly and she'd be throbbing, tingling and dripping within seconds, yearning for his deep thrusts and would have to get her toys out, giving herself release! He'd literally turned her life, heart and desires upside down, in a good way and she loved him deeply and now yearned to just be with him. It didn't matter if they didn't make love. Just being near him was enough!

Still devouring him, Scarlet reached down, taking his pulsating, dribbling shaft in her hand and began massaging it, making sure to rub his head too as she'd learned that it sent him into a frenzy.

As she was slowly working him into a fevered state, she heard him moan breathlessly 'I want you, Scarlet!'

She didn't care where they were, if he wanted her, he could have her. She'd do ANYTHING for him!

'Then you can have me!' she replied.

She stood up, removed her boots, jeans and knickers then offered him her hand.

'I don't need to get up, just come back down here!'

'No, I have an idea. Come with me.'

He took her hand and stood up and she led him to his bike that was to the side of the tree.

'Can you move it under the bough?'

He frowned but obliged.

'Get on,' she commanded.

He obliged again, leaving his booted feet on the grass.

'You sure this'll work, luv!'

'Of course. You'll just need to hold me tight around my waist and make sure your legs are firmly braced against the ground!'

Then she climbed on, straddled him and the bike, facing him and placed her feet on the back footrests.

She started kissing him again, with more fervour this time and, taking his hands in hers, placed his arms firmly around her waist.

Once she was sure she was secure, she reached down, gripped his pulsating cock and eased it inside herself, wrapping her arms around his neck tightly.

They both gasped and moaned as she began to grind her hips against his which were rocking beneath her.

She threw back her head with wild abandon, leaning backwards and holding onto his neck. He followed her, reaching his mouth towards her and as it found the translucent skin on her neck, she felt him lick and bite which ignited flames within her soul.

She was on fire – on fire for HIM. She allowed herself to get carried away as she rocked harder and with more urgency. His thrusts became more forceful as he drove himself within her as deeply as he could.

They were like a pair of rutting wild beasts, releasing all their pent-up passions to each other recklessly. And this was reckless; she was half naked and they were howling away on the back of a Harley in a public place before dark! But neither of them cared. It was the right place and time for THEM and they weren't about to let societal reservations get in their way!

They kept up their rhythmic momentum, taking each other higher and higher as they crunched each other's hips together, getting faster and more powerful.

She repeatedly leaned back, letting her head drop backwards with his arms supporting her back then she'd come back up to kiss him deeply, pull his ponytail and lick his neck before leaning back again.

She could feel her tidal wave approaching as the bike began to shake so she leaned back one last time and gave him all she had, powerfully pounding against him and whimpering loudly.

She sensed his climax too when he tensed and his grip on her got tighter.

Their rhythm sped up until the divine happened in tandem.

Her walls were breached so powerfully as she contracted around him and he burst, shooting his hot lava into her and their liquid love merged and flowed as one as it seeped out, coating his balls and his saddle with sticky sweetness.

She let out a high-pitched, piercing shriek at the exact same time he released a warrior's roar and together, they made the most heavenly chorus, making the angels blush.

Both their necks were craned backwards as their orgasms refused to relent. They were so powerful!

When they both started to come down, Stewart pulled her up and into him, engulfing her trembling body in his strong arms. She reciprocated and they held onto each other for dear life as they were both quivering wrecks and neither of them wanted to tumble off the bike, ending up in an entanglement of sticky hips, limbs and leather beneath a heavy Harley.

They both panted, whimpered and shook for ages and once they both started to return to normal, Scarlet extracted herself and got off, in a surprisingly elegant fashion and cleaned herself off before putting her clothes back on.

Stewart just sat there, dazed for a few seconds more then he too dismounted and plopped down on the grass, laying his head back against the trunk with his eyes closed. 'Fuck me, Scarlet. You're so brazen! That was madness… but bloody amazing!'

She giggled while wiping his cock for him before popping it back inside his leathers.

'I can do that myself you know!'

'Oh I know,' she shrugged, 'but I wanted to do it for you!'

'No. You just wanted to touch it again!'

'Haha, that too! I do so love your cock, Stewart!'

'Yeah, I noticed,' he replied, grinning from ear to ear then added, 'well, I'm glad we didn't eat beforehand 'cos I'm famished now and want to stuff my face!'

He reached for the basket, took out the plates and began to dish out bread, cheese, grapes and strawberries. He handed over her plate and they both devoured their food, going back for more as Stewart poured more wine for Scarlet.

'Aren't you having any?'

'I'm driving remember?'

'Oh yeah,' she giggled back.

'And you should only have one more as you've got to stay steady on the back!'

'Yup. That's fine!'

They ate some more, scarfing down brownies and truffles too and Scarlet finished her wine while Stewart drank water.

It was now five forty-five p.m. and darkness had settled about them when Stewart said, 'Time to go I think. Let's pack up and head home.'

They packed away the plates and cups and put their rubbish in a plastic bag, shook off the blanket, folded it away and secured the basket onto the bike.

Just as Scarlet was going to pop her helmet back on, Stewart pulled her in and kissed her. A deep, warm, loving kiss. When he came up for air, he looked into her eyes and exclaimed, 'I wanted to tell you this here, in this place, under this particular tree.'

'Tell me what?'

'I love you, Scarlet! I don't THINK I do, I KNOW I do.'

Her eyes welled up again and small tears started to meander down her rosy cheeks as she reached up and held his face. 'You've just made my heart soar, you beautiful man. I love you too, with all my heart!'

He gathered her up in his arms once more and kissed her again, with as much love as he could muster then just held onto her tightly as they languished in their declared love for one another until he softly said, 'We'd better go!'

She nodded sweetly as they both secured their helmets and climbed atop his bike, Scarlet now cuddled into his back and they headed for home in the darkness, the wind cooling their fevered bodies.

*

It took a couple of hours to get back to Stewart's garage. They put their helmets away and locked up, taking the picnic basket with them.

As they approached his front door, Stewart noticed a package on the doorstep. 'I'm not expecting anything.'

Scarlet knew exactly what it was. 'It's for you from me, darlin'.'

'Oh really?'

He bent down to retrieve it and read the shipping label "MR. S SLOANE". A broad smile spread across his face, 'What it is?'

'You'll have to open it to find out. Let's go inside and I'll make you a cuppa then you can open it!'

'OK'

He opened the door and, once inside, Scarlet headed for the kitchen, made them both some tea and joined him on the sofa.

'Can I open it now?'

'Of course.'

'It feels quite heavy,' he exclaimed, as he tore open the packaging.

Once inside, he was left with a heavy, flat parcel that was wrapped in black gift wrap with a gold damask pattern. He proceeded to carefully open it, noting that the paper was gorgeous and he didn't want to tear it. Inside, he found an 8"x10" ornate, silver photo frame and within the frame was what looked like a poem, printed in an Eighteenth-Century style script. He looked at Scarlet quizzically.

'Read it,' she said.

He reached for his glasses and read the following:

My darling Stewart,

'I tremble in your presence.

Quivering in awe at your divine magnificence

All the demons you've vanquished with the flaming sword you valiantly brandished

All the obstacles you've overcome and the battles you've fought and won

All moulding you into the beautifully stunning, powerful creature you have become.

And I want to fiercely love you; body, heart, mind and soul

You're the bravest, most galant warrior I know.

And I'll not rest my heart in any other home.'

With love always
Scarlet xx

Stewart was deadly quiet and she could see the emotion on his face. It looked like he was rereading it over and over. When he finally looked up, there were tears in his eyes. One had broken free and was slowly running down his cheek.

'Did you write this, Scarlet?'

'Yes, I did. I wrote it for you especially for tonight. The night we begin a new chapter, the night that marks the fact that you trust me enough to let me further into your life.'

He just stared at her for a few moments, clearly very emotional. He tried to speak again but his voice cracked so he cleared his throat before saying, 'I had no idea that you could write so beautifully. I knew you wrote as a hobby but I've never seen any of it! I'm rather speechless.'

'But do you like it?'

'LIKE it? No. I ADORE it, Scarlet! It's simply beautiful, heartfelt and full of praise! I feel honoured and deeply loved and

I don't think that 'Thank You' is enough to express how profoundly this has touched me. So, if it's all right with you, I'd like to show you instead.'

'It's definitely all right with me, my love!'

He stood up, took her hand, and, carrying the frame with him, led her to the bedroom where he put his gift on his nightstand in a place of honour, dimmed the lights, undressed both himself and Scarlet and proceeded to make the most passionate of love to her, continuing into the wee hours of the morning, taking them both to paradise on the precious, fluttering wings of love!

Part 9 – The way to his heart!

They'd been making love all night but not their usual kind of lovemaking. Stewart had been very gentle, tender and caring with plenty of warm, missionary rocking, deep eye contact and passionate kissing. His reaction to her gift had confirmed her deep love, affection and devotion to him which had, in turn, confirmed to himself just how much he already loved her. He didn't quite understand it yet as he'd never fallen in love so quickly before; he'd been extremely cautious of women for the longest while due to a couple of severe heartbreaks earlier in his life. He'd been misused, mistreated and cheated on and he'd built strong walls around his heart to ensure it would never happen again. He'd met other women along the way and had had liaisons but none of them had made him feel the way Scarlet did.

She worshipped the very ground he walked on and made it her mission to lift him up, support him, care for him and love him in every way she could. She loved him endlessly, selflessly, unconditionally and completely and he felt it within his soul so he'd decided to trust her and let her in but he still had his defences raised and there were times he unwittingly shut her out as he'd lived this way for so long, it was going to take time for him to learn to totally let go.

She'd been battered and bruised in love too, quite literally as her first husband was a controlling bully and had treated her despicably which actually angered Stewart to his core. How any man could treat a lady like that was beyond his comprehension, but how they could do it to someone like Scarlet baffled him even more as she was such a sweet, kind, compassionate, loving and magical creature who deserved to be cherished. It also baffled him as to how she could be so trusting and loving with any other man after being so badly brutalised. But here she was, loving and trusting him anyway and he considered it an honour to be the object of her devoted love.

Stewart had awoken before Scarlet, and after watching her slumbering so sweetly and peacefully, had decided to just let her sleep until she awoke naturally. After all, he'd made love to her for hours and hours, bringing her to orgasm a good handful of times, if not more, and had worn the poor lovely completely out.

He'd showered, dressed and gone out to buy a few breakfast bits from his local mini-mart, returning home to eat and check his emails in his office.

It was Sunday but as he was the owner and CEO of his company, he had to keep an eye on things no matter what the day was.

Upon opening his email account, he'd seen an email from his secretary and had read it. There were yet more problems but this time, they were worse and it infuriated him as they were bloody avoidable and unnecessary. In reaction, he'd shouted loudly 'For fucks sake!' which had jolted Scarlet awake.

She called out to him, 'Stew, are you OK, love?'

The response she received wasn't very desirable. 'I told you NOT to call me that so fuckin' DONT!' He bellowed back, followed by 'Go back to sleep, I'm fine!'

She sat there a bit bewildered for a few seconds then decided to get up and go to him.

She brushed her teeth and tidied her hair then went to his office where she found him glaring at his iMac screen.

'What's happened, darlin'?'

'I thought I told you to go back to sleep?'

'Well, I'm awake now and don't want to, so talk to me!'

'There's nothing to talk about; it's work stuff!'

'OK. Can I get you anything? A cup of tea?'

'No. I'm fine. I just need to sort this out and need space Scarlet!' he barked.

'OK. No worries then. I'll leave you alone!' And she left, making her way back to the bedroom where she showered, dressed in soft, gold coloured joggers and a long-sleeved black t-shirt. It was very chilly outside and she wanted to be cozy.

Stewart's outburst towards her was a first though and it had left her feeling a bit emotional. She knew he had moments like this as he'd told and warned her about them so she didn't allow herself to get too upset but she did feel slightly tearful. Not wanting him to see that though, she'd not hurried in the shower, wanting to give herself time to compose her emotions.

She went to the kitchen, made herself breakfast and coffee then plonked herself at the dining table where she ate and checked her phone for any updates or messages. She'd then cleaned up her plate, made herself another coffee and settled on the sofa with a movie, deliberately staying out of Stewart's way!

Halfway through the film, she heard him moving about then he appeared in front of her, looking ready to go out. 'Erm, sorry I yelled at you like that. There's an issue at work and it's totally pissed me off. Forgive me?'

'Of course,' she replied. 'It's OK, love!'

'I've got to go to the office to straighten things out, so are you happy to stay here on your own or do you wanna go back to yours? Either is fine.'

'No, I'm fine. I'll stay here, if that's OK with you.'

'Course it's fine. I've no idea how long I'll be but I'll keep you posted OK?'

'Yep. That's fine. Take your time and don't worry about me.'

'OK, Thank you!'

He bent down and kissed her then left, getting into his waiting taxi.

*

She'd spent the next few hours alone with her feet up, cosily languishing on his incredibly comfy sofa, covered in a fluffy blanket, watching her favourite movies and nibbling on dark chocolate, one of her favourite treats.

It was two thirty p.m. when her phone pinged and it was a message from Stewart to say he'd be home by three thirty and was there anything she wanted him to bring in.

She replied, **Nope. Just you. See you soon**

She was slightly concerned as to what kind of mood he'd be in when he got back but she had enough time to prepare herself mentally.

At three twenty she heard the key in the door so she switched off the telly and went to the kitchen to put the kettle on. She anticipated his need for a huge mug of hot, sweet tea.

She heard him go to the bedroom where he changed then he appeared in the kitchen, looking frazzled and on edge.

'Tea for Milord with an extra spoonful of honey. Figured you'd need it.'

'Aahhhh, you're a star, Scarlet. Thank you. But it needs something extra today.'

He opened a cabinet and retrieved a bottle of whiskey which he poured generously into his mug. 'That'll take the edge off!' and took a long swallow.

'Do you want to talk about it yet?'

'No. I don't wanna bore you with the details, luv. Plus, I'm liable to swear gratuitously which isn't very galant when there is a lady present.'

'Stewart, you're AT HOME. The one place where you can let everything go and say whatever you want without judgement. I'm not a delicate little flower, am I?'

'Erm, NO! Far from it.' He giggled at her.

'Well then, just be yourself and let it all out, gratuitous profanity and all.'

He did; he told her everything with lots of swearing and gruffness, and as he did it, she could see some of the frustrations melt from his face but it wasn't enough. He needed to seriously unwind and she knew exactly what to do.

He was still seething inwardly and, even though he was much calmer, he was still a bit snappy and sarcastic with her which she handled with graceful compassion and love. She didn't get upset with him, didn't take it personally or allow it to affect her deep feelings for him. Her love was unconditional. Stewart was her soul mate, her twin flame, she was positive about that and she considered it her duty to be a calming, loving influence so she decided to focus her attentions on helping her beautiful man through this chaotic episode and take matters into her own hands.

She put on his favourite jazz music, dimmed all the lights and told him to go relax on the sofa.

She went to the bathroom, ran a hot bubble bath with a very large dose of magnesium salts and lavender oil, lit candles and set Alexa to play the same jazz playlist as the living room.

Then she went to get Stewart who was lounging comfortably.

'Right my lovely, come with me please.'

'Why? I'm comfy.'

'Just come with me. You'll be even comfier where we're going, I promise you!'

He stood up, she took his hand and led him to the bathroom where she undressed them both, climbed into the tub and offered him her hand.

'Join me.'

He nodded and smiled as he too climbed in and slipped down into the steaming, soothing water in front of her, his back towards her and laid his head against her cushioning breasts.

She proceeded to sponge him down gently, his chest, arms, neck; gently drizzling the water over his skin while he relaxed into her, sighing.

As she continued to lather him up, she placed soft kisses on his shoulders and neck, then his face, his stunningly chiselled face.

She felt her adoration for him fire up her soul and her heart swelled, making her want to take all of his pain away so she decided to do what she knew he needed, what would help him the most.

She placed the sponge on the side and slid her hands around his front and began massaging his cock and balls, making him inhale through his teeth with his head still laid back against her chest, continuing to rub him all the while kissing him and nibbling his earlobes until she sensed he NEEDED servicing properly.

Thankfully, his bath tub was very spacious with plenty of room for two people so she got him to kneel up facing her and she used her mouth to suck out all the demonic forces plaguing his mind. She sucked him powerfully while she kneaded his buttocks with her hands and scratched his back with her sharp fingernails.

When she brought him to climax, she didn't stop but continued to engulf him. His cock relaxed then hardened again as she refused to release him.

Once he was perfectly rigid once more, she turned her attentions to his balls, sucking them individually as she pulled the skin of his cock back and forth along his shaft, growls emanating from his throat.

As soon as she felt him tense, once again ready to burst, she took him in her mouth again and sucked him all the way home, pulling with as much force as she could muster.

She was getting very skilled at this, one of his favourite sexual exploits and she wanted to make him howl.

And she did!

With one final strong pull, he exploded into her mouth and let out one helluva roar which ended in a high-pitched wail as his voice crescendoed.

His hands had been in her hair the whole time, and as he orgasmed, he made fists, grabbing handfuls which she loved and he held on for ages, his body rigid and quivering as waves of euphoria washed through him.

She then felt him start to relax as the waves relented and he lolloped onto her, depleted, and finally, relaxed.

And there he lay, face down in the tub with his head on her bosom, panting and wheezing, until he managed to speak. 'You're like a drug,' he confessed. 'A relaxing enchanting drug that numbs all the pain and calms the mind. An erotic opium, of sorts! How do you do it? How do you manage to bring me peace so cleverly and beautifully with that one single act? I've obviously had women do that to me before but it's never left me in this kind of state!'

'Well, maybe it was never done selflessly! Maybe it was just a carnal act before, whereas with me I do it out of love and with only you in mind. My own physical satisfaction is neither here nor there, it's just for you but it does give me huge emotional satisfaction when you collapse afterwards. That's when I know I've done my duty well! Plus, I do get physical satisfaction too as hearing you moan, groan and whimper makes me climax. It's the most arousingly erotic sound I've ever heard. It's a beautiful melody Stewart and I could listen to it for hours!'

He giggled, making her boobs jiggle. 'Erm, I think if that went on for hours, my poor cock would drop off. That suction of yours is incredibly powerful. I'll have to nickname you Cleopatra!'

'Cleopatra? Why?'

'Well, she had a reputation with the Roman Centurions, didn't she? Wasn't she known to service a hundred or so after dinner each day, using very powerful suction?'

'A FEW HUNDRED AFTER DINNER? EVERY NIGHT? Bloody hell, her cheeks must have been permanently numb! And what a brilliant gag reflex she must have had! Fuck me, all those sturdy cocks in one night! Mind-boggling.'

'I'm sure you could match it, with your lusciously wide mouth and talented tongue!'

'What? A few hundred different cocks each night? Stewart! What do you take me for?'

He laughed and laughed.

'NO NO, you plank, I meant with me! We could see how many times you could service me in one night!'

'So you're happy for me to suck your cock right off then are you? *Hmmm*?'

'Well, no but it would be rather interesting to try, ay?'

She couldn't stop laughing and his head was bouncing up and down on her boobs and belly as she cackled!

'You're bloody priceless, my darling!'

'I'm actually quite serious. We should see one night just how much we could both handle. You enjoy giving it and I enjoy receiving it. Would be a very cathartic evening, especially for me. Haha.'

'If I do it too much, my cheeks might stay sucked in then I'll be walking around looking like a fish for days!'

More rapturous outbursts of laughter ensued.

'I guess I'd be willing to give you a 'suck-a-thon' as long as I had PLENTY of red wine to guzzle!'

'Well that's a given. I'll make sure there's plenty for you to drink. And just think of all the extra protein you'd be gettin'!' He looked up at her, droplets dripping from the silver bristles on his chin with a massive cheeky grin and his eyebrows raised.

'Protein?' she quizzed with a frown.

'Think Scarlet, THINK!'

She furrowed her brow, thinking then the penny dropped.

'Eewww, Stewart. Don't be revolting!' she berated with wide eyes, slapping his wet shoulder.

He just laughed again.

They had so much fun together. They could literally spend hours just talking and laughing. They had the same filthy sense of humour and very similar interests, and what one didn't know, the other taught. Not only were they very closely connected lovers, they were also best friends. It was a beautifully natural relationship. Again, she was positive they were twin flames!

'So how about Saturday night then?'

'For what?'

'Suction Night!'

'Oh for fucks sake, you're serious then?'

'Of course I am, and I'm gettin excited just thinking about it!'

'Well, I'm happy to give it a go. Just don't be disappointed if I can't manage as much as you think or hope I can!' she shrugged back.

'You could never disappoint me darlin',' he retorted as he kissed her belly.

'OK. It's a date! And in addition to buckets of red wine, I'm gonna need lots of eighty five percent dark chocolate and Coke Zero too please.'

'You can have whatever you want darlin' but why eighty five percent specifically?'

'Because I'm gonna need something strong to remove the taste of cock and sperm from my mouth! Although YOU taste delicious, the aftertaste isn't very pleasant, you know!'

'Erm, well, I don't know actually but I'll take your word for it! I'll make sure you have everything you need, Milady!'

She kissed the top of his wet, bandana covered head and leaned back against the bath as they relaxed together.

'Scarlet?'

'Yes.'

'I am sorry for today. I hope you can forgive me!'
'There's nothing to forgive, my love. Nothing at all!'
He looked up at her and gave her the most beautiful smile.

*

They'd lain in the bath for about half an hour, just soaking and relaxing with Scarlet adding extra hot water. When they got out, Scarlet had insisted on smothering him with home-made Magnesium and Rose Essential Oil. She let him drip off a bit first then began to slather him, starting at his feet.

'Hang on, Scarlet, that stuff smells like flowers! I'm a bloke.'

Scarlet looked at the protruding appendage in front of her face and replied, 'Erm yeah. I had noticed.' And with a giggle, 'I made this concoction myself. It's a blend of coconut oil, magnesium oil and rose essential oil. Both the magnesium and rose are perfect for reducing anxiety and stress. They'll give you a wonderfully calm feeling.'

'Oh really? I never knew that. Well, I knew magnesium was good for relaxing tense muscles and pain as you always have it in your bath but I didn't know about the rose!'

'Yep, one of the best essential oils for it when used topically! So, even though you may smell like your old Granny, you'll feel bloody amazing haha!'

'Well I guess me smelling like an old Granny is a good thing!'

'Why's that?'

'Because I may get a bit of peace. If I smell like an old lady, you won't wanna grab at me and lick my privates!'

'Hahahaaaaaa! Sorry, old man, NOTHING will EVER put me off of your private parts!'

He raised his eyes with a grin and a slight shake of his head!

She had reached his midriff by now and had bypassed his manly parts and was making her way up his tummy towards his chest, then up to his shoulders and down his arms.

As she was rubbing the oil into his upper arms, she whimpered slightly and bit her bottom lip.

Stewart quizzed her, 'What? What was that noise for?'

She looked at him, flushed in the face, still biting her lower lip and grinning.

'Oh no. Here we go again! If it ain't me bulge in me leathers, it's me ponytail and if it ain't me ponytail, it's me tattooed arms! Will you get a grip, woman!'

'A grip?' she asked. 'Sure, I can get a grip!' And she grabbed his cock, squeezing it tight.

'Whoa! Fuck me! I meant 'pull yourself together' not cut off me blood supply!'

She wailed with laughter.

'I know what you meant but I just had to.' She shrugged. 'Now, I can't bloody help it if I find your arms and tats arousing, can I? Would you prefer it if I didn't fancy the pants off of you? *Hmmm*?'

'No no. I'm very happy you find me so thrilling. I just wish you could touch me without having an orgasm!'

'I didn't have an orgasm, I had an ovary cramp and a delicate dribble. There's a difference.'

'Delicate dribble... hahahaaaaaa!'

As she made her way over to his other arm, she decided to make the most of the situation and she licked all his tattoos before applying the oil.

Stewart was laughing as she did it.

'I can't believe you just slobbered all over my arm!'

'Mmmmmm, it was yummy,' she retorted as she quivered slightly.

'Did your ovaries cramp again?'

'They did indeed and the dribble wasn't so delicate this time.'

'Shall I get a mop for the puddle you're about to leave on the floor?'

'May just have to I guess! You're too divine for words and I just can't help myself. I could honestly eat you alive! Now shut up and let me finish!'

'Yes, ma'am!'

She smothered his back and sexy bottom with the oil then went to get his soft pyjamas, dressed him and popped him into bed.

'Why am I going to bed? It's five o'clock!'

'You're gonna relax and let the oils work, watch telly or read while I go and cook dinner.'

'Oh no. I want to spend time with you though. We can order in.'

'How many times have you told me how much you miss having a roast dinner?'

'Oooo, you're making a roast?' he retorted with a gleeful look.

'Yep! Roast chicken, roast potatoes, yorkshires, lots of yummy veg and gravy with a special pudding for afters, all from scratch.'

'Sounds bloody perfect. That'll take you ages though!'

'You've got that movie you wanna watch right? The one I'm not interested in seeing. You watch that while I cook and I'll pop in now and then to gawp at you.'

'You like gawping at me, don't ya?'

'Oh I do. You're a breathtaking sight, you sexy fucker and I could quite literally stare at you twenty-four seven and not get bored! Now, here's the remote. I'll go grab you a cuppa then get crackin' in the kitchen.'

'Actually, instead of tea, can I have some wine?'

'Absolutely. I was gonna open a bottle anyway. I like to drink red while I'm making a roast. I'll bring you a glass.'

'You like to drink red no matter what you're doin'. You're a lush, luv!'

'Cheeky sod!'

She kissed his cheek and wondered off to the kitchen where she cracked open the wine, poured two glasses and delivered one to Stewart who was already engrossed in his movie.

Back in the kitchen, she set the oven to preheat and made a rub for the chicken with butter, fresh garlic, chicken seasoning and pink Himalayan salt, smothering it all over the skin and poking holes it in with a knife. Then covering it with foil, she popped it in the oven to start cooking. It was a small chicken so wouldn't take too long. Once the potatoes were peeled, she put them to boil slowly in salted water and turned her attentions to the pudding. One of Stewart's favourites was rice pudding which she'd never made before so she'd gotten a recipe from her Mommy whose own home-made rice pudding was very delicious as she put raspberry jam in the bottom of the dish before baking.

She combined the pudding rice, sugar, milk, cream and vanilla in a bowl then transferred it into a glass baking dish with a thick layer of jam on the bottom and set it aside to bake later.

She'd boiled the potatoes slowly to give them a fluffy texture and just before they were ready, she'd put oil and salt (the added salt gives them a crunchier coating) in the bottom of a roasting tin and popped it in the oven to get hot. Once bubbling, she strained the potatoes, gave them a shake in the saucepan to fluff up the edges then transferred them into the oil which sizzled nicely.

Having done all she could for now, she left the chicken and potatoes to cook and went to join Stewart in the bedroom, taking the wine bottle with her.

As she entered the room, he paused the telly. 'How ya gettin on darlin?'

'Good. Everything's on track.'

'I can't bloody wait. I haven't had a home cooked roast in ages! When I asked you to come over more, I had no idea I was getting a personal chef as well. You don't have to cook you know, I've always ordered in and I'm quite happy to continue. I want you to relax while you're here.'

'Stewart, we cannot live on take-away. It's not healthy!'

'There are all kinds of take-aways, luv. We can have whatever we want delivered, even roasts!'

'Look, I don't find cooking a task at all. I enjoy it. I find it relaxing and rather rewarding. Especially when the people I'm cooking for enjoy what I've made. We're both very busy people and need proper healthy nourishment. And I'm used to a certain diet of freshly prepared, whole foods and if I don't stick to it the majority of the time, my digestion gets sluggish and I start to feel fatigued. I need to take care of myself and while I'm at it, I'll take care of you too! It'll be good for you to eat properly!'

He reached over, pulled her close and kissed her deeply and, because she'd had half a bottle of red already, the feel of his tongue in her mouth set her lady parts ablaze.

She set her glass down, launched herself at him, straddling his hips and snogged him ravenously.

She loved to snog with Stewart. He had the most luscious tongue and the juiciest pink lips and was the best kisser ever!

His arms were around her, caressing her back and gripping her bottom as they kissed passionately and loudly for a good while.

She was incredibly aroused as was he, evidently, as his cock was huge and hard, pressing against her from beneath the duvet and all she wanted to do was strip him of the bed covers and ride him with wild abandon but she couldn't or dinner would burn so she had to pull herself together.

She withdrew from him. 'I'd better go and check the chicken and tatties.' And she hopped off before he could protest and pin her down.

'Just turn the oven down and get back here quick!'

'Nooooo, you'll have to wait darlin'. We'll finish what we started later.'

She gave him a wink and trotted back to the kitchen where she removed the foil from the chicken, draining off the juices into a jug, turned the potatoes, popped the rice pudding into the oven and set the vegetables to boil.

Now it was time to set the dining table which she did along with pretty wine glasses, candles and soft music.

She could have gone back to the bedroom for a bit but decided not to as she knew they'd not be able to contain themselves a second time so she cracked open a fresh bottle of wine and sat down with her phone to have a browse on Social Media.

About ten minutes later, the vegetables were ready, so she strained some of the water into the jug with the chicken juices and set them aside then whisked up the batter for the yorkshires. The chicken was ready with a lovely crisp skin so she removed it and, in its place, put a Yorkshire pudding tin containing a small amount of oil.

She gave Stewart a ten-minute warning as she made the gravy out of the chicken juices and vegetable water, adding in chicken and onion gravy granules, put the batter in the Yorkshire tin and began to assemble the plates.

Stewart arrived, sniffing the air and making approving noises and she told him to go sit down which he did.

The Yorkshires now well risen and crisp were added to the plates and carried to the table along with the jug of gravy. She popped his plate in front of him.

'Fuck me, Scarlet. That looks and smells bloody divine!'

She smiled and sat down having put her own plate in her setting, then proceeded to pour gravy on each of their plates.

'More please,' he urged. 'I LOVE my gravy!'

'Weird that, so do I.'

Both their plates were swimming in it!

Stewart poured them fresh glasses of wine and they tucked in with Stewart making the scummiest of noises each time he filled his mouth.

They chatted throughout their meal and got through the entire bottle of wine and once their plates were scraped clean, Stewart said, 'I can't remember the last time I had a roast as bloody delicious as that! You are one very clever lady!'

'Awwww thank you, my love.' She winked back at him.

'I'm so stuffed though. Well and truly stuffed.'

'Don't forget there's pudding but it won't be ready for another half hour or so.'

He then made a rather unfortunate noise with his bottom, looking enormously shocked and Scarlet roared with laughter.

'I'm SO sorry. How rude of me. Please excuse me.' He gushed, a bit red in the face.

Scarlet was still laughing with watery eyes but managed, 'It's fine, you silly old sod. It's only a fart. Everyone farts.'

'Yeah, but not at the table!'

'Farting is a natural bodily function. I honestly don't care. Fart away. It's hilarious!'

With that, he let another one rip which sent Scarlet into hysterics. She was holding her belly with tears streaming down her face when another loud one clapped through the air. 'I think I need the loo,' he said as he jumped up very quickly and scarpered for the bathroom, leaving Scarlet rolling about, wailing.

He was gone for a good twenty-five minutes and when he came back, Scarlet had cleared the table and was in the kitchen washing the dishes.

'I'll do those, luv. You cooked so I'll clean up. Please leave 'em.'

'I'm almost finished. Do you feel better after your number two?'

He went bright red then grinned.

'Yes, thank you!'

'Why are you embarrassed?'

'Well, it's not the kind of thing I'm used to discussing!'

'Don't be a twat darlin'. It's only poo!'

He shook his head. He shook his head at her a lot!

'What?' she asked him.

'You're such a child.'

'Oh I know and I don't care. Does it bother you?'

'Nope. It's endearing!'

'Good. Have you made room for pudding?'

'Haha, yes I have!'

'Lovely. Off you pop then and I'll bring it through.'

He disappeared off while she got the pudding out of the oven and carried it to the dining room, placing it on a mat in the middle of the table. His face lit up like a Christmas Tree!

'RICE PUDDING! You made rice pudding?'

'I did indeed!'

'I fucking LOVE you lady.'

She beamed while she served him a generous portion and gave herself a much smaller one.

'What's the sticky red stuff though?'

'Raspberry jam!'

'Ooooo, my mum always put a dollop of jam in mine when I was little but I've never had it baked together.'

He spooned himself a mouthful and made more 'mmmmmmm' noises.

'That, my darlin', is to die for. You did good, Scarlet. Well bloody done!'

'Thank you kindly. Now eat up like a good boy!'

He did. He devoured it!

'May I have some more?'

'Of course you can. You don't need to ask, you daft thing. Help yourself!'

He served himself another decent helping and devoured that too, savouring each mouthful.

When he'd finished, he leaned back against the back of his chair, rubbing his full belly and looking very satisfied. 'What with your care in the bathroom, an afternoon in bed and that amazing meal, I feel so very relaxed and satisfied! Thank you, Scarlet.'

'It was my pleasure. The whole idea was to get you to relax so I'm very happy!'

'Well, there's only one thing left to do now.'

'What's that?'

'To finish off what we started earlier!'

'Oh yeah. How exciting. But I think we need to let our dinner digest first or we'll both be vomiting which won't be pleasant.'

'Let's watch a bit of telly then. It's only eight o'clock. We have plenty of time. You go off to the bedroom and get comfy and I'll sort out the rest of the dishes. I'll join you in a few minutes!'

'I can do 'em, Stewart. I want you to relax!'

'Nope. I insist. Off you go,' he said, as he patted her bottom and sent her on her way.

So she accepted gracefully and did as she was told.

She brushed her teeth and got into bed, sitting up against the pillows and looked for something to watch while she waited for Stewart. She felt incredibly happy and fulfilled. She'd achieved quite a bit today but the major thing was she'd succeeded in her task of getting Stewart into a calmer state of mind and that made her little heart sing and she sighed!

Stewart finished cleaning the kitchen, switched off all the lights and returned to the bedroom where he found Scarlet sat up in bed, snoozing away. She'd fallen asleep, bless her! She'd worked like a trooper today, all for him and his heart had swelled with pride and gratitude. She was a keeper, this one. A true gem and he was determined to make her just as happy as she was him.

He didn't want to wake her as she looked so beautiful and serene plus he'd awoken her rather abruptly this morning by shouting out obscenities, the poor lass, so he decided to leave her alone and let her sleep.

He gently removed a couple of pillows from behind her head, lowered her down as softly as he could, tucked her up nice and tight, kissed her lips delicately and left the room.

He looked back at her once more as he closed the door, feeling overwhelmingly in love with the Sleeping Beauty in his bed.

Part 10 – Cleopatra

Scarlet had slept like a baby the previous Sunday night after a busy day. She'd fallen asleep very quickly and Stewart, being the sweet hearted, caring man that he was, had left her alone!

They'd awoken Monday morning, breakfasted together and had gone out for a few hours to walk, talk and spend some quality time together in the outdoors. They were both outdoorsy people. They loved nature, wildlife and green spaces so had made the most of the crisp autumn day. And walking was important to Stewart, he could walk for hours and hours and often did!

Whilst they were strolling arm in arm beside the river, Stewart broached the subject of Scarlet's birthday which was just under three weeks away, on a Saturday. 'It's your birthday soon, young lady! Is there anything particular you'd like to do to celebrate?'

'I hadn't thought about it really,' she responded, shrugging her shoulders.

'Well, I have and I was thinking of taking you back to Paris. Fancy it?'

'Oh my, I'd love to,' she offered back, with a beaming smile.

'Good. That's settled then.' He confirmed as he kissed her rosy cheek. 'We'll leave on the Friday and stay till Monday like we did last time!'

'Perfect! I can't wait darlin'. Thank you!'

'It'll be my pleasure,' was his response with a glint in his eye. 'A rather kinky one, I might add.'

'Oh, I see. It's not just a trip for my birthday. It's also a trip to satiate your perverse appetite. Are you getting bored, old man?' she enquired with a giggle.

'No. Of course not, but it would be nice to add some spice to the mixture!'

'Oooooooooo.'

'Oh no. You've got that wicked look in your eyes. What's 'oooooooo'?'

'I was just imagining you, deliciously naked, smothered in a spicy cake mixture with a 'melting candle' protruding from your hip area, just waiting for me to 'blow' it out then lick and gobble you up! It's making me rather excited!'

Stewart burst into hysterics, then added, 'I'm sure that could be arranged!' with his trademark cheeky grin.

'Oh goodieeeee. Yaaaay.' She reacted gleefully with a bounce in her step. 'But I have just one more request!'

'I don't suppose it involves leather, does it?'

'How did you guess?'

'I can read you like a dirty book, Scarlet! Yes, I'll be packing my leathers especially for you!'

'Yaaaay.' She excitedly bounced again, clapping.

They both guffawed as they kept walking then Stewart asked her another question.

'Talking of trips, how do you fancy spending Christmas with me; somewhere cold and snowy?'

Her eyes widened. 'Really? Where?'

'Well, remember you told me that your dream was to spend Christmas and New Year in Lapland?'

Her eyes widened even more as she replied, 'YES!'

'Well, if you can get the time off work, I'd very much like to take you this year.'

She stopped dead in her tracks and looked at him. 'Whaaaat? THIS year?'

'Yeah. This Christmas!'

She was so shocked. 'Are you serious, Stewart? Won't that cost a bloody fortune?'

'Erm, one I'm very serious, and two the cost is no concern of yours, young lady!'

'I'm blown away, honestly!'

She was feeling very overwhelmed and started to tear up as she just gazed at him.

'Don't cry, you silly mare,' he replied, as he wiped away a trickling tear that had escaped from her eye.

'Sorry, this is making me quite emotional. It's not something I ever expected. No man has ever treated me the way you do or made me feel so special. It's quite overwhelming. You're such a sweet, kind, generous man with a big, beautiful heart and I'd be honoured to go with you!'

They hugged and kissed beside the river and carried on walking, with Scarlet glowing with happiness and love and Stewart beaming from ear to ear at her humble, sweet and grateful reaction. He wanted to make her feel as special as she actually was because she more than deserved it!

They continued their walk, discussing their plans and arrived back at Stewart's at four p.m. where they passionately made love before he sent her back to her place in a taxi. She had work the next morning and wanted to get an early night as weekends with Stewart were always rather energetic and she needed some rest. She didn't want to turn up at work looking, quite literally, shagged out!

*

It was a chilly Friday evening and Stewart had gone out for a bikers' group ride, coming home late.

He wasn't expecting to find Scarlet at home as she had a late meeting at work, so was going back to hers and coming over in the morning. But her meeting had finished much earlier than expected and since she had a key, she'd let herself in and texted him to advise she'd be waiting for him at home but not to rush. She wanted him to stay out and enjoy himself.

He'd returned home quite late and as he was hanging up his keys and taking his gloves off, unbeknownst to him, Scarlet approached him from behind and slid her hands around his waist, down his belly and grabbed his bulging bollocks through the tight leather, massaging them gently and grabbed his growing cock with the other.

She'd been waiting for this exact moment for ages – Stewart, in his tight leathers, a bit sweaty, a bit tipsy and smelling all naturally masculine just so she could grab him and be indecent with his spectacular private parts as they bulged out of his hip-hugging leather trousers. She was obsessed with him in leather biker gear and couldn't ever get enough of it.

His head turned slightly towards her face that was nestled on his shoulder and he licked her cheek.

She too turned in, licked his mouth, and sucked on his bottom lip as she unclipped his belt, unbuttoned his leathers, gripped his cock that was starting to pulsate and started slowly massaging his shaft. He groaned deeply as she continued to bite and suck his lip.

She used her other hand to cup his heavily laden bollocks, rolling them through her fingers as she continued her manual assault on his dribbling cock.

He reached one hand behind himself in search of her mound.

She was only wearing a long, plum coloured t-shirt and black knickers so he found her lips with ease and started to rub her, arousing her instantly. She was already aroused at the sight of him and the feel of him in her hands but he was such an expert with his fingers and knew exactly how to excite her very quickly.

She couldn't bloody wait! She wanted him to take her NOW, fully clothed!

'I want you to fuck me as hard as you can. Give me your roughest shots – no need to hold back or be gentle! Let me have it. Fuck me NOW!'

He spun about, not uttering a word and backed her up to the dining table where he turned her around, bent her over, spread her legs, pulled her knickers to one side and rammed his rock-hard cock deep inside her with warrior force, his leathers hanging about his hips.

He reached out, grabbed her hair, wrapped it around his hand and pulling it back hard, rode her like a wild animal, releasing all his pent-up stress from the week on her like she'd asked him to, all kinds of wild noises emanating from his beautiful mouth. She howled!

She loved his animalistic side; she craved it. She'd never experienced sex like it before, but he'd opened her mind and introduced her to new possibilities and sensations. She was addicted! But he was never gratuitously rough with her, never treated her with anything but the utmost of respect and love and she would never allow anyone else to do these things to her, only him. Only ever him!

He continued his hot, fiery assault on her, pounding her insides with fierce ferocity, growling all the while.

It was so powerful, so rough, so forceful that the table was moving, jolting forward beneath her and she was holding on for dear life.

Some may have thought that this was too brutal, may have wondered how she could call this respectful and loving but this was what HE needed and what SHE wanted. When his frustrations mounted, this was what helped him release it. It was his therapy and she was more than happy to facilitate his release as it quite literally broke her heart to witness him so stressed so she took it, happily! No, she hadn't seen him since Monday evening but she knew from video chat conversations that he'd had a tough week. But also, she didn't see it that way; he wasn't hurting her or mistreating her, it was just rough sex and if it got too much to bear, she'd let him know and he'd stop as he'd never, in a million years, deliberately cause her any pain. The only pain she could feel was the one his cock caused when it thrashed against her cervix but that was a sweet, pleasurable pain which she actually loved. It drove her mental and ensured her own powerful release! It was cathartic for them both!

They'd found a perfect rhythm and were both in sync. Stewart held nothing back but continued to bang into her as she thrusted backwards against him, matching his intensity.

The table had moved clear across the room and was now up against the wall, making a rather loud banging noise.

Good grief, this man was strong! Very, very strong!

She could feel the fire mounting up inside her and knew she was about to pop as Stewart let loose, giving her everything he had in these last few moments.

Then bam, one final, forceful bash from behind and they both howled as they exploded, their respective floods spilling out onto the floor in a hot, steaming puddle.

Scarlet's howl was more like a scream and Stewart reached around, covering her mouth with his hand to stifle the volume, shushing her as he huskily panted.

He was leaning over her back, completely spent as she flopped down onto the table in a sweaty, trembling heap but he still had a fist full of her hair and was still pulling.

'Stewart, my hair!'

'What?' He panted.

'My hair. You're still pulling it!' She giggled through gasps.

'Oh fuck. I'm sorry, love!' He offered as he let go, rubbing her scalp. 'I didn't realise.'

They stayed bent over the table until they caught their breath then Stewart helped her stand up and they went off for a shower, Scarlets legs quivering like jelly as she walked.

Upon climbing into bed with steaming mugs of hot chocolate, Stewart piped up. 'So, tomorrow, we're going to a fancy dress place I know.'

'Fancy dress? What for?'

'Well, it's our Suction Night tomorrow, isn't it? So I thought we'd make it even more exciting by dressing up for the occasion; you as Cleopatra and me as a Roman Centurion!'

'Oh my giddy aunt, you mad man! That's outrageously funny.' She cackled back then frowned. 'We cannot RENT costumes for Suction Night, Stewart. They'll get covered in bodily fluids! You can't give them back after that. It's puerile and nasty! *Ewww*!'

'We're not renting, we're buying. I've already contacted them. They sell stuff too and they've got a couple of different ones to choose from, so we'll go and try 'em on and buy the ones we like. Then we've got 'em for whenever we want to role play!'

'Oh, I see, this is gonna be a regular thing then, is it?'

'I certainly hope so, darlin'!'

Stewart was beaming as Scarlet laughed her head off. 'You're a naughty, cheeky fiend, Stewart Sloane!'

'Oh, I know but from from the look on your face, you approve wholeheartedly.'

'Oh, I most definitely do!'

They drank their hot drinks, turned off the lights and snuggled down for the night. Tomorrow was gonna be a busy day.

*

They slept in on Saturday morning which was unlike them. They were normally up and about by nine to nine thirty but they'd both had a hectic week and with last night's shenanigans on the dining table, they'd wiped themselves out so they didn't awake until eleven thirty a.m. Unheard of!

They'd stayed in bed a while, cuddling, talking and laughing and had finally gotten up at twelve thirty, dressed and gone for lunch at one of Scarlet's favourite cafes where she bought him lunch for once. He'd made a fuss as he was very old-fashioned and was of the mind that a lady did not pay for anything but Scarlet had insisted, most emphatically, so he'd reluctantly given in!

They'd taken their time over their meal of poached eggs on a bed of garlic parmentier potatoes, steamed spinach and smashed avocado with lots of mocha for Scarlet and buckets of tea for Stewart and had hailed a taxi to whisk them off to the cosplay shop.

Upon their arrival, they'd been greeted by a rather lovely looking young lady who greeted Stewart by name, smiling sweetly and making googly eyes at him. Scarlet's antenna went straight up!

She trusted Stewart but *what was this one up to? Hmmmm?*

'Hi, Emma. How ya doin'?'

'I'm good, thank you, Stewart. You look amazing as usual.'

'Aww thank you kindly,' he replied, giving her a kind smile.

Emma gave Scarlet the once over with an odd look on her face. 'And who do we have here?'

'This is Scarlet. My lovely girlfriend. Scarlet, this is Emma.'

Scarlet reached out her hand to shake Emma's but Emma didn't offer hers. Scarlet looked at Stewart quizzically who quietly said, 'Don't worry. I'll explain in a bit!'

Scarlet's mind was racing – *explain what exactly? What did he need to explain?* Jealousy started rising but she pushed it back down, not wanting to be THAT kind of girlfriend so she just smiled, nodded and followed Stewart's lead.

Emma then began to speak to Stewart again, ignoring Scarlet completely. 'So after you called on Wednesday, we pulled out a couple of costumes; two Cleopatra and two Roman Centurion and here they are!'

She led them into a private side room where they were displayed. When Scarlet saw her choices, she beamed. 'Oh my. They're beautiful. So intricate.'

Stewart agreed with her, adding. 'The changing room is just there, so pop in and try 'em on while I go into the other one and try mine and we'll meet back here for inspection.'

Scarlet nodded approvingly, grabbed her costumes and headed for her changing room.

As she was making her way, she heard Emma say to Stewart, 'Would you like some help getting into them, Stewart? They're a bit fiddly with all the different bits and bobs. You might need a hand!'

'No, no. I can manage, thank you!'

'OK, well I'll wait here then, just in case.'

'No. That's OK. You can leave us. We can manage.'

'Oh, but I don't mind. I'm happy to help you with whatever you need. Honestly! Anything for you, Stewart.'

Scarlet stopped in her tracks and turned back around to see Emma pink cheeked and fluttering her eyelashes at Stewart, her hand on his upper arm. Shocking! *Was she REALLY making a play for him with his girlfriend in the same room? The brazen hussy!*

So she decided to step in and protect her man from being fondled by this dainty yet very forward young lady. 'That's OK, Emma. I've got this. If MY MAN is in need of assistance, I'm more than capable of helping him. You can wait outside and we will call you if we need anything further!' And she grabbed Stewart by the hand and half dragged him into his dressing room and away from Emma's tarty clutches.

Emma went red and looked fuming but Scarlet didn't care. They were the customers and she needed to back off and be a professional. Emma turned on her heels with her pink nose in the air and left. Stewart was laughing!

'Oh, Scarlet. That was so funny.'

'Was it indeed!'

'You don't need to worry, you know. I'm not remotely interested in her. She's always been like that with me. She's just a kid with a crush and I've rejected her advances many times but she doesn't seem to catch on so I just ignore it!'

'Darlin', you can't just ignore that. She was fondling your arm and clearly throwing herself at you. It's inappropriate! Even if you were single, it's still inappropriate! But you're not single which makes it even worse. She's shameless! You need to make it clear that she cannot do that.'

'Don't you trust me?'

'Of course I do. Implicitly! But I don't trust her! If she touches you again, she'll get the sharp end of my tongue!'

'Can I get the sharp end of your tongue too? Sounds kinda nice,' he blurted, flashing his eyes, biting his lip and fluttering his eyebrows.

'Certainly!' and she licked his neck.

'Oooooo, I think my soldier wants to come out to play!'

Scarlet wailed and slapped his arm. 'He'll have to wait till tonight!'

'Now who's the spoil sport?'

She shoved him into his dressing room, saying, 'Go and change!'

She went into her room too and changed into the first of her costumes. She wasn't keen as it didn't fit her right. It was a bit tight in some places and loose in others. And as she knew she'd be on her knees and in all kinds of positions, she knew it would rip so she took it off and popped the other one on. Perfection!

It was a white, full length, figure hugging dress with gold embroidered accents that curved over her hips and met at the front with flowing white, gold and turquoise panels that were attached at the back and draped over her arms. Turquoise and gold beading with the same embroidery delicately accentuated the bust and neckline and gold and turquoise cuffs went over her wrists. Golden sandals graced her feet and a black wig with a golden headdress finished it off! She felt positively exquisite and couldn't quite believe how she looked in it! It was perfect and the white material had a slight stretch to it so she could move freely. She called out to Stewart, 'How are you getting on, my lovely?'

'Almost ready, how about you?'

'I'm ready!'

'OK. Hang on!'

She heard him shuffle about then, 'Come on out then. I can't WAIT to see this!'

She pushed back her curtain to see Stewart waiting impatiently and when he saw her his jaw dropped, leaving his sexy mouth wide open!

'Scarlet! You look beautiful! Stunningly beautiful. That fits you like a bloody glove! Fuck me! I'm… erm… Fuck Me!'

'Well, I would but I'm not sure this is quite the place darlin'!'

'What?' He looked at her, confusion on his face.

'You said 'Fuck Me'. I mean, I'm game for a bit of dangerous behaviour as you know. Remember Paris under the table? But fucking in a dressing room is a step too far!'

'Oh, you minx. You know what I mean!'

She laughed. 'I take it you approve then?'

'Oh yeah. I DEFINITELY approve! You're a spectacular sight!'

'As are you!' she replied, salivating.

In all the excitement of seeing his face light up at the sight of her, she hadn't quite noticed his costume and then it grabbed her attention. Quite brusquely!

There he was, a finely chiselled specimen in a blood-red tunic, black chest armour with a gold lion appliqué, gold shoulder straps and trimming, an attached belt with gold trimmed black armour flaps, a draping black cape and wrist gauntlets. A pair of gold Roman sandals wrapped up towards his knees and he held a gold Spartan helmet under his arm with a sword in his hand. What a sight!

Scarlet was frozen to the spot. She could quite literally drop to her knees and give him the suction he was waiting for right here in the cosplay shop and it took every ounce of decorum to resist the temptation!

They both stood there, shocked into silence, gawping at each other, filthy thoughts swirling about their heads!

Stewart finally broke the silence. 'Scarlet?'

She snapped back to reality. 'Yes?'

'Well?'

'Well what?'

'Get a grip, woman! Is it to your liking?'

'Oh!' she giggled. 'Sorry, luv. I'm in a bit of a daze! YES. FUCK YES! You look positively edible and I am going to gobble you all up tonight!'

'Ah, that's the reaction I was hoping for. GOOD!'

He started to approach her with his arms open, going in for a cuddle but she stopped him 'NO. NO! Stay away from me or I'll not be held responsible for being indecent in public! You are too divine for words, Mr Sloane. I suggest you get out of that thing before I lose my mind and all control of my ladylike propriety!'

He strutted off laughing and they both changed back into their clothes.

They exited the private room to find Emma waiting for them outside the door, very red in the face and wide eyed. *Had she been standing there the entire time, listening to them?* Oh dear, no wonder she looked so shocked!

'I take it you're both happy with your costumes then?' she enquired.

Scarlet responded, 'Yes, thank you Emma. Very happy indeed!' and she gave Stewart a cheeky wink and he responded by kissing her firmly on the lips. Scarlet was thrilled that he'd done that as it was the best way to let Emma know that he wasn't interested in her one bit. He had his woman and needed nobody else! He was well and truly taken!

They went to the cashiers desk, Stewart paid for the purchase, thanking Emma from a safe distance and they left, feeling incredibly excited for the evening they were about to have – their filthy Roman Suction Night!

*

On the way home in a taxi, they stopped off at the supermarket to get what they needed for tonight: eighty five percent dark chocolate and Coke Zero for Scarlet and Stewart wanted some grapes to dangle into Scarlet's mouth like the Romans used to do which Scarlet found rather amusing!

They'd arrived home at five p.m. and decided to order dinner early. Indian Korma again!

It arrived at six p.m., they ate and drank wine with Stewart going for his shower first. Scarlet wanted him out of the bedroom while she was getting ready, so she'd banished him to get himself ready in the living room.

They'd decided to host their special evening in the living room as there was more room for shenanigans so while Scarlet showered and beautified herself, Stewart lit candles, set out the grapes and wine plus Scarlet's personal requirements and popped on some soft music.

Back in the bedroom, Scarlet had dressed herself after abluting and smothering herself in body oil with a golden shimmer and had applied her makeup Egyptian style to complete her look, finishing off with a spritz of Dior.

She called out to Stewart to make sure he was ready which he was and upon her arrival in the living room, she found him lounging back on the sofa, looking all virile and sexy in the candlelight.

'Fuck!' she blurted out.

He smiled, got up and walked towards her. 'Mmmmmmm, look at you. I'm not sure who's gonna end up eating who 'cos you look positively delicious, Scarlet.'

'You can eat me if you want. I certainly don't mind.'

'Erm, I don't think I'll get me head up that dress though,' he said, eyeing her up and down.

'Dresses can easily be slipped off, my darling.'

'They can indeed but first, I want those perfect, pouty, golden lips of yours around my soldier who has honourably stood to attention in your presence, my Queen!' and he looked down at his crotch.

Scarlet's eyes followed his and then she realised he hadn't worn the red tunic under the armour and he'd done that deliberately so as when his cock inevitably rose, it would poke through the armour flaps which was exactly what it was doing now. A very clever move!

'Oh yes, I see. He's peeking at me expectantly and he's all pink and glistening,' she said seductively, licking her lips as she backed Stewart further into the candlelight. 'And he's such a handsome soldier. I think he deserves a kiss!'

She lowered herself to her knees and gave his glowing tip a kiss.

Stewart sighed.

She continued kissing him; soft, feathery kisses all over his head as she gently took a hold of him and started massaging his shaft. Stewart's head was flopped backwards as he held her head, delicately stroking the hair of her wig and making the most arousing of sounds.

Hearing him moan urged her on as she began to lick him; stroking the length of him from base to tip and back again, her lady lips beginning to tingle.

His grip on her head got slightly firmer as his hips started to slowly gyrate.

Then she heard him say in a low, raspy tone. 'Darlin', I can't wait. Just take me now and suck me hard. I need to be in your pretty, wide mouth NOW!'

She looked up at him, her face sparkling in the candle glow and replied, 'Your wish is my command, brave warrior,' and she immediately engulfed him; every inch of his pulsating hardness and began to suck with all her might. She sucked powerfully, as she pulled back and forth, not releasing him for a second.

He gripped her head tightly and she held his hips firmly as she pulled him in to meet her, getting faster as she went, making him gasp and hiss as she whinnied and whimpered.

She was throbbing down below now. Servicing him always brought her immense pleasure. It was such an erotic act between them and he was just so very delicious. His taste was sublime!

He now set the pace as he hissed out. 'Faster, harder and deeper. Please!'

She opened her throat and took him deep, increasing the pull and urged him to thrust his hips which he did. He thrusted himself into her as he pulled her head towards him at breakneck speed, all the while looking down at her to witness her golden lips taking him in. Her cheeks looked hollow as she sucked harder than she ever thought possible and that sight finished him off.

His neck craned and he howled 'Fuuuuuck' heavenwards, as he shot his glorious seed deep into her throat, repeating it again, this time with her name 'Fuuuuuck, Scaaarlet.'

Their pace slowed to a gentle rock, his beautiful cock pulsating within her mouth as she took everything from him.

She kept him within the warm confines of her mouth until his body relaxed and his hardness softened then released him, kissing his lower belly gently and holding him around his waist.

He dropped to his knees in front of her and kissed her deeply, their tongues rolling. He broke free. 'I want to taste myself on your lips.' And he went in for more, sucking her tongue into his mouth.

She began to quiver, whimpering softly into his mouth as he engulfed her tongue and lips then she too came, but gently. She didn't explode; she just released a warm stream of delight into her white, lace Brazilian panties.

She pulled away, plopping back to sit on her heals and he held her head against his armour-clad belly while she trembled.

'Fuck me, Scarlet. Where did you learn to do that? It was fucking perfect!'

'I don't know. I've not really done it properly before meeting you!'

'REALLY? What, never?'

'Well, yes but not like this as I never enjoyed it before. It was just an act really. An act I didn't look forward to but, with you, I find myself wanting to do it so very badly. It makes me feel powerful. And I just love pleasing you. And you taste bloody divine too!'

'Mmmmmm, I do rather, especially on your lips.'

She giggled!

'Want some wine, darlin'?'

'Yes please, and some chocolate and a large glug of Coke Zero!'

'Coming right up.'

He poured her some bubbles which she gulped then handed her a glass of wine and some chocolate which she ate slowly on the floor with Stewart sat next to her.

'How many times do you think you can manage it tonight then?'

She smiled. 'I have no idea. My cheeks are already feeling a bit tingly and numb after that so give me some time and we shall see. Maybe the first one of the evening should have been a bit gentler!'

'I know but I couldn't wait. Just feeling myself in your beautiful mouth and watching myself disappear between your lovely lips drove me crazy and I couldn't wait or hold back. It's your own fault for being so elegantly good at it! Oooo, you've got chocolate on your lip,' and he leaned over and licked it off. 'Oh wow. That's yummy. I've never tasted chocolate that dark before.'

She reached for the table, grabbed another square, popped it into her mouth, pulled him in close and said, 'Here, have some more!' and kissed him, sharing the melting ooze in her mouth with him. They slobbered and licked each other, making yummy noises and getting melted chocolate all over their chins and they licked that off of each other too.

She handed him her wine. 'Now sip that with choccie still in your mouth. It's heavenly.'

He did and his eyes widened. 'Blimey. That's bloody lovely together! You're a wealth of culinary information, Scarlet!'

'My speciality is sausage actually. I'm a bit of an expert with sausages!'

'Really? What kind of sausage?'

She looked at him, her eyebrows raised, waiting for the penny to drop.

'What?'

She continued staring at him, until, 'Oh for fucks sake, Scarlet,' and he burst into hysterics.

'That took you a while! Have I sucked out your brain as well as your seed?'

'Hahahahahaaaaaaaaa!'

'Right, valiant soldier, up you hop onto the sofa. It's time for round two!'

'Oooooo, so quick. Lucky me!'

He excitedly climbed onto the sofa and sat back as she pushed his powerful legs wide apart, nestling herself between them and started biting his inner thighs. She nibbled her way up the inside of his left thigh, licked her way across his balls then down the inside of his right thigh then back up, across and down. She repeated this a few times then started nibbling, gently, on the tip of his cock too, on her way around.

Because he was into kink, he didn't mind a bit of tooth action on his cock so she was free to nibble away and she did, delightfully!

His moans and groans exiting his plump, pink lips were as divine as usual – he was revelling in the sharpness of her teeth as they grazed the delicate skin of his heavenly private parts. She allowed her bites to get a little stronger, causing him to buck and flinch, inhaling sharply through his clenched jaw then exhaling deeply with a growl. She loved hearing him growl as that meant the beast within was awakening and that, in turn, meant that she'd probably end up getting pounded maniacally into the floor which excited her immensely! He'd bloody better give her a thorough jolly rogering after all this hard work!

As she continued teasing him with her teeth he, once again, piped up with, 'Scarlet. Stop teasing and suck me!'

'No. Wait! Just relax and enjoy the build up!'

'Not tonight, luv. I can't. I'm too horny, too wound up, too desperate. All I want is your lips around my cock!'

He was looking at her through fevered eyes and she could actually see the desperation in him, so she decided to give him what he wanted and went to town on him for a second time, repeating what she'd done before except, this time, she used her teeth too, grazing him as she slowly yet powerfully pulled backwards with that deep, powerful suction he craved so much.

As her cheeks were feeling a bit numb, she needed to heighten his sensitivity with her teeth or it'd take too long and she'd end up disappointing him. But, if the grunts, growls and thrusts we're anything to go by, he was loving every single sharp scrape.

As she continued to suck, pull and scratch, he started to thrust upwards, once again, grabbing her head. She was worried about not being able to control the teeth grazing so stopped as he built the intensity. 'Teeth, Scarlet. Keep using your teeth!'

She obliged willingly!

Now things were getting rough and she felt her gag reflex weakening. She'd only ever performed this once a night for him before so hadn't a clue how she'd react to more but with a long, hard, thick object being thrust down your throat multiple times, you're bound to get a reflex reaction at some point. And sure enough, on his next thrust, she gagged but he didn't notice and she kept going. Then again, she gagged harder this time but choked it back as he kept on pushing himself into her. Then again but this time, she wretched powerfully but still managed to keep a hold of him and still, he didn't notice. He was too enraptured, too deeply in the throes of mad passion so with watery eyes, she kept going until he spilled once more, hollering and howling but she couldn't swallow it. She'd had enough so she let him go and licked his leg, releasing his seed onto his skin with her tongue while she massaged him with her hand, bringing him down gently. He was writhing beneath her, none the wiser that she'd smothered him in his sticky ejaculations.

He shook and trembled as she climbed on top of him and kissed him deeply, all the while stroking his arms tenderly.

They remained there, holding onto each other until Scarlet spoke up. 'You OK, darlin'?'

'Yes, sweetheart. Are you?'

She giggled.

'What's funny?'

'You didn't notice, did you?'

'Notice what?'

'Me gagging on your soldier!'

'NO!'

'Darlin', until I get more used to it, you can't thrust yourself so deeply into my throat! I ended up almost choking and had to spit your fluids out onto your leg!'

'Did ya? Oh fuck. I'm sorry darlin'!'

'I thought you were gonna kill me!'

He cuddled her up, apologising again, not quite believing how he'd not noticed!

'You were on another planet I think,' she exclaimed.

'You should have just stopped, babe!'

'No way! I wasn't gonna spoil it for you.'

'But ya know, watching your lady gag on your cock can be rather arousing, Scarlet. It ain't a bad thing!'

'I am aware of that but I'm afraid it's one thing I find unpleasant, Stewart. I don't like it! My ex used to purposefully choke me with his parts and it brings back awful memories!'

'I'm so sorry luv. I had no idea the bastard did that to you! Next time, just stop!'

'No! Next time, I'm tying you down so you can't fucking move mate!'

They laughed and cuddled and Scarlet explained she was done. She couldn't handle any more and needed to drink coke.

She climbed off, went to the coffee table and downed a load of fizz. The bubbles felt so nice in her mouth.

She turned around and Stewart was still sat there, flopped on the sofa, legs wide apart, his cock all limp and soft laying on his sticky thigh, fast asleep! Awwwww, she'd knocked him out! She felt rather proud then realised this meant that she wasn't going to get her stiff rogering!

Darn!

Oh well, at least he'd had what he wanted. What he deserved! Tomorrow was another day after all!

She gently roused him and helped him to his feet. 'Where are we going?'

'To bed, luv. You're done in!'

'Yeah but I haven't sorted you out yet!'

'Erm, in the state you're in, I don't think you'd be capable of giving me the jolly rogering I'm after.'

'Jolly rogering?' he quizzed with a sleepy smile. 'You do come up with some quirky quips, darlin'!'

'Off to bed with you, Mr Sleepy Sloane.'

She helped him to the bedroom, took off his costume, wiped off his groin area and leg with baby wipes which she always kept in the bathroom, popped him into bed and kissed him. By the time his head hit the pillow, he was out like a light, gone into a deep, sated sleep which gave her a very warm, fuzzy feeling deep inside her soul.

She'd done that! She'd knocked him out instead of the other way around and, once more, she swelled with pride but hoped to high heaven she hadn't knocked him too far out that he couldn't perform tomorrow because her parts were still throbbing and she'd be needing some relief of her own!

Part 11 – Paris

The weeks were passing by with Scarlet staying at Stewart's from Friday to Monday. She'd been with her company for many years and had been PA to Stephen Archer for three quarters of that time and had always put in the overtime when required. They had a very strong working relationship and were also friends. She'd been over to his house for dinner on a few occasions and had developed a friendship with his lovely wife, Savanna, so when they'd had lunch together one day, which they did twice a month, Scarlet had broached the subject of reducing her days to four per week, wanting to no longer work Mondays so she could spend more time with Stewart. He was so happy that she'd finally found the man of her dreams, that he agreed to it without hesitation! Plus, she had her own assistant too so she could cover for her on a Monday.

As a result of this, they'd spent so much more time together; half living together and their relationship had solidified even further, their love strong, steadfast and true. They had become a deeply connected couple!

*

One evening as they were getting ready to settle down for the night, Stewart was already in bed, awaiting her lovely warm body to cuddle up in his arms while they watched some telly!

They loved nothing more than to snuggle up in bed and

watch TV of a quiet evening and Stewart enjoyed it even more after Scarlet had performed her regular evening beauty ritual which he adored witnessing. She took such beautiful care of herself, her body and her skin. She was incredibly old-fashioned about it, believing a lady should always look, feel and smell elegant. Her skin and hair should be soft, delicately scented and well nourished!

As she exited the bathroom, looking ravishing in nothing at all, just her glowing birthday suit, he snuggled back onto his pillows to watch her perform her ritual.

She began by slathering her body in his all time favourite whipped body butter that contained precious oils and smelled like brown sugar and vanilla. She then slinked into her silky soft, dusky rose-coloured night shorts and cami top, trimmed with ivory coloured lace, washed her hands then returned to sit at the dressing table he'd bought for her to apply her various layers of face serums and creams.

Having cleansed her face, neck and décolleté in the shower, she applied toner to a cotton pad and gently removed any traces of left-over cleanser, patting it dry with another cotton pad. Then came her skin smoothing and tightening serum which she pressed in, holding her skin taught as she did it, giving her visage a 'lifted' look. Her eye area came next as she applied youth awakening eye serum to her lids and under eyes, followed by a brightening eye cream, which she gently tapped into her skin using her ring finger.

Once that was complete, she moved on to her anti-ageing Marine face cream which she, again, worked in using upward strokes until fully absorbed, finishing off with a light spritz of refreshing moisture dew and brown sugar flavoured lip balm ~ she looked radiant! Glowing!

Hair next: she stood up, bent forwards to allow her locks to drape towards the floor, spraying them with moisturising hair perfume and combing it through with a wide-toothed comb. She never used a brush as brushing her hair when dry always made it frizz which she hated!

Skin and hair nourished and smelling like a warm sugar cookie, she finished off with a light veil of Dior perfume which just added to her opulence and slid into bed beside her gorgeous man whose arms were awaiting her!

He hugged her in tight and breathed deeply, inhaling her scent with much satisfaction, 'Mmmmmm, my word, you smell and feel divine, as always! One of my favourite parts of the day is you climbing into my arms after your beauty ritual, looking and smelling so very exquisite. You are the definition of a true Lady which is something of a rarity these days. I'm honoured to call you 'mine'. Truly honoured!'

'Awwww, Stewart. You always say such beautiful things. I'm honoured to call myself 'yours' too! The thing is, I don't just take care of myself for me, I do it for you too as I know how old-fashioned you are. If you could go back and live in the Eighteenth Century with your Eighteenth-Century brain, you would and I try to be the kind of 'lady' you'd have had in your arms back then!'

'I never knew that!'

'My darling man, you are the epitome of a true gentleman and you deserve to be loved by a true lady. It's as simple as that!'

'I love you, ya know, Miss Adams!'

'I love you too, Mr Sloane!'

They kissed, with Stewart making scrummy noises as he tasted her lip balm then sank back to watch telly!

It wasn't too long before Stewart turned towards her, 'On the subject of me being loved by a true Lady; earlier in the doorway,

I saw a gloriously naked lady! She had NO clothes on, the brazen hussy! Do you think said lady would be willing to love me tonight, in all her nakedness?'

'Hmmm! I do think she could be tempted into making another appearance! She may need some encouragement though!'

'Oh! What sort of encouragement, I wonder?'

'Ummm, well, I don't want to be crude, but if YOU were nude, she may very well come bursting out, in all her brazen glory!'

'Oooo. I'd best strip then!'

He reached beneath the covers, wriggled about a bit then flourished a pair of boxers in her face before throwing them purposefully across the bedroom, 'Is the lady tempted yet?'

'Marginally!'

'Only MARGINALLY?'

'You may be nude but you're still covered!'

'Ah. Easily remedied!' and he ripped off the duvet, revealing his delicious nudeness, including his dutiful soldier that was standing to very rigid attention!

'Mmmmmm. Scrumptious!'

She jumped up, hurriedly slinked out of her silky jammies, also throwing them across the room and hurled herself at him, aiming for his staggeringly generous cock which she intended to make a fulfilling meal of before riding it into the night.

'There she is!' he exclaimed with a twinkle in his baby blues and a lopsided grin, 'My very own nude, crude, true Lady ~ all Elegantly Filthy and Delightfully Improper!'

'And she intends to live up to that description with as much vim and vigour as she can muster. So I suggest, you sexy fucker, that you brace yourself!'

He reached his arms up behind him and grabbed the headboard, 'Braced and ready, my Lady!'

'Good boy!' she uttered with a wink and a wicked smile before powerfully engulfing his glorious cock in her mouth, making him squirm, groan and twitch uncontrollably.

This was just the beginning. He had indeed tempted her and wound her up into a very hot, dripping state and tonight, she was gonna make damned sure she left him hot and dripping too; hot, dripping and whimpering like a puppy in her arms!

And she did; she always knew just what he needed and how to deliver it successfully.

He'd needed her to take *him* to the stars for once and riding him there was the best way as he, now and then, needed *her* to take the reins, needed *her* to be the one setting the pace.

And it wasn't always a galloping pace he needed either, sometimes she just needed to make love to his soul as well as his body, with lots of loving devotion and gentle tenderness but this night, he'd needed his body rocked by her undulating curves, rhythmically and rather savagely, riding him like a blazing unicorn, streaking across the night sky ~ and a stellar job she'd done too as, just as she'd promised, he was left hot, dripping and whimpering like a puppy in her arms; curled up beside her, sweaty and shaking like a leaf, making the most adorable noises!

Then he'd fallen asleep in that same position and that's when she knew she'd served him well; when she heard his gentle snores rattling up from her bosom, her heart had melted and she felt very satisfied indeed, knowing that her beautifully scented, nocturnal endeavours had taken him to a place of serenity!

And serenity is what he desperately needed as his dark episodes were becoming more frequent and, even though these rollicking escapades of hers helped, he very much needed more;

he needed to release his kinky beast but was so persuaded that he had to keep that side of his life separate, he would only allow that to happen in Paris. No matter how hard Scarlet had tried to tell him nobody would be any the wiser, he just wasn't ready to actually live the life permanently, at a detriment to himself!

*

The weekend before they were due to go to Paris, Stewart had awoken on the Sunday morning under a very dark cloud. No reason for it. He was just moody, distant, curt, angry and very cutting!

She'd tried everything to cheer him up but had failed miserably; however, she was determined not to give up on him. She couldn't. She adored him way too much.

He was steaming about the house with every little thing setting him off. Even her!

He'd raised his voice and had sworn at her a few times, telling her to leave but it didn't put her off for she knew it was just one of the mild Intermittent Explosive Disorder episodes he'd warned her about. He'd told her about his IED which causes irritable, irrational, angry outbursts for no known reason. They just come out of the blue. Luckily for Stewart, his case was mild so he never became violent, threatening or dangerous but he'd warned her that it could be quite scary. He'd explained that his episodes were also few and far between and he'd noticed over the years that an episode usually came after periods of stress, overwork and lack of sleep which he'd been experiencing recently due to work. He'd added that a long, quiet walk usually helped him to handle it and regain control but that he'd be pretty knackered afterwards. What he hadn't told her, though, was how SHE was to handle it while it was happening!

He was in the kitchen making himself a cup of tea when she'd tried to connect with him again.

'Stewart, is there anything I can do?'

He spun about to face her with darkness in his eyes. 'Will you just fuck off!'

'No, I'm not fucking off! I'm going nowhere! That's what others have done. They've quit when the going got tough. But I'm not them and I won't give up on you because I love you way too much! I'm here for it all. Whatever you throw at me, I can take, so deal with it! I will NOT walk out on you.'

'But I want you to! I want you to fuck off and leave me alone!'

'Yeah see, I know you don't mean that. I know that's not the real Stewart talking. So no matter how harshly you speak to me, I'm going nowhere!'

She thought she saw a tender glint in his eye, so she raised her hand to gently stroke his cheek and he grabbed her wrist and held it tight in the air, hissing his words at her through clenched teeth.

'Are you deaf or just stupid? Don't fucking touch me and go home!'

'NO. For the last time, I'm not leaving you alone in this state!'

She was facing him down, staring back at him with as much intensity as she could muster.

He released her wrist and turned away, flinging his arms about, mumbling, 'Fine. Stay, go, do whatever the fuck you want!'

'Thank you,' she replied softly but firmly. 'I'll be in the living room when you're ready.'

'Ready for what exactly?'

'Ready for whatever it is that you need!'

'You can't fix me, Scarlet!'

'OK. If you say I can't, I can't but I'm certainly not gonna walk out on you 'cos when this black mood lifts and I'm gone, I'll just be another one who left you when you were down and I WILL NOT be that person! You're stuck with me, baby.'

The battle was clearly raging in his mind; she could see it in his eyes. One second they were dark and the next there was a glint and back and forth it went as he tried to fight through the darkness and it broke her heart into a million shards to witness it. It was almost unbearable. But bear it she must!

She left the kitchen and went to the living room to sit on the sofa.

A couple of minutes later, she heard the front door open and slam shut. She got up to look out the window and there was Stewart, marching off up the street and she let him go!

He needed space and that was fine. Yes, maybe she should have left and gone home so he could have space inside his own house but she knew what it would do to him if he snapped back and found her gone. It was unthinkable! So she'd had to stand her ground.

He'd been gone for three hours when she heard the doorbell.

She looked out of the window to see who was there and it was Stewart. He must have forgotten his keys.

She opened the door and greeted him with a smile. 'Hey you.'

'Hey!'

He wondered off to the bedroom and she went back to the sofa.

A few minutes later, she heard his voice quietly say 'Scarlet?'

She turned around and he was standing by the living room door looking broken, lost and forlorn.

She got up and went over to him. 'Yes, my love?'

He had his head lowered. 'How come you're still here?'

'You didn't actually expect me to leave, did you? Leave you alone in this state?'

'I did though! I thought you'd be frightened and run!'

'Frightened? Of YOU? Never in a million years! And why would I? I had no reason to leave, darlin.'

'But I was so bloody rude and aggressive! I spoke to you deplorably.'

'Ah, but that wasn't the true you, that was your dark side and I know the difference. Don't ask me how I know, I just do! So anything you do or say when that side of you takes over goes straight over my head!'

'You weren't upset?'

'No, not because of anything you said or did. What upset me was seeing you battling within yourself. That ripped my heart open!'

'I'm sorry!'

'Don't be. Please don't be! This is something you have no control over and I do not hold you responsible. IED is a monstrous beast! And you didn't really do anything bad. You didn't hurt me; you were just loudly and verbally unpleasant. It's nothing I can't handle, I promise you. Do you remember Paris? The night you wrecked me? I was in the tub, you were sat on the edge and I told you that I loved you, that I would never hurt you and that I wasn't going ANYWHERE but would be by your side for as long as you allowed me to be, right?'

'Yeah, I remember.'

'I meant it!'

He nodded sheepishly.

'Stewart, may I touch you?'

'Oh don't be silly! Of course you can!'

She closed the gap between them and took his face in her soft, gentle hands. 'Darling, beautiful man, look at me!'

He raised his eyes to hers which were now glistening with tears.

'You have NOTHING to be ashamed of. Nothing! So please stop averting your eyes. I love you with my entire being and I am right here to support you always. I have your back and, hopefully, your heart.'

Tears now welled up in his eyes too as they gazed at each other. He was trying to fight them back but it wasn't working so she engulfed him in her arms so he could cry without being looked at. And he did, he wept quietly on her shoulder while she held him close to her heart and stroked his back, tears streaming down her own cheeks too. When his gentle sobs relented, he stood up straight. 'I'm exhausted!'

'I'm not surprised, sweetheart. Did you walk for three hours solid?'

'Yeah. I needed to. But it's not the walking that exhausts me. It's the episodes. They always leave me completely drained.'

She wiped his face with her hands and said, 'Would you like a bath?'

He nodded. 'Yeah. That would be lovely.'

'OK. Come with me, my darling.'

She led him to the bedroom where she sat him on the bed and suggested he undress, then went into the bathroom to prepare his bath, setting the lights and calming music.

She returned to the bedroom, took his hand and directed him into the bathroom then into the water which was warm and smelled divine.

He sunk down and asked her, 'Aren't you joining me?'

'No, my love. You need to soak, relax and stay quiet, I think. You know what'll happen if I get in with you – we'll get all touchy-feely which will lead to other things that I'm not sure you're in the right frame of mind for just yet. Am I right?'

'You are. I'm so tired and that's the last thing on my mind.'

'As I thought so just chill, baby. Would you like a cuppa?'

'Yessss! Yes please.'

'I'll go make you one!'

She went to leave the bathroom when Stewart called after her, 'Scarlet?'

She turned back around. 'Yes, love?'

And in a very quiet, tired voice he said, 'Thank you. Thank you for staying!'

She walked back over to him, stooped down, held his adorable face in her hands and replied with, 'You are so very welcome my darling.' And she placed a soft, lingering kiss on his forehead.

She made her way to the kitchen to make him a steaming mug of sweet, honeyed tea, took it back to him, kissed his head tenderly again and left him wallowing blissfully.

Thirty minutes later, she returned to find he'd dozed off in the bath which was quite worrying as it was incredibly dangerous.

She roused him gently. 'Stewart, sweetheart. Let's get you out. You can't sleep in the bath!'

He came around and nodded, so so sleepy. Bless his heart, he was well and truly depleted!

She helped him out, dried him off and got him into bed, stark naked. Making him put jammies on was just another task, so she decided not to bother. The simpler the better today.

She tucked him up with extra blankets and said, 'I think Paris is gonna be crucial. It's not just gonna be a celebration for me but some well needed therapy for you! I know sex, especially kinky sex, is an outlet for you and I believe the timing is perfect. I just want you to know that whatever it is that you desire that weekend, I'm more than willing to submit to it, my darling, because I trust you implicitly and love you more than words could ever express, so if I need to toughen up so you can release, I will. I will do anything for you, anything! Whatever it takes!'

He looked at her through puffy, droopy eyelids and said very sleepily, 'You have no idea how much that means to me. I love you too, endlessly!' and dropped back off to sleep as she stroked his beautiful face with tears rolling down her cheeks.

Seeing him so totally broken was heart-wrenching but as he'd told her earlier, she couldn't fix him!

Maybe he was right and she couldn't BUT she could be a constant for him; someone to stick by him through thick and thin; someone to love him through his darkness; someone to bravely face his demons down and not run; someone who'd bring some light into his life and the person who'd be able to match and handle his kinky side when he needed it most!

Paris could not come quick enough!

*

The following morning, Scarlet had awoken to find Stewart was already up and in the kitchen.

Still sensitive from the previous day, he was in a right fluster, 'What's wrong, baby?'

'There's no bloody milk for me tea and I've already made it too!'

He was so fucking sexy when he was flustered and all he was wearing was his tight, grey boxers and Scarlet couldn't help but eye him up and down as she had a filthy idea; one she hoped would sort him out good 'n' proper!

She walked over to him, backed him up against the countertop, yanked down his boxers and engulfed his deliciousness in her mouth. 'Mmmmmmm,' emanated from her throat as Stewart inhaled sharply.

To get him hard and ready, she gently flicked her moist tongue over and around his head then along his shaft to the base where she sucked the skin between her teeth. Within seconds, his succulent cock bounced up like it was on hydraulics and she wasted no time in sucking him powerfully while he groaned deeply, his hands in her soft hair, holding her head firmly.

She gave him everything she had, making her own cheeks numb as she continuously pulled him in harder and deeper until he popped, releasing his warm, creaminess into her mouth.

She quickly retreated, jumped up, leaned over the counter and spat the contents of her mouth into his tea mug, licking her lips and grinning at him wickedly, 'Your milk, my darling!'

'Uuuggghhh, you dirty, filthy, nasty little heathen. That's disgusting!' he shot back at her. He was trying so bloody hard to be serious and had a genuine look of disgust on his precious face, but it wasn't working as his boxers were still around his knees, his wet cock was hanging out and bouncing around as he moved and he just looked so very funny. Scarlet couldn't help but laugh – a lot!

'No no Scarlet. It ain't funny, it's nasty. YOU'RE nasty,' he jibed as he picked up his mug, shuffled over to the sink and emptied the thick, lumpy liquid down the plug hole.

'Hey. That was my daily protein allowance, you wastrel!'

'Well, it wasn't for you, was it? It was for me and I ain't drinking Cum Tea. You're so nasty sometimes, Scarlet!'

'Ohhhh! OK. I'm so sorry I've offended your delicate sensibilities, my angel. I promise to never do it again!'

'That I DO NOT believe. Filth is in your DNA; you just can't help yourself. You're a very naughty young lady indeed. Very VERY naughty!'

Scarlet was still laughing as his cock just wouldn't stop boinking every time he moved.

'What is so funny?'

'You do realise you've been telling me off this whole time with your cock hanging out, right?'

He whipped his head down to look, 'And you didn't think to say anything? Hmmm? Opted to just stand there laughing at me instead, you wicked female!'

'Why on earth would I do that? It's been way too entertaining watching you try to be all serious with your wet willy flapping about the kitchen and your boxers round your knees! Besides, how could you NOT realise that they're still around your knees? Did I suck out your ageing, addled brain as well as your cream?'

'Right. That's IT, you cheeky bloody mare!'

He wriggled out of his boxers, swiftly grabbed her, spun her about, pushed her up against the kitchen wall, yanked her hips backwards, slid her knickers to one side and rammed himself inside her as hard as he possibly could.

Scarlet let out an unbridled, high-pitched wail as he bashed her cervix and continued to do so, his sturdy hips delivering blow after mighty blow.

Oh boy, did he let her have it! He held nothing back at all and showed her no mercy as he hammered her into the wall. And she was loving it!

Every Herculean hip wallop made her scream as they sent lightning bolts shooting up through her core and she had a smile on her face the entire time. This, to her, was sheer perfection – rough, tough, wild perfection!

Stewart ramped up the speed, literally going at her hammer and tongs, building them both up into a maniacal frenzy then WHAM, one final, bone shattering bash sent them both tumbling over the edge and off the cliff where they collapsed onto the floor in a trembling, twitching, pulsating, squirting heap of boneless limbs!

Stewart was on his back, legs spread, desperately gasping for air and Scarlet was on her side, her head on his chest with her left leg draped over his sweaty, heaving body, panting madly.

Although her pelvic convulsions had begun to relent, sticky juices were still meandering out of her tender lady lips, making her shiver.

And there they lay, unable to move; a pile of wrecked bones and twisted body parts. Ruined!

Once he'd got his breath back, Stewart said, 'You may be a naughty little minx, Scarlet but you're also a very clever one!'

'What do you mean?'

'Well, it's literally just dawned on me what's happened here this morning!'

She turned over and raised her head to look at him, 'Do tell, darling man'

'You saw an opportunity and you took it, weaving your magic so you'd end up getting exactly what you wanted thus enabling me to release my frustration! When you came in and found me annoyed about there being no milk, you knew that, if you played your cards right, you'd get a well-deserved hammerin' and you played each hand beautifully! I salute you, my queen. Very well played indeed!'

'Why thank you, kind sir. Us queens always aim to please!'

'And you always seem to succeed too – except for today!'

'Oh? What haven't I succeeded at today then?'

'I'm still bloody gaspin' for a cuppa and there's still NO FUCKING MILK!'

They rolled about on the slippery wet floor in floods of laughter until Scarlet sat atop him, kissed his nose and said, 'I'll get dressed and go get you some milk, my wild, untamed king. I do believe you've well and truly earned it!'

*

Paris – Saturday

They'd caught the Eurostar on the Friday evening just as they'd done before, arriving at Stewart's flat quite late in the evening, both of them bone weary from their respective busy schedules.

They'd dined on the train so had nothing more to do other than unpack, shower and sleep.

Having not set an alarm, they'd slept in.

Stewart had awoken first and had gone out to source food for a light, late breakfast and some flowers for Scarlet.

Back at the flat, he'd made tea, popped the Pain au Raisins, her favourite, on a plate and went to wake her up.

'Wakey wakey, Scarlet,' he whispered in her ear, gently tousling her wavy locks. She roused and flickered open her pretty hazel eyes to see him perched on the edge of the bed, beaming at her. 'Mmmmmm, what a sight,' she sleepily offered.

'Happy birthday, you beautiful creature,' he replied as he flourished a stunning bouquet of Black Baccara Roses, leaned in and kissed her softly, inhaling her scent at the same time.

'Oh my, Stewart. They're beautiful! Thank you.'

'Black Baccara! Your favourite, yes?'

'Yesssss! But how did you know?'

'I have my sources.' He grinned back at her.

'What a resourceful boy you are!'

She reached out, took the bouquet and smelled them, sighing deeply.

'They're so very delicately scented. I love them, Stewart. So very thoughtful of you!'

'You're most welcome, lil lady. And now, brekkie and tea!'

He reached for the tray he'd rested on her nightstand and placed it on her lap. 'Another of your favourites.'

'Ooooooooo yay. Pain au Raisin. You've been busy this morning.'

'It's your birthday. I need to make sure you have everything that makes your precious lil heart happy.'

'Awwww. You're so adorable. But just being with you is enough. You're all I want and need. Nothing else!'

He smiled, shrugging and said, 'Oh well, in that case, I'll cancel dress shopping on the Champs-Élysées and dinner atop the Eiffel Tower, shall I? And we'll stay here, order pizza and watch telly instead!'

'Whaaaaaaaaaat?' she hollered gleefully, bouncing on the bed, knocking the tray flying. Thank goodness the mug wasn't in her hand! 'Don't you bloody dare! I can't believe this, darlin'! I'm so happy and very excited! Yaaayyy.' And she launched at him, hugging him tightly and kissing him all over his gorgeous face. Stewart hugged her back, laughing. He loved her wide eyed, excited little girl reactions. It was so endearing!

'I wanted to make today as special as possible so I made plans way ahead of time.'

'I don't know what to say except thank you! I'm deeply touched baby!'

'You're so very welcome, my love. Now, finish your breakfast then we can get ready and leave. We have a full schedule so make haste, young lady!'

He kissed her cheek and went to the bathroom, leaving her covered in crumbs, beaming from ear to ear.

She hurriedly devoured her pastries, drank her tea and shot out of bed, very eager to get the day started.

Stewart came out of the bathroom after having a shower, a towel around his waist and still glistening with tiny water droplets which caught Scarlet's eye 'Ohhhhh. Mmmmm' escaped her lips as she licked them, walking towards him slowly.

'Now now, don't you start, woman!'

She was biting her lip. 'I'm afraid, you sexy, virile, hunk of a man, that I cannot help myself. I need to taste you.' And she closed the gap between them, grabbed him, pulled his ponytail hard and licked his neck. 'Yum. You taste like sex on a stick!'

He laughed. 'You're mad. Now get off me and get dressed!'

'I need to shower first. Down there needs a definite wash now, thanks to you!'

'ME? I haven't done anything. It's all you and your overactive ovaries. Now, off with you!'

'Couldn't we have a quickie before we go?' she begged as she pawed at him.

'NO. There's no time for you and your naughtiness,' he retorted, batting her hands away, giggling. 'You're incorrigible. Get off!'

She laughed as she walked away.

Scarlet showered, smothered herself in oils, popped on her bath robe and returned to the bedroom, where she found he'd lain out her clothes for the day.

Wine coloured jeans, a black sweater, her black leather, fur-lined jacket and her chunky black leather boots and on top of the pile of clothes was a black gift box, wrapped in gold ribbon.

'Stewart?' she called out.

He re-entered the bedroom dressed from head to toe in a black suit with a long jacket that had a slight sheen to it. His burgundy waistcoat graced a black shirt and a burgundy cravat was tied about the collar with a black bandana and peak cap adorning his head. 'You called, my lady!'

'FUCK!' was all Scarlet could manage as the sight of him floored her. 'You look so handsome and very dapper!'

'Well thank you, darlin'!' he gratefully replied with a wink.

'What's this?' she asked as she pointed to the box.

'That's one of your gifts. Open it.'

She smiled and did just that, removing the ribbon.

Inside, wrapped in gold tissue paper was another intricate set of lace and silk undies but silver this time.

'Oh, Stewart. These are incredibly elegant. Wow!'

'Incredibly elegant undies for an incredibly elegant lady!'

'You're way too generous!'

'A gentleman should always spoil his lady, especially on her birthday.'

She kissed him gratefully and put them on while he disappeared off again, making a phone call.

The deep-plunging bra gave her voluptuous bosom a beautiful boost and the high-waisted Brazilian knickers set off her curves perfectly. She felt exquisite!

She went off to find him so he could see her in all her glowing glory. He was in the living room, still on the phone so she politely coughed to gain his attention.

He turned around and his whole face lit up. He beamed at her and his blue eyes twinkled as he licked his lips, leaving them wet. He beckoned her over with his forefinger. She obliged as he asked the person he was talking to to hang on a second. He held the phone to his shoulder with one hand as he pulled her in with the other and kissed her, whispering in her ear that she looked perfectly ravishing.

She skipped back off to the bedroom where she dressed, fixed her makeup and hair, popped on her boots and rejoined him in the living room where he was waiting for her, his call finished.

'Right, luv, let's get cracking. Our car will be here in a few minutes.'

'I'm so excited. What is the plan and where to first?'

'Firstly, a lovely walk in the Jardin des Champs-Élysées, followed by a light lunch, a visit to a salon for a make-over, dress shopping then an early-ish dinner at Le Jules Verne in the Eiffel Tower all finished off back here where I'll be tantalising your tastebuds and blowing your delicate little knickers off!'

'Blimey! My heart is positively racing and I'm feeling rather giddy!'

'Good! But I have two requests, Scarlet, please. One, I don't want you gushing thanks at me all afternoon. This is how a lady should be treated and it's my pleasure to spoil you. I don't need repeated offers of thanks and neither do I want you commenting on the prices of anything. How much I spend on you is my affair! Clear?'

'Yes, my darling. Crystal!'

'And two, NO Scarlet Coloured Filthy Chaos in ANY restaurants today! No fumbling under the tablecloths, grabbing at my privates and certainly NO accidentally-on-purpose dropping cutlery just so you can scurry about on the floor in search of dessert between my legs! Is that clear too, you salacious young lady?'

Scarlet bellowed out a cackle. 'Oh my gosh. That was hilarious!'

'Yeah, I know it sounds funny,' he replied, also laughing, 'but I'm actually serious darlin'. You've got to promise you'll behave UNTIL we get home!'

'I promise I will. You have my word!'

He sighed with relief. 'I've been a bit worried. I know what you're like when you've been on the red wine. You get hornier and hornier and filthier and filthier and eventually turn into a sex-starved maniac! And I know you say it's all my fault and I do love that side of you. I more than love it actually but not today where we are going. I need you to act like the elegant lady you are. Naughty, cheeky banter is fine but you get so physical with it and you just can't today. Save that for when we get home!'

'Again, I promise you, I will behave like the perfect lady!'

'Thank you. I can relax now.'

They had a quick cuddle and kiss then made their way downstairs and hopped into their car which whisked them off to their first stop, Le Jardin des Champs-Élysées!

*

After a chilly but very romantic walk around the gardens, they'd gone for lunch at a small, intimate restaurant.

Stewart had suggested they keep it light as dinner later would probably be quite rich so Scarlet had ordered French Onion soup with Lobster Bisque for Stewart, both accompanied by a basket of fresh, crunchy baguette and a bottle of red wine.

They'd eaten, drank, talked and laughed for over an hour, thoroughly enjoying themselves when Stewart looked at his watch, realising the time.

'Bugger, we gotta go, luv, or we'll be late for your appointment.'

He requested the bill, paid and they left, making their way along the Champs-Élysées to the beauty salon where they were greeted by an adorable stylist named Marcel who ushered Scarlet to his station. After Stewart advised him of the look he was after and with Scarlets wholehearted approval, Marcel and his team of beauty therapists got to work.

She had her hair washed and conditioned while young ladies beautified her hands and feet. Her squeaky-clean tendrils were then smothered in a smoothing keratin mask, wrapped in a hot towel and she was laid back so yet another young lady could begin her Instant Glow 24k Gold facial. Her rosy face was cleansed, toned, and gently exfoliated and while 24k gold mask sheets promised to give her eyes a relaxed, dewy and brightened look, she was given a calming neck and shoulder massage with rose essential oil which Stewart had specifically requested. Her facial complete and her hair thoroughly rinsed, she was returned to Marcel for her make-over.

Stewart had been very specific about the look he was after for his beautiful lady; chic, classic elegance with a cheeky twist! After all, even though Scarlet was a classy woman, she was also a very naughty, cheeky minx so her look had to reflect her personality and Marcel did not disappoint.

Stewart had left the salon to go shopping for more gifts for Scarlet. He'd looked online and had seen what he wanted and had ordered them for collection today. He'd returned after an hour and had been waiting, drinking champagne. After Marcel had finished Scarlet's hair and make-up, she walked out to greet him.

'Well, well, well, would ya look at that! Gorgeous Scarlet. You look simply gorgeous! Marcel, it's perfect. Well done!'

'I'm very happy to hear that, Monsieur. You are welcome. But, if I may say, your lady is naturally radiant, elegant and chic so I didn't have to do much. She already glows from within.'

'You may say that. Indeed you may. And you're right; she is and she does!'

Stewart's eyes hadn't left Scarlet for one second, even when he was speaking to Marcel. He walked towards her, kissed her cheek softly and said, 'Breathtaking!'

She smiled, both inwardly and outwardly. She felt so incredibly special and it was taking her aback for she'd never had anything like this kind of treatment before or the endless stream of compliments. It was quite overwhelming.

Stewart settled up, took her hand and they left as it was now time for dress shopping!

They made their way to the place Stewart had chosen to buy her a dress. That's who he'd been talking to on the phone at the flat. He'd wanted to make sure everything was set before their arrival. The window was dressed opulently with the most stunning of ladies dresses gracing the mannequins, making Scarlet's eyes twinkle. Good heavens, it all looked incredibly expensive but she'd promised him she'd not say a word about that kind of thing so she contained it as they entered the building.

A very beautiful older lady named Elise welcomed them at the door and took them to a large dressing room, decked out with a sofa, mirrors and a curtained off changing area. All very posh indeed!

On a small table next to the sofa was a bottle of red wine with two glasses and Elise offered to pour for them.

'No that's OK, Elise. I'll take care of that while you take care of my lovely lady.'

'As you wish, Monsieur! Madame, please come with me.'

Scarlet followed Elise to the space behind the curtain where she found four dresses hanging up. She gasped. 'Oh my word. They are exquisite!'

'Oui, Madame. I chose them for you according to Monsieur's requests.'

Scarlet was lost for words!

'Are you all right, Madame?'

'Yes, Elise. I'm fine. I'm just a bit shocked!'

'I will help you undress. Which one would you like to try first?'

'They're all beautiful but my eye is drawn to this deep red and silver one. It's just so beautiful!'

'Ah, yes. I think this will suit you well. Especially with your dark hair.'

Elise assisted Scarlet with undressing, taking extra care not to ruin her hair, then helped her into the dress which was an elegant, vintage style deep, ruby red number with silver trimming accentuating her bust, cinched in at the waist then softly fluttering wisps of chiffon cascaded from her hips to her feet with matching bolero and simple silver stilettos.

There were no mirrors behind the curtain as the whole experience was geared around a surprising reveal once the curtain was pulled back, so Scarlet had no idea how she looked. But she felt like a goddess!

Elise left and Scarlet heard her say, 'Monsieur, are you ready?'

'Definitely!' he replied.

She returned, pulled back the curtain and Stewart's jaw dropped at the sight of Scarlet, looking regally stunning with her dark, raven locks all swirled on top of her head with one single long ringlet gracing her neck over her left shoulder and her face aglow with the radiant make-up Marcel had painstakingly applied, her ruby red lips a contrast to her pearly teeth as she beamed with sheer delight. She looked like a Golden Era Hollywood Star and it was as if he was struck dumb - standing there, gazing at her lovingly and longingly, totally speechless!

He approached her as his eyes drank in this heavenly vision before him and Scarlet noticed his suit trousers protruding slightly. *Ooops!* She looked down then up again, grinning as he flashed his eyes at her, biting his lip.

He quite hurriedly asked Elise to give them a few moments alone and she quickly left, obviously aware of what was happening between them.

Once she'd shut the door behind her, Stewart slid his hand around Scarlet's waist and pulled her into him, pressing his hardened arousal into her groin and releasing a low growl into her ear.

'All I can say right now is that I cannot bloody wait to get you home, rip off this dress and make a complete mess of you! But I'll have to wait and mark my words, young lady, once I get you home, you're in for the ride of your life so I suggest you brace yourself!'

'Be careful, old man, as you're making me trickle which means damp knickers which then means a wet patch on this lavish dress. NOT the ladylike look you've so carefully planned for tonight!'

'Mmmmmmm,' was all he could muster as he went in for a deep kiss. Pulling back, he checked her over again. 'You, my lady, strike a heavenly, ravishing picture and I will be very honoured to have you on my arm tonight!'

'Thank you, my darling. Am I to take it that I don't need to try on any of the other dresses then?'

'As far as I'm concerned, that's the one but it's up to you entirely.'

'Well, I haven't actually seen myself in it yet.'

'Oh shit. Of course you haven't. I'm a twat. Come here and see.'

He guided her to the mirrors which were placed at different angles and she gasped at the sight of herself.

'Oh, my giddy aunt fanny! I can't quite believe it. Erm, wow!'

'Yep. Stunning!'

'I think I could, quite literally, shag meself!'

He laughed as he wrapped his arms around her waist from behind, peering at her in the mirror from over her shoulder. 'Well, luckily for you, you don't have to. That's my job and I will enthusiastically be performing my less than honourable duties later!'

She sighed deeply. 'The anticipation is killing me and continues to make me damp.'

'Well, I suggest we get ourselves off to dinner. The sooner we eat, the sooner we can get home and the sooner I can take you to the stars where you belong!'

She spun about in his arms and hugged him tightly. 'Lead the way then, Mr Sloane!'

'Gladly!'

He took her hand and they exited the dressing room with the rest of the staff and some other clients all gawping at this perfectly matched, beautiful couple. Stewart paid for Scarlet's items and they left, her other clothes and boots kindly packed into a bag by Elise.

As they approached their car, Stewart lifted Scarlet's hand up to his mouth and kissed it. 'I don't think I've ever been in the presence of royalty before. Tonight is for you, my Queen,' and he opened her door, still holding her hand as she swung herself in. He got in the other side and they were off for dinner at the Eiffel Tower.

*

The drive was a very short one. In fact, they could have walked but Stewart didn't want Scarlet having to walk too far in the heels she was wearing.

Le Jules Verne was on the 2nd floor and accessed by a private elevator from the Eiffel Tower South Pillar entrance.

Stewart already knew that Scarlet had a dizzying fear of heights so he kept her very close to his side as they exited. He wanted to make sure she didn't have a panic attack. She'd told him about her panic attacks in the beginning. Heights and flying set them off and, sometimes, crowded spaces, especially if it was very noisy! The restaurant this evening was going to be a bit of a challenge as it was up high and busy; very busy, so Stewart needed to make sure he kept her calm.

Once at their table, Stewart ordered their wine. When it arrived, Scarlet was given the honour of tasting it before it was poured. She approved wholeheartedly.

They ordered their starters and main courses then Stewart disappeared off, saying he needed to visit the gents.

When he got back, he removed his jacket, sat down and rolled up his shirt sleeves a bit, revealing his lower arm tattoos.

'Oh don't, Stewart. Put them away!'

'Put what away?'

'Your tats. You know what they do to me!'

'You'll just have to put up with it and behave then won't ya 'cos they're staying on display!'

'You rogue!'

He knew exactly what he was doing. He was purposefully winding her up, having made her promise to behave. This meant she'd be ravenous for him later. What a clever rapscallion!

The wine flowed, the food came and went and they talked, laughed and wound each other up with lots of cheeky innuendos, naughty talk, lip bites and winks, all whilst listening to the lovely live piano music.

As their main courses and current bottle of red were polished off, a waiter appeared with another bottle and to clear their plates and Scarlet noticed Stewart give him a nod!

What was he up to now?

It didn't take long for her to realise exactly what as no sooner had that thought crossed her mind, the pianist started playing the tune to Happy Birthday and Scarlet felt herself go beetroot!

Noooooooooooo! How embarrassing!

Everyone started singing as a waiter walked over carrying a tray with two desserts on it, both of which were graced with sparkling candles. Stewart was also singing away and stood up as the waiter reached the table and put the tray down.

The singing continued for a couple more seconds followed by rampant applause and cheers from the other diners and it all ended with Stewart laughing at the look of shock and horror on her face and giving her a well-deserved cuddle.

'You look mortified.'

'I am... but also incredibly touched. That was so sweet!'

As he sat back down and Scarlet turned back round to face the table, she noticed two wrapped packages had been placed next to her dessert.

She looked up at Stewart who said, 'Open the smaller one first!'

'Don't you think you've done enough?'

'Don't start! And no, I haven't. Open it!'

She did, rather carefully as it was wrapped so perfectly. Inside was another bottle of their favourite Dior perfume.

'You can never have enough of that stuff and I've only ever seen you with a small one, so now you've got a big bottle!'

'Thank you, darlin'!'

'Now open the last one! This one is extra special.'

She took a long swallow of red wine as she was feeling overwhelmed again then took a deep breath as she opened the final package. Under the intricately designed wrapping paper was a square, flat, black leather jewellery box that closed with a single popper. Her heart began to race as she realised he'd gone to yet more expense. He really didn't need to!

She looked up at him one more time before opening the box and, as she lifted the lid, she saw the most magnificent items inside - a matching set of sterling silver, Marcasite and Garnet jewellery; necklace, bracelet and chandelier earrings. Her absolute favourite in the world. She adored vintage style, Victorian era jewellery and this was quite perfect indeed! The look on her face was a picture; her mouth formed into a large 'O' shape as she gazed into the box, tears in her eyes!

When she finally managed to pull her eyes away, she realised Stewart had gotten up and was beside her, crouched down by her chair. She turned towards him. 'You've made me so happy, Stewart. I adore them. They're just perfect and I can't put into words how grateful I am!'

'You don't need to; I can see it on your face. Happy Birthday Scarlet!' and he kissed her softly. 'Let's pop these on, shall we? Take off your earrings darlin'!'

She removed her earrings as he unclipped the necklace she was already wearing and, as he put her new necklace on, she fixed her new earrings in place with him finishing off by fastening her bracelet onto her wrist.

He then took a step back. 'Let me look at you! Mmmm. Divine perfection wrapped up in you, my lady! They suit you beautifully!'

'Do you mind if I visit the ladies to have a look?'

'Of course not, silly. Off you pop!'

She did. But it wasn't just to look in the mirror. She was feeling very overwhelmed at all the attention, gifts, compliments and displays of love and affection that she needed to get some air too.

She went to the loo as she also needed a wee then took in the resplendence of her body adorned with the shimmering dress and her skin and neck graced with the majestic jewels. She was, again, speechless! She gulped back tears of emotion and headed for the door to the balcony, feeling refreshed as the chilly air hit her face.

Then the height hit her right in her core and she froze. Her breath quickened, her chest tightened and palpitations started. *Fuck! She was having a panic attack and she was alone.* She couldn't move!

Luckily though, someone had witnessed her being gripped with fear and had advised a member of staff who had, in turn, advised Stewart and he arrived, gently holding onto her arm and urging her to step backwards through the door.

'No, I can't move!'

He put his arms around her waist from behind again, held her tight and said, 'Yes you can, baby. I've got you. You're safe. Just step backwards with me.'

Although she was in the grips of a severe attack, she did feel slightly calmer already, just having his strong, capable arms around her so she followed his lead and stepped backwards, continuing until they were through the door. Once he'd shut it, she flung her arms about his neck and sobbed on his shoulder.

He engulfed her quaking body in his arms once more and just held her as she cried, just as she'd done for him before when he'd had his attack of IED. This was his chance to support HER and her own mental health battles. Although she was a very strong, confident, powerful woman, she still had scars left over from her years of abuse and this was the evidence of it and he needed to be her calming force now!

'I've got you, baby. I've got you. It's OK. Ssshhhhh!' he whispered to her, as he stroked the back of her neck softly.

She managed to pull herself together and, with her sobs subsiding, she looked up at him.

'Oh dear, you've smudged your make-up!'

She giggled. 'I'll go clean up then meet you back at the table!'

'I'll wait for you!'

She smiled as she went back to the ladies, blew her nose, dried her eyes and face and tidied up her make-up. Marcel had used her own foundation which she had in her handbag which was a relief as she looked like Rudolph the red nosed Reindeer after a piss-up!

Stewart held her hand as they walked back to the table, they ate their very rich, chocolatey desserts, had some coffee, paid the bill and headed for the elevator.

On the way down, they'd stolen a deep kiss from each other. 'Time to head home and for you to make that mess of me you promised earlier!'

'It most certainly is little lady! Are you quite ready to be thoroughly manhandled and jolly rogered?'

'Hahahaa! Definitely!'

'Good!'

They snogged some more before the elevator door opened, both of them gagging for more!

*

Back at Stewart's flat after a car ride that seemed to last forever, Stewart had wasted no time in getting Scarlet out of her dress, licking her as he stripped her.

As she was standing at the end of his bed in just her silver undies, he left the bedroom, returning with two bottles of wine and glasses, poured for them both and sat her on the end of the bed. 'So, you know what happens next, don't ya darlin'! We're in Paris and this is where I let my kink out and I've got new things to teach you. You still trust me, right?'

'Of course. I've already told you that!'

'And you remember the safe-word?'

'Kiss me!'

'Good. And before I introduce each new thing, I'll ask for your consent! Remember, anything you're uncomfortable with, just say no and we won't do it. And I mean that. Please don't accept something you don't like just to please me or satisfy my needs! This is about both of us, not just me! Understood?'

'Understood!'

'But before all that, there's just one more thing. Wait here!'

He got up, left the room and was gone for a short period while Scarlet gulped down more red. She knew she was gonna need it as Mr Kinky Sloane was on the rampage!

After a few minutes, she heard the words 'Close your eyes!' She obliged.

She heard the light switch flick then 'Open!'

She opened her eyes and there was Stewart, stood before her butt naked and smothered in a white substance.

'Oh my gosh. Is that icing?'

'It is, my lady. Your birthday cake is ME and you can eat it all!'

She wailed with glee. 'Oh you perfectly delightful, filthy, naughty man! Priceless.'

He'd applied the icing to his arms, chest, neck, belly, bollocks and cock and she was gonna lick every last drop of it off of his scrumptious body!

Scarlet skipped off to get a towel which she placed on the bed, urging him to lay atop it. Once in position, she climbed aboard her very own human freight train and began to lick him.

'Mmmmmm, it tastes like cinnamon!'

'Yep. Remember on our walk a few weeks ago, you mentioned a spiced cake mixture? Your wish is always my command, Madam!'

'Mmmmmmm mmmmm mmmmm.' She continued to lap every inch of him, starting with his neck and working her way down until she reached his cock which was hard and glistening.

'And there's my very own dripping candle. How perfect!'

She made him wait a bit longer before devouring it, clearing the icing from his balls first then licked and lapped at his soldier, making him groan and writhe beneath her. Then she took him; took him deep inside her mouth and sucked the life out of him.

As she was voraciously gorging herself on every inch of his appendage, she heard him softly say between grunts and pants, 'You're all mine, Queen Cleopatra!'

That made the hunger she had for him even wilder and she took him home powerfully. He gushed into her mouth, the icing sweetening his essence blissfully, all kinds of rapturous noises escaping his lips. Music to her ears!

She continued to softly lap him, waiting for his hardness to ease but it didn't. He bolted upright, reached over to his nightstand, opened the drawer and retrieved his little Clitoris Air Stimulator. He then grabbed her, spun her about and sat her between his legs, her back to his chest, his arms reaching around her to the front. His hands dived between her legs, his fingers pushing her knickers aside and he started to gently rub her pearl, making her grind against his hand, softly whimpering.

After massaging her for a few minutes, he positioned his little gremlin machine over her clitoris and switched it on, increasing the power immediately as she was already heavily aroused and swollen. A whelp escaped her mouth as her grinds got harder.

He hadn't set it to intermittent pulses this time; it was a continuous suction with little puffs of air. It sucked and blew, sucked and blew, driving her mad with desire. 'Stewart, I want you!'

'Not yet!' he whispered back.

He increased the intensity a notch and her legs began to twitch. She could feel an orgasm coming as she leaned back into him, bucked her hips upward and contracted, warm stickiness oozing out onto the sheet.

But that didn't stop Stewart. No! He increased it again.

'Fuck! Stewart. I want you!'

'Nope!'

Her whinnying got louder, her hips thrusting, her insides throbbing and Stewart managed to keep his evil little device in place, never letting it move.

Then another orgasm built and popped. This one more powerful than the last. She threw her head back onto his shoulder and cried out, bucking upwards, more abundant, warm trickles flowing.

And yet again, he didn't stop but increased the intensity even more!

'Oh gosh, Stewart, please just fuck me!'

'No, my love. Not yet!'

She grabbed a handful of sheets as he flicked the switch one last time, her jewel being delightfully and powerfully whipped about inside the tiny vortex. This was gonna be a big one!

She must have been holding her breath as she heard Stewart urge her to breathe. She gasped, moaned, groaned and cried out as he built her up to boiling point, always kissing her neck and nibbling her shoulders. Then she cried out loudly again, thrust upwards and backwards as another powerful orgasm ripped through her body, making her tremble and squirt all over his bed, her insides spasming ferociously.

She flopped down again, breathless as he finally switched off the device, releasing her engorged clitoris. And he held her while she quivered, still kissing the back of her neck, stroking her hair and rubbing her arms.

'Did you enjoy that?'

'Mmmmhmmm.'

'Good. That was just the beginning!'

'Are you gonna fuck me now 'cos I desperately need you to—'

'No, my love. Not yet!'

She let out an infuriated grunt which made Stewart chuckle.

He slid out from beneath her, lay her against the pillows, reached into his bedside drawer and removed a key. He went to a cabinet, unlocked it and opened its doors, revealing its contents.

Scarlet's eyes widened!

'What on earth?'

She was going to make him chuckle quite a bit tonight so it would seem as he just laughed again!

'What are all of those? Some look monstrous!'

'They all have their uses. They may look foreboding, luv, but I promise you, when used properly and with care and attention, they are positively delightful!'

He made his choices for tonight: the usual blindfold and whip plus cuffs for her wrists instead of ties, shackles for her ankles, nipple clamps and a pair of black gloves with tiny spikes on!

'What the bloody hell are those?'

'These are Vampire Gloves!'

'They're spikey!'

'I know,' he responded with a giggle. 'Honestly, luv. Stop worrying. I won't ever hurt you. And if you don't like something, I'll stop. Do you want me to put them away?'

'No. It's OK. I trust you. But make sure you're gentle with those spikey bits please!'

'Oh you're gonna make this so much fun, darlin'.'

He approached her, still laughing. 'Are you ready?'

'Yes!'

He removed her underwear, secured her to the bed with the cuffs and shackles, covered her eyes with the blindfold then lifted her head. 'Drink darlin'!'

He held her head while she gulped down a full glass of wine then settled her back against the pillows.

Silence!

More silence!

Still more!

'Stewart?'

'Sshhhh! Don't speak!'

She finally felt him mount the end of the bed, followed by the coolness of leather on her skin, trailing from the pulse point on her throat, down beneath her breasts, over her belly and settle on her mound.

The room was silent apart from their breathing. His was husky, hers gentle but quick.

The leather left her mound and trailed back up to her chest where she felt it circling around her right nipple then over to her left. It felt amazing and was making her hardened peaks throb.

He suddenly removed the whip from her breasts and began licking her nipples instead, sucking them gently at first.

He still held the whip but had it pointed downwards now, dragging it up and down her inner thighs.

He was being ever so gentle and Scarlet was wondering why! *Was this to be a gentle kink session?* It relaxed her a little. Those evil, spikey gloves of doom had really given her a fright and she'd been expecting him to go at her hammer and tongs. Something he'd said he was going to do earlier in the evening so this was a very pleasant realisation for her!

Boy, little did she know though!

Stewart had sensed her anxiety and had seen the fear in her eyes so he'd decided to lighten up in the beginning. He'd also toyed with the idea of just putting the gloves away but he knew what he was doing and knew he'd not hurt her. He'd only cause enough pain for pleasure! But he also knew that if he lulled her into a false sense of security, her reactions to his more questionable efforts would be hilarious to witness so, with all of that in mind, he was taking it slow and gentle. For now!

Scarlet felt him tense up. She sensed his eagerness as he started biting her breasts, gently nibbling around the areola of one while he kneaded her other then he switched. He was becoming more and more ravenous with each suck of her nipples, with each bite of her womanly flesh!

He suddenly stopped again, leaving the bed and coming back with nipple clamps.

'I have nipple clamps – do I have your consent, Scarlet?'

'Most definitely!'

He affixed each one in place causing Scarlet to inhale sharply and moan loudly. She felt the need to writhe but couldn't due to her restraints and her frustrations mounted as her nipples caught fire; a pleasurable, throbbing heat igniting other fires within her.

Stewart dropped lower, positioned himself between her trembling thighs, parted her lips and began to lap within her folds. The laps here frenzied as his gentleness began leaving and he brought his teeth into play as he gnawed at her like a hungry wolf devouring its prey.

'Stewart, I want you inside me!'

'Not until I've had my fill.'

'You're driving me insane.'

'Good!'

'*Aaggghhhh!*'

She heard a muffled giggle come from between her lady lips which made her even more frustrated, the sadistic bloody sod!

And all she could think of right now was how badly she looked forward to the day when she could turn the tables and get him back. She'd give him a taste of his own medicine!

She felt him reach over the bed and heard light shuffling then 'Time for the gloves, little lady. May I proceed?'

She exhaled. 'Yes'

He started on her inner thighs, gently scraping the tiny spikes up and down her delicate skin. It was a mild sensation at first, akin to how exfoliating gloves felt in the shower and not painful. She relaxed!

He grazed the rest of her aching body, every inch of her, ending back between her thighs when he started rubbing her already tender clitoris with his be-spiked thumb!

'*WHOOOOOAAAAAA.*'

More bloody giggles came from Stewart. 'Want me to stop?'

'Laughing? YES! You horrid man! Rubbing? No.'

That made him laugh even more!

The flicks of his thumb got a little harder and although it was painful, it was also so very arousing and she began to pull at her restraints as she tried writhing.

Her poor little gem was now as inflamed as her nipples and she couldn't hold back her cries. She wasn't screaming – yet, but she was getting very vocal! A good thing this room was soundproof or every single one of Stewart's neighbours would have known every English swear word there was!

She was cussing loudly while he laughed at her. He'd known this was going to happen and he was relishing in it. This was the part that helped him so much. The part of his kink that helped him release the anger and pent-up emotions. And Scarlet's hilarious outbursts were an added bonus. He was loving every sadistic minute and becoming very aroused and, although she was frustrated and cross with him, she was also incredibly happy to facilitate his release!

She had been tugging on her cuffs and shackles so much that they started to burn and it got too much. 'Kiss me. Kiss me!'

He stopped. 'What's wrong, luv?'

'My wrists and ankles are burning!'

'I'll loosen them.'

'Thank you.'

He adjusted her restraints before she felt his tongue trail up her belly, between her breasts and up her neck to her chin, ending with a very sloppy, dirty tongue kiss!

'Will you be my Queen Cleopatra for me again?'

'Of course. Always!'

He straddled her torso and she felt the tip of his cock on her lips which she willingly parted, allowing him to slide into the warm moistness of her mouth.

For the first time though, he had full control. She couldn't touch him or hold him back nor could she set the pace. She was entirely at his mercy.

He gently thrust himself into her mouth, hissing and inhaling sharply. She sucked on him as powerfully as she could and when he rested his tip by her lips, she knew he just wanted her to use her tongue.

This entire erotic act was driving him wild with lust and he knew he couldn't thrust into her too deeply as he'd choke the poor lass but he needed to let loose. 'Time for you to get that jolly rogering you've been after!'

'FINALLY!'

He went to the end of the bed, released her ankles, grabbed her hips, lifted them up and entered her with as much force as he could muster. He NEEDED it. He needed roughness!

And he battered Scarlets insides, driving himself into her deep and hard, making her scream on each forceful thrust.

She was so thankful for this. She'd been aching for him for ages. He'd wound her up tight and now she needed to maniacally uncoil.

She relished in every ferocious crash of his hips, each one sending electric shocks through her sweaty, dripping body.

'Yesssss! Yesssss! Fuck me, Stewart! Give me everything you've got!'

She dug her heels firmly into the mattress and began meeting his intensity, driving her hips upwards as high and hard as she could.

Her arms were tired and aching as they were the only anchor she had but she didn't care. She wanted this as much as he did! He'd introduced her to this and now she had a yearning taste for it.

He'd started his deep, guttural growls now which she knew meant he was close. She was close too but even if she hadn't been, hearing that always moved her along.

She felt her walls start to contract on their own, squeezing the life out of his precious cock which finished him off and he, for the first time ever, screamed! He'd howled before. He'd roared before. *But screamed?* Never! And it made her orgasm even more powerful as she knew what it meant! She knew that, together, they'd achieved not just his release physically but also emotionally and mentally! It was such a beautiful sound too. So much so, it made her cry!

His orgasm lasted longer than hers. She'd howled with him and flooded his cock and sheets with her sweet essence but he'd gushed and gushed and gushed; his neck craned backwards, his body taught, veins popping out everywhere while he screamed and howled, letting it all out!

Once his body let up, he collapsed on top of her, panting and wheezing. And she noticed something else – Gentle sobs!

Awwww gosh. Her heart literally melted!

His emotional release was so much bigger than she'd realised and he was crying on her breasts. And she couldn't hug him, she couldn't stroke his back… Nothing! BUGGER!

'Stewart, sweetheart. Release my arms please. I want to hold you!'

He struggled up slowly, trembling, got the key, unlocked the cuffs and plopped back down on top of her. Her arms were as heavy as cement blocks and aching awfully but she had to muster up every ounce of strength to hold him. She managed to get her arms around his back and they just lay there, Stewart's tears trickling down her belly as she softly caressed and scratched him, sushing him quietly. It was a good fifteen minutes before Stewart lifted his head to look at her, his eyes red and puffy and he just smiled as he gazed into her loving eyes. She smiled back, no words necessary. They were saying everything with their eyes! He squirmed up higher and kissed her. They kissed each other for a while, just loving one another with their lips and tongues. It wasn't too long before Stewart asked her, 'Shall we have a bath together? We can top and tail, drink wine and reminisce about today!'

'Yay. I love that idea!'

'I'll go get it started.'

He kissed her nose and popped off, leaving her lying in a warm wet patch.

Once the bath was ready, they took their wine and got into the bath, Stewart at one end and Scarlet at the other. They chatted about the stunning day they'd spent together and just relaxed.

Then Stewart broached the subject of Christmas. 'So, did you square away your time off for Christmas?'

'Oh sorry. Yes. I forgot to tell you. I booked off three weeks. I had more time saved up than I thought so I took a chunk of it. I finish work on the 16th of December and don't go back until the 9th of January!'

'Oh, well done you. So that means that we can leave for Lapland on the 22nd of December and stay until the 2nd of January with extra time at both ends. Brilliant! I'll get on my laptop tomorrow and get it booked!'

'Are you sure about this though, my love?'

'If you mention money one more bloody time, I'm gonna get cross! Stop concerning yourself with my finances. I actually don't get what your issue is with it!'

'I don't want you ever to think I'm with you for your money, Stewart. I earn a decent wage and am comfortable but I'm nowhere near as well off as you and couldn't possibly ever do the same for you. Plus, you hardly ever let me pay for anything and I just don't want you to ever think that I'm taking advantage of you! I'd be mortified.'

'For fucks sake, Scarlet. Listen, I'm gonna say this once and only once. You are part of my life and I do not agree with ladies paying their own way. It's just who I am. When we are together, you're looked after by me because that's the way I want it. You haven't asked for anything. You never ask for anything. And, it's MY money. I can do what I bloody want with it. So, if I wanna go on an expensive holiday with the woman I love, I'm going to. If I wanna buy said lady gifts, I will. For once in your life, someone is looking after YOU so accept it and get used to it! OK?'

She nodded. 'Yes OK, but may I make a request?'

'What's that?'

'Will you please allow me to treat you now and then? It's important to me!'

'I let you buy me lunch once!'

'Hahahaa, yeah. ONCE! Big whoop.'

'OK OK. Fine. If it'll make you feel more comfortable, then yeah. That's fine.'

'That also means while we're on holiday. You've gotta allow me to contribute in some way!'

'OK. You have a deal!'

'Yay!' and she splashed him. 'And one more thing.'

'Go on.'

'Because you're just so fucking sexy, virile and downright munchable, I'm changing our definition of IED!'

'Oh no. Here we go. To what exactly?'

'Irresistibly Edible Disorder!'

He howled, holding his belly.

'Fuck me, you're mad. Simply mad but fucking hilarious! But if I'm so irresistibly edible, why aren't you over here eating me, hmmm?'

'That can be rectified,' and she launched at him, sending water splashing over the edge of the bath onto the floor.

Needless to say, Queen Cleopatra wasn't hungry for a while after that night!

Part 12 – Lapland – Volume 1 Finalé

Almost a month had gone by since their Paris weekend.

After the high-octane shenanigans on Scarlet's birthday night, they'd decided to stay put on the Sunday. They'd spent the day in their pj's, watching movies and making love which had surprised Scarlet as Paris was where Stewart's kinky beast came bursting out to play but that Sunday, the beast was satisfied and was happily at rest. Instead, she just got Stewart's skillful love-making side.

He'd managed to make her feel like his Queen – what, with all his carefully planned attentions and events on her birthday and his tender treatment of her the day after, their relationship had progressed even further. It had become more steadfast, more grounded and they were now even more in love than before.

It wasn't just Scarlet worshiping him any more – he too worshiped the very ground Scarlet walked on. It was now equal!

Stewart was more relaxed these days too!

Having heeded Scarlet's warnings about his taxing work schedule, he'd reduced his load and did more work from home than at the office. He was a very work driven individual and had to keep busy. He hated being bored but Scarlet had explained to him that he could still do work at home but that NOT being in the noisy, chaotic atmosphere of the office would make all the difference to his stress levels. And he'd listened to her and, after only a week, he'd noticed a positive change. It did make all the difference as he was much calmer and more centred. Wasn't she a clever little thing!

This also meant that their Christmas trip promised to be even more enjoyable as she wouldn't have to worry about him possibly being highly strung for the first few days. They'd be able to arrive and immediately breathe and relax!

But there still remained one thing between them – Stewarts very protective attitude towards his receded hairline and, if they were going to properly relax and just be themselves comfortably, Scarlet just had to broach the subject.

One morning at the breakfast table, while Stewart was reading his newspaper, she did just that!

'Stewart?'

'What luv?'

'When am I gonna get to see you fully naked?'

He frowned, 'You've seen it all darlin; every filthy inch!'

'Oh no I haven't. There's one part you always keep hidden!'

Still frowning, he quizzed, 'Which part?'

'Your head!'

A wicked look descended upon his glorious face as he chimed back 'You probably know that better than me – you've not only seen it; you've touched it, licked it, sucked it AND measured it, if I remember correctly!'

'I mean the head sitting on top of your neck, you filthy bastard!' she loudly replied, laughing 'and you have remembered correctly. I did measure it one night when we were in a drunken stupor. How that monstrous appendage of yours fits inside me is mind-boggling – anyway, we are digressing!'

'It fits because, my love, you have very stretchy walls!'

'Well, THANKS for that, Stewart. Thanks for making me feel like an old bag lady with a saggy minge!'

He laughed so hard he almost fell off his chair whilst choking on his mouthful of Belgian Waffle and Maple Syrup. 'NO NO NO, I didn't mean it like that! Fuck me, I'm sorry, I'm sorry,' he spluttered out as she batted at him with her hands. 'Can we please get back on topic!'

'Yes, we can. My covered head, right?'

'Indeed. We are soon to be together solidly for three whole weeks and I have still yet to see you without a head covering. Why?'

'Well, initially, it was because it embarrassed me and I didn't want you to be put off and run a mile but now, it's because I'm just so used to wearing one all the time, I don't even think about it. Wearing a bandana or a beanie hat has become a habit, even around the house and in bed!'

'So that means you're now happy to take it off so I can see you without it?'

'I am. Want me to take my bandana off now?'

'I'd like to remove it myself, if I may?'

He beamed, 'You may but I must warn ya ; I look very old without it – like a right old git!'

'That, my darling, is impossible. You're way too stunning to look anything like a right old git!'

She got up and approached him, reached around the back of his neck, untied the knot in his bandana and slid it off gently while taking a very deep breath.

She'd been waiting for this moment. He'd told her about his severely receded hairline from the beginning and she'd told him that she didn't care a jot but he needed to be ready and comfortable enough and now he was!

And what a sight to behold – his hairline had receded almost to the crown on the top of his head but he had a little tuft of hair at the front and his scalp was fresh and pink but the hair that flowed down from there was the thickest mane of platinum white waves that he braided from the nape of his neck. Her mouth was agape in awe of just how gloriously beautiful he actually was – and he was hers. All of him, including his stunning head!

She bent down, interlaced her fingers in the thick white hair at the back of his neck and kissed the top of his scalp tenderly – then licked it!

'Oh, you didn't. Fuck me woman! Do you HAVE to lick everything?'

'When it's a part of your delectable self, then yes! I do indeed and now I've licked and tasted both your heads!' she shrugged, 'and, by the way, you are too beautiful for words, my darling man! It honestly just makes you even more irresistible!'

'Awwww, thank you. That's actually such a relief but, if you don't mind, I'll still be wearing it around the house as I'm just more comfortable that way!'

'I don't mind one teeny bit BUT the next time you make love to me, it'd better be nowhere in sight. Deal?'

'Deal!' he agreed with a wink.

Scarlet slid off her chair, into a crouching position and shuffled towards Stewart's knees which she pushed open.

'What the bloody hell are you doing now?'

'My tongue is tingling from licking your head and it's made me quite ravenous so I'm gonna satiate myself on your other one!'

He giggled, 'You're literally obsessed with my willy!'

'Ohhh. I am and do you know why?'

'No, but I'm sure you're about to enlighten me – go on!'

'Well, for one, it's YOUR willy and any body part that's attached to you is simply divine. Two, it's a very, very, VERY pretty willy; a delightfully soft, baby pink when it's sleeping then a vibrant hue of crimson with blue, veiny streaks flashing through it when it's standing to dutiful attention – a true work of art! And three, IT TASTES LIKE HEAVEN and I could happily feast on it twenty-four/seven. Mmmm mmmm mmmmmmmm!'

He was beaming at her with that radiant smile of his, his eyes sparkling, 'I have never heard a cock described so eloquently before – a work of art! Thank you kindly, my elegant little willy worshiper! But I'm afraid you cannot feast on it twenty-four/seven as that is physically impossible, ain't it?'

'It is which is why I get my lips around it any chance I can and this is one of those chances so sit back, relax and let me have my fill, you scrumptious creature!'

And that was that – she'd now seen every inch of her beautiful man and he could rest easy, knowing that she would never 'run a mile' because of his hair, or lack of it. She still found him as exquisite as before, if not more and there was no need to hide any further!

*

London – Wednesday, 21st December

It was the day before their scheduled flight to Lapland and Scarlet was especially excited. She was bouncing about, giddy with glee but also a bit worried about the flight. She HATED flying and usually needed tranquillisers to knock her out and prevent her from screaming her head off at every bump and jolt in the air but Stewart, disapproving of mind-altering drugs, had urged her to not take them this time but to let him help her stay calm with breathing techniques and lots of wine and she'd agreed. But her tummy was doing somersaults just thinking about it – excitement and fear all mixed together!

It was late afternoon when they'd finished packing for their impending snowy adventure. They'd been out shopping the day before to buy new clothes, footwear, thermals etc. as it promised to be extremely cold with temperatures predicted to be as low as -11 degrees Celsius in the day and -18 degrees Celsius at night which delighted Scarlet. She LOVED the cold, especially snow. One of her all-time favourite pastimes was snuggling under a cosy blanket in the winter.

Stewart had made all the arrangements; he'd booked their accommodation and had chosen a hotel with private log cabins that came pre-decorated, including a Christmas Tree. Although he could have chosen self-catering, he'd decided to go for all-inclusive so neither of them had anything to do at all. No sourcing groceries, no cooking, no cleaning. He wanted them both to have nothing to do except enjoy themselves. He'd also hinted at some other special things he'd booked but refused to divulge what exactly until they'd arrived.

As they needed to be up quite early in the morning, they'd ordered dinner from their favourite Indian Takeaway and headed to bed at nine p.m. to get an early night but Scarlet was on tenterhooks and couldn't settle. She was being a right little fidget, tossing and turning.

As she lay on her back in the dark, Stewart turned over towards her and draped his arm over her tummy. 'Is tomorrow's flight worrying you, darlin'?'

'Yeah. I'm trying not to think about it but my mind keeps running away with me. It just won't let me settle!'

'Come here, I've got a remedy for that.'

He pulled her towards him, climbed on top of her, slipped off his bandana and began to kiss her. They were only in their undies so he reached down, slipped her knickers to one side, lowered his boxers and made love to her; slowly, passionately and lovingly, his aim to calm her nerves and make her feel safe. It worked as, no sooner had they finished, she'd passed out in his arms!

*

London – Thursday, 22nd December

They awoke that morning in the same position they'd fallen asleep in, Scarlet still in Stewart's arms. He'd held her all night, not wanting to disturb her. He knew that a decent night's sleep was going to be crucial for her nerves the next day!

He'd booked their car to take them to Heathrow T3 for eight a.m. Their flight on Finnair was scheduled to leave at ten twenty a.m. and Stewart, not one for online checkins, wanted them to check in by nine. He detested hiccups so had decided it best to check in a bit early.

He'd awoken Scarlet with a mug of tea and a plate of toast smothered in her favourite almond butter which she declined at first as she was feeling a tad nauseous. She always did the day of a flight but Stewart insisted she eat. She painstakingly managed one piece, telling him she'd be sick if she forced any more down but one piece was better than nothing!

They showered, got ready, had a lovely long cuddle and kissing session then headed for the airport with Scarlet feeling very nervy indeed.

Stewart held her hand throughout the car journey, frequently kissing her cheek and reassuring her which helped.

At the airport, they checked in, dropped their luggage and proceeded to the gate, passing through security with surprising ease and stopping for a glass of red at the bar. The flight was scheduled to leave on time so they only had twenty minutes to wait until boarding.

Once on board, they found their seats with Stewart wanting Scarlet by the window and him on the outside. They sat down, got comfy and Stewart started to gently talk to Scarlet, wanting to keep her mind on anything other than the flight.

As they started to taxi, Scarlet placed her hand on her abdomen and started to shake. This was Stewart's cue to begin breathing techniques with her. He held her hand, saying, 'Right, baby. Close your eyes and breathe in through your nose slowly, letting your belly expand as much as you can and hold for three seconds then out through your mouth until all the air is gone. And repeat. I'll do it with you!'

She nodded and they began, repeating the exercise a few times. Every time she stopped, he'd urge her to continue, holding her hand and stroking her arm the entire time. Sometimes, he'd let her breathe by herself just so he could speak reassuring, loving words to her, reminding her that flying was the safest way to travel, statistically and to just remember the wonderful time ahead of them. He constantly kept her focused on her breathing and happy thoughts!

She felt so calm. Her heart rate was normal, her nausea was gone and she'd stopped trembling. Wow, he was good!

'Open your eyes, Scarlet, and look out the window!'

She did and suddenly realised they were already in the air!

'Bloody hell! We're up already. I can't believe that!'

'We've been in the air for fifteen minutes, darlin',' he replied, smiling.

'You're a bloody wizard! I'm honestly shocked. I'd normally either be drugged up to the eyeballs or screaming by now!'

'Belly breathing is brilliant for calming fear and nerves. So, if we get any turbulence or bumps, just BREATHE like I taught you and you'll get through it without panicking. OK?'

'Yes.'

'Good. When the flight attendants come around with refreshments, I'll grab us some wine. That'll help too! But it's only another two and a half hours till we change in Helsinki and it'll go by quickly. I promise,' and he kissed the back of her hand like the true gentleman he was. A sweet, kind, gracious and true gentleman!

They had a two-and-a-half-hour stopover in Helsinki, where they had to change planes for their flight to Rovaniemi, Finland which was much shorter at one hour twenty-five minutes and Scarlet was now persuaded that, with Stewart's help, she'd get through it calmly. And she did!

They drank wine, talked, breathed, drank more wine and repeated all the way to Lapland where Scarlet actually watched the landing with a big smile on her face. A first for her as she'd normally have her eyes squeezed shut with her fingers in her ears! He was proving to be a very calming force for her indeed and she was eternally grateful!

After collecting their bags and exiting the airport, they grabbed a taxi to their hotel, checked in and were escorted to their chalet which looked adorable from the outside, all covered in snow with smoke billowing out of the chimney. Chocolate box perfection!

As they entered, they both gasped and exclaimed at exactly the same time 'FUCK ME!' then looked at each other, laughing.

It was simply stunning!

The front door opened up into a large lounge/diner with wooden panelled walls, wooden floors, soft, squishy sofas with fluffy blankets draped over the backs, a large, flat screen TV and sound system and softly lit lamps in the corners. But what took their breath away was the stone fireplace that had a fire already roaring away within and a giant, plush hearth rug laid in front.

After they closed their mouths from gawping in amazement, Stewart leaned in and whispered, 'I can already envision you lying naked on that rug with me writhing on top of you.' Winking at her cheekily.

'Mmmmm, yes please,' was her salivating response.

The porter then gave them a tour of the rest of the chalet. The bedroom was just as grand with the same wooden walls and floors, a Super King-sized bed, sumptuous, fluffy bedding and more rugs. The bathroom was next and was the room that excited Scarlet the most as Stewart had told her there was a hot tub.

They walked in and my oh my, Scarlet bounced up and down, clapping and repeating the word 'Yay' which made Stewart laugh and he cuddled her in to his side. There was a stunning walk-in waterfall shower but the pièce-de-résistance was the hot tub. It was so big!

'I can see us having some lovely times in there darlin'. Can we start tonight?'

'We sure can but maybe we should wait for the porter to leave. Don't wanna embarrass the poor lad, ey?'

They laughed and tipped the young man who took his leave.

And they were alone – finally!

'Right, let's make a plan,' Stewart said. 'Why don't we unpack and get comfy, order room service and relax a bit. Then when we've digested our dinner, we can slip into the hot tub with a bottle of wine and get filthy?'

'Sounds the perfect plan! But first, come here please!'

He approached her and she wrapped her arms around him, hugging him tightly. 'Thank you, my darling. Thank you for getting me through today and for being such a loving, big-hearted, adorable man!'

'You don't need to thank me, baby! It's my duty to look after you and I do it with love and pleasure. Just as you hate seeing me go through my IED episodes, I can't stand seeing you full of fear. It breaks me. I'll never let you struggle alone!'

She kissed him, tenderly, on those pillowy lips of his then on the end of his cute nose. 'Right. Let's get crackin' 'cos that hot tub beckons!'

He smacked her on the bum as she skipped away singing Christmas songs, leaving him shaking his head at her childlike sweetness.

They unpacked, changed and ordered dinner – Chicken Burgers and fries – and had plopped down on the comfy sofa to eat, Stewart at one end with his feet up and Scarlet at the other with one leg draped over his so his feet were between her thighs.

'So, Mr Secretive Sloane, now we're here, are you gonna tell me what surprises you have in store?'

'Oh yeah. I did promise you, didn't I! Well, here's the rough itinerary. On Saturday, we're going to a posh Christmas Eve shindig at an Ice Bar, Monday, we're off to a local Christmas Market, Tuesday, we're booked into the hotels spa for a couples massage and a spiced chocolate mud bath, on Thursday, we're going on a very romantic sleigh ride, complete with blankets and brandy-laced hot chocolate, all beneath the Aurora Borealis, hopefully, then finally, next Saturday, New Year's Eve, we're here at the hotel for their New Year's party and fireworks!'

'Yaaaaayyy!' She clapped, bouncing – Again!

'Fuck me, Scarlet. You're such a big kid!'

'Oh, I am. I know. It's the sleigh ride that did it. I'm a sucker for that kind of thing!'

'I know, that's why I booked it.'

'And the couple's thing sounds bloody divine. Spiced chocolate mud bath. No idea what that entails but I can't wait to find out.'

'When I was reading about it, it said you go into a private stone room where you get showered with this spiced chocolate mud mixture which you rub on each other. Apparently, it's exfoliating, softening and very nourishing for the skin but also has natural magnesium in it so also relaxes the muscles, mind and senses. So I figured that was perfect for us being the highly-strung pair we are!'

'Oooooooo. We'll be slipping and sliding all over the place and, hopefully, each other!'

'Well, it is a private room so we can get up to whatever we want. The thought had crossed my mind too.'

'Of course it did. You're a lech!'

'Ah yes, but you like it because you're a filthy wench.'

'Hahahaa, I do and I am but only with you. You bring out my inner vixen, Mr Fox.'

He jiggled his eyebrows at her, grinning like a school boy and wiggled his toes, tickling her lady lips. She jumped and almost choked on her final mouthful of food. 'DON'T do that when I've got a mouthful, you twat. I nearly choked.'

'I can think of much better things for you to choke on,' and he wiggled his toes again, making her squeal.

'Right, that's it. You've done it now!' and she launched at him, licking his divinely chiselled face while grabbing his cock.

He was beaming as he said, 'Hot Tub!'

They jumped up, almost running to the bathroom, stripped off and hopped in, eagerly.

Stewart grabbed her and sat her on the bench in the tub with her back against the rim and started to use his fingers on her. She threw her head back, grinding forward against his hand while he kissed and nibbled her neck.

The bubbles in the tub were caressing their aching bodies, heightening their arousals as Scarlet reached under the water and began massaging Stewart's hardened cock. He responded with a sharp intake of air with Scarlet watching his facial response. She loved seeing what she called his 'cum' faces. He was such a handsome, erotic creature and she loved to watch all the emotions cross his face as she pleasured him. He entranced her! He also had a very cheeky habit of making them for her when they were NOT in the throes of passion, just to wind her up, the naughty man!

As they were both grinding and moaning, Stewart suddenly said, 'Enough foreplay. I need to be inside you!' And he took her with one swift move.

The water was cascading about them as Stewart lifted her legs and wrapped them about his waist, Scarlet holding him around his neck, gazing into his sparkling, blue eyes and they rutted together, thrusting, grinding and moaning in perfect harmony.

They had to remember that this cabin was NOT soundproofed so they couldn't be too loud. A point they'd actually discussed the week before. Stewart had broached the subject, telling her that they couldn't be their usual highly vocal selves. He'd said, 'You cannot scream, Scarlet!' and she'd replied with, 'Well, don't attempt to penetrate my womb with your cock then!'

He wasn't pounding her now. He was forceful and precise, a very talented, skilful and experienced lover, gently but powerfully taking her to the brink.

It was a meaningful experience. They were intrinsically linked. Two star-crossed lovers who'd finally triumphed over the curse that had kept them apart, finding each other later in life but not too late. And they intended to hold on to each other for dear life!

He reached beneath her, grabbing her buttocks and began pulling her up towards him, driving himself just deep enough to make her cry out but not scream. He found the perfect angle and took them home, both of them exploding in waves of euphoric desire and love, Stewart kissing her to muffle both of their vocal reactions. And they held each other's trembling bodies as they allowed the surges of heat to dampen in the comforting water.

'I love you, baby.' Escaped from Scarlet's mouth.

Stewart looked at her. 'I love you too, beautiful one!'

After holding each other close for a few minutes while the soothing water bubbled away, Stewart pipped up, 'You do realise we just changed the bathroom function, right?'

'I don't follow?'

'Well, the function of a bathroom is mainly to get clean and we just got very dirty indeed!'

'Oh we did. Positively filthy and I so love being filthy with you!'

'I'm rather partial to it too. How about we get even filthier?'

'As filthy as possible, please Mr Sloane!' and they proceded to make the water boil with the heat from their steaming hips.

*

Saturday – Christmas Eve

Friday had been a relaxing day. They'd donned their snow boots and warm winter clothes and had gone out for a walk during the two hours and thirty minutes of daylight and had played monopoly for the remainder of the day, just enjoying each other's company.

This is when they both learned something new – Scarlet learned that Stewart liked to TRY to cheat because he was super competitive and just had to win and Stewart learned that Scarlet had a very devious, sneaky side and was very wily. Stewart lost both games that evening!

*

Christmas Eve had arrived and they were due at the Ice Bar at five p.m. It was an annual event that saw the crème-de-la-crème come out for a cocktail party with hors d'oeuvres.

Although it was an auspicious event, it didn't matter what you wore as you were provided with fur hats, coats and long boots before entering. Stewart had made sure they were fake fur though before booking as neither of them would want to wear the real thing being animal lovers.

Scarlet had chosen red, obviously and Stewart had opted for white which he looked divine in, especially with his platinum ponytail loose at the back and they'd entered the bar which was decked out with white fairy lights, quite a few intricately carved ice sculptures, ice tables and ice stools with white, fur covered cushions and soft, white, sheer, sparkly curtains hung over the walls of ice, twinkling in the lights.

It was exquisite and very festive indeed!

They made merry and a few friends, having a whale of a time and getting quite tipsy!

They'd left the party at eight p.m., arriving back at their cabin starving as neither of them had eaten much. They were told that a few of the hors d'oeuvres had Reindeer meat in them, and because they didn't want to eat Rudolph, they'd only picked at the other snacks on offer.

They giggled about, taking a shower together. Lord knows how they didn't slip and bang their heads as they were truly messing about like a pair of drunk teenagers!

After their shower, they ate the room service they'd ordered and literally stuffed themselves.

Sat at the dining table feeling very replete indeed, Scarlet had her feet up on Stewart's lap who was massaging them for her. He abruptly stopped and rubbed one of them on his bulge.

'Fancy letting Cleopatra out to play tonight? This centurion requires her wide-mouthed attention!'

She pulled her foot away. 'No. It's Christmas Eve. No naughtiness allowed!'

'Why not?'

'Because Santa won't come if I'm naughty!'

'Oh really? We shall see about that.'

He got up and went to the bedroom, turning the lights down as he left, leaving the only light coming from the Christmas Tree and fire. Scarlet remained where she was with her feet on his chair when she heard *Ho Ho Ho* from behind. She got up and spun around to see Stewart, wearing nothing but a fluffy Santa hat, grinning from ear to ear. 'Santa WILL most definitely CUM if you're naughty!'

Scarlet howled, 'Oh my gosh, you priceless man!'

She walked over to him and gently squeezed his soldier.

'How naughty does Santa want me to be?'

'Filthy. Santa wants you to be a filthy girl! And if you jingle his bells, he'll let you lick his lollipop!'

More howling from Scarlet!

'Ah, I see. So he's a lecherous Santa this year, is he?'

'Oh yeah. He's a filthy lech this year!'

'Well, I s'pose I'd better be a very naughty girl then. Follow me, Santa!'

She led him to the Christmas Tree where she got on her knees and began to 'jingle his bells' with her tongue and fingers, rolling them about and flicking them, Stewarts gruff vocal reactions ringing in her ears. She began to trickle down below as those noises made her juices flow!

'Suck them, Scarlet!'

She obliged by taking them into her mouth, one by one, giving him what he wanted, all the while massaging his throbbing soldier.

'*Aaaggghhh*' erupted from his mouth 'Harder!'

She wasn't sure what he wanted harder, the suction or massaging so she powered up both, making his knees twitch.

As she continued her drooling assault on his tight bollocks, she felt him steady her head and heard him say as she looked up towards him. 'You can lick Santa's lollipop now!'

She smiled up at him and took her reward deep into her hungry mouth. She was always hungry for his rugged appendage. She adored it!

She pulled and sucked him powerfully, not stopping to lick as she felt he needed just this. Just her impressive suction.

He was making a melody with his throat – a deep, husky melody which told her she was right about what he needed.

She increased the pull as she opened her throat and took him deep, his tip touching her tonsils. He tensed as the sensation brought him to boiling point and he released; his sweet yet salty seed oozing into her mouth.

He controlled his wailing and growled instead; growled and hissed through clenched teeth, repeating the word 'Fuck' a few times.

He finally relaxed and plopped down in front of her, the light from the tree illuminating his resplendent body. 'You're so very talented, my Queen!'

'It's such a pleasure, my King.'

'I know it is. I know'

He hugged her, kissed her neck and stroked her hair. 'You've sucked me dry though!'

'Are you feeling depleted, my darling?'

'Yeah. Just a bit.'

'Off to bed then. I'm pooped too. But first, we have to put the gifts under the tree and hang up our stockings!'

They'd both purchased gifts for each other and had also bought stocking fillers. Nothing extravagant as Scarlet had made it clear that Christmas was to be an equal affair.

They stuffed each other's stockings and hung them up by the fire, placed their gifts under the tree and went to bed, both of them sound asleep upon their heads hitting the pillow!

*

Sunday – Christmas Day

After copious amounts of alcohol the night before, they both awoke with slightly sore heads so while Scarlet made a strong pot of tea using the English tea bags Stewart had insisted they bring with them, Stewart ordered breakfast; fried eggs, bacon, fried potatoes and toast with a café mocha for Scarlet. They both wanted carbs, grease and caffeine! They'd eaten, retrieved their stockings and began opening them. They'd decided on six stocking fillers each and were opening them one person at a time.

They were silly, funny things. Scarlet had gotten Stewart a pair of Christmas boxers with her face all over them which he found exceptionally amusing, and the oddly weird thing was, he'd had the same idea and had gotten her a pair of silky, French knickers with a picture of him with his tongue sticking out right on the crotch area. It was hilarious! He'd also got her her own set of red leather handcuffs and she'd bought him a cock ring with an attached clitoris stimulator. There was also flavoured lube, crotchless knickers, cock shaped chocolates with creamy white centres in a cock shaped box, nipple shaped jelly beans – filth galore!

The other guests on the property must have thought they were quite mad at the raucous laughter coming from their cabin. It was quite maniacal!

They stopped for more tea then proceeded to the tree, with Scarlet giving Stewart one of his gifts first – a new handmade, leather-bound diary. It was burgundy with the initials SS engraved in gold into the centre of the front cover at the bottom for Stewart and Scarlet. He adored it!

He gave her her first gift – a pair of deep wine coloured, high-waisted, figure-hugging leather trousers. 'Ooooo fuck meeeeee! I LOVE these, darlin'.'

'Try 'em on!'

'Now?'

'Yes, please.'

She toddled off and came back to show him.

'Every time I buy you clothes, all I wanna do is take 'em off of you straight away. You look VERY sexy indeed, young lady. Go and get 'em off before I end up ripping off all the buttons!'

She giggled as she changed back into her jammies.

They had two more gifts for each other – a new black sweater with leather trim and accents and some very erotic smelling cologne for Stewart that had taken Scarlet an age to find and a pair of thigh-high and very kinky black leather boots for Scarlet, with the final gift for her being very special.

He handed her the wrapped box. 'Merry Christmas, darlin'!' he said softly, kissing her cheek.

She carefully removed the wrapping and opened the box within to see a Silver and Marcasite oval locket with SS engraved on it.

'Ohhhhh Stewart, it's beautiful.'

'Open the locket!'

She did and inside, was a tiny photo of them, taken at the Eiffel Tower on her birthday. She burst into tears.

'I love it, Stewart. I'll wear it always,' and flung her arms about his neck.

He held onto her, rubbing her back. 'My pleasure, beautiful!'

She pulled herself together and as she wiped her eyes, he put it on her. 'A perfectly exquisite necklace for a perfectly exquisite neck!'

She rushed off to look in the mirror in the bedroom, returning red eyed but full of joy.

'I'm never taking it off. EVER!'

'Good. It looks magical on you. But have you noticed how we both engraved the SS on gifts? Kinda weird!'

'Yeah it is, but it's because we're so connected, my love. We have a soul connection!'

He nodded. 'I'd given up hope, you know. Completely given up hope of ever finding the right lady. Then you burst into my life, turned my world upside down and blew my leathers off. Haha!'

'Fate darling. Fate!'

*

That evening, after having a Christmas Dinner delivered to their chalet, they snuggled up to watch Christmas movies with wine and chocolates.

During a romantic scene in the movie, Stewart turned in and kissed Scarlet. 'That hearth rug looks rather inviting, don't you think?'

'Mmmm. It does!'

He switched off the telly, stood up and offered her his hand, leading her to the fireplace where he proceeded to undress her, standing back to look at her flawless skin, set aglow by the firelight, her long, deep raven tendrils of hair sweeping over her shoulders and covering her nipples.

'Do you know how breathtaking you are, Scarlet?'

'Why don't you show me!'

He stripped himself off and Scarlet gasped suddenly. 'My word.'

'What?'

'You're magnificent, Stewart, and I can't quite believe you're mine!'

He knelt on the rug and took her hand, pulling her down to join him then placing her hand over his heart.

'I am yours, Scarlet. All of me! Every inch of me and every beat of my heart belongs to you and only you, for the rest of my life!'

The emotions welled up within her. What he just said with her hand on his heart moved her deeply. She swallowed hard as he added, 'And now, I'm gonna show you just how much I deeply treasure you!'

He lay her back softly, nestling her head in the softness of the rug and began to kiss her skin ever so gently. He took his time to kiss every inch of her; from the top of her head to the tip of her beautifully pedicured toes. No nibbling, no biting; just sweet, gentle kisses with the silkiest flicks of the warm, moist tip of his tongue. Once he'd smothered the front of her body, he turned her over and repeated it all on the back, carefully tracing his lips and tongue down her back, over and under her buttocks and down her shapely legs to her feet. As he reached her toes, he slid his hands up the inside of her thighs, pushed them apart and began to kiss her tingling lady lips, gently licking them between feathery kisses.

She began to trickle as he used the flat of his long tongue to part her lips and went to town within her now dripping folds, lapping up her streams as they escaped. He reached beneath her and lifted her hips slightly and trapped her throbbing pearl between his lips, sucking it in and teasing it with his teeth. She moaned and pushed back to meet him, starting to grind slowly against his face.

She was in a fevered delirium as he relentlessly sucked her into his mouth, flicking with his tongue and gently biting with his teeth. She was peaking. Electric pulses were flashing up through her lady parts into her belly as he built her up and she began to twitch and writhe, moaning his name. She felt it coming as she went mad with passion and she popped, releasing warm rivers, convulsing uncontrollably and crying out ecstatically. He released her, lay atop her back, and, holding her lips apart, drove himself deep within her walls that were still pulsating from her powerful orgasm. He leaned over her shoulder. 'Kiss me, Scarlet.'

She turned her head to meet his and did what he'd asked, their tongues marrying perfectly. She was hungry for his tongue so she sucked it into her mouth and released, repeating over and over. She couldn't get enough of it.

After a while, he pulled back, got onto his knees, lifted her hips upwards and slipped deeper, her whimpers becoming more high pitched as he hit her cervix. This was immensely pleasurable for her. She loved it when he got deep enough to touch her cervix with the tip of his cock. It was painful but a good pain, a pleasurable pain that she could endure and did, very gladly!

He could have gotten rough right about now but didn't. He had no intention of treating her roughly. He wanted to make her feel deeply loved and very beautiful. He planned to bring her to only one more orgasm and leave it there. There was to be no ruining of this lady tonight. Just love!

He held her hips firmly in place as he expertly stretched her walls with his staggering ruggedness, driving her wild with the sensations. He switched positions again as he closed her legs and placed his own on the outside to make her sensations even stronger and kept stroking her insides, heat now building from the friction. Her moans turned to whelps and her breath quickened as he sped up, his own climax nearing. He got faster and faster until they both let out a cry and flooded each other with their waves of bliss, her insides spasming powerfully around him and his cock pulsating deep within. He released her hips and lay on top of her, kissing her back as she whimpered, still convulsing. They lay there, basking in this majestic afterglow, the flames from the fire crackling in the background. It was the most romantic of interludes and one they'd never forget.

After a few minutes of silent tenderness, they got up and went to bed, not caring that they were sweaty and sticky. Neither of them wanted to rid themselves of each other's essence. They wanted to sleep with it and they did, their bodies entwined as they blissfully slumbered!

*

Tuesday, 27th December

The trip to the Christmas market had been a happy one. They'd enjoyed hot Glögi (Finnish mulled wine), hot dogs with fried onions and freshly fried Munkki; small sugar-coated Finnish donuts! They'd amused themselves with filthy jokes. These two could never go a day without streams of filth oozing out of their mouths! They'd bought a few mementos and had returned to their cabin in the late afternoon and had just rested, relaxed and dozed, quite heady after drinking one too many mugs of the hot, spiced wine.

Tuesday morning had arrived and their appointment at the spa was at eleven a.m. They'd been for their couples massage and were now awaiting their mud bath, wearing just robes. It was advised that you went in naked. As they were waiting, one of the beauty therapists came along to explain the process and what they should do with the mud. They had an hour to massage each other with it and could do what they liked, making as much noise as they liked as nobody could see or hear them as they could lock the door from the inside with the key which she handed to them 'Enjoy!'

They entered, hung their robes on the hooks in the entranceway then entered the mud chamber. A low rumbling noise became evident as a dark mud-like substance began to squirt out of the walls. It was warm and literally smelled just like it was described – Spiced Chocolate. How bloody divine was this!

They gleefully started picking up handfuls of it, smothering one another in the warm, rich substance until they turned into a pair of children and had a mud fight, slinging it about and getting it everywhere, laughing uncontrollably as they went. They had the time of their lives!

After a few minutes of mud wrestling, they sat down panting, trying to catch their breaths. They both sensed the mud start to warm their muscles and felt suddenly relaxed.

Stewart piped up. 'You do realise that we can make as much noise as we want, right? No-one can hear us!'

'Yeah. That's what she said!'

'So I can fuck you into next week and make you scream without anyone hearing!'

'Ohhhhh yes. I hadn't though of that. Aren't you a clever thing!'

'Mmhmm. I have my moments!'

'Well, what are you waiting for? Get over here and fuck me senseless, big boy!'

He grabbed her, stood her up, turned her around, pushed her against the wall, pulled her hips backwards and fucked her to within an inch of her life! He thrusted so hard, she thought he'd break her hips AND crack the wall! And she was howling!

This wasn't the love from Christmas Day, this was his deep-seated need for rough sex. He loved her deeply and wanted to treat her tenderly but, sometimes, he needed to roughly dominate. But Scarlet needed it too! She wasn't just 'letting' him do it, she CRAVED it!

She lowered her torso, braced her hands against the wall and drove herself backwards to meet him, mud flying everywhere as they crashed into each other with savage force. He reached up as he let out a very loud, animalistic growl, grabbed a fistful of her mud-caked hair and pulled it backwards, hard!

Oh, she loved it; revelled in it even!

They crashed, banged and walloped each other for what seemed like hours until the inevitable happened and they burst, both of them releasing loud, earth-shattering noises!

Gosh, they'd needed that! It was perfect.

As Scarlet went to stand up, her legs buckled but Stewart was there to catch her, as he always was. He grabbed her about the waist and held her against him as her legs shook and twitched.

'I think I've ruined you again.'

'You have indeed, and I bloody loved it. I'd ask you to do it again except I'm slightly broken, therefore, won't work properly.'

'Haha. Let's sit down.'

He helped her to the bench where they sat cuddling for the remainder of their hour, showered off the mud, put on their robes and left the chamber, handing the key back to the therapist as they left the spa.

'I think we need lunch and a nap, young lady!'

She was still giddy from the entire mud experience so didn't answer, she just smiled and nodded. She was depleted. Not in an exhausted way but in a delightfully relaxed and thoroughly rogered way and all she could think about was snuggling up with Stewart on the sofa and falling asleep on his chest!

*

Thursday – 29th December

The day had arrived for the Sleigh Ride and Scarlet was beside herself. She'd woken up, bounced out of bed and hadn't stopped bloody bouncing. She was beyond excited! Stewart had witnessed her child-like behaviour on several occasions but not quite to this extent. He'd never witnessed the side effects of it which were Scarlet becoming scatter-brained and clumsy.

She'd almost burned herself with the kettle, had forgotten to put tea bags in the tea pot so when Stewart poured himself a cup, he just got hot water, she was dropping everything and couldn't quite focus on more than one task at a time. A total basket case!

He actually thought it was funny except for when she almost gave herself 3rd degree burns with boiling water, then he got slightly concerned.

'Scarlet, luv, calm down!'

'I'm fine!'

'No, you're not. You're being a mental case.'

'Oh, I know,' she replied embarrassingly putting her face in her hands. 'I'm sorry. I get scatty when I get over-excited.'

'I can see that! Scarlet Coloured Chaos!'

'No, no. I haven't been filthy once today!'

'I didn't say Scarlet Coloured FILTHY Chaos, just Scarlet Coloured Chaos, without the filth!'

'Oh. Oh dear. You've named it already! For fucks sake, how humiliating!' And she covered her face again.

'No, don't do that. Don't be embarrassed! It's hilarious. You literally go from being a strong, capable, well-educated woman with her act firmly together to a blithering idiot in a snap. It's night and day and very funny! BUT, what ain't funny is you almost scalding yourself with boiling kettle water. That's concerning so no more responsible jobs for you until you put your brain back in!'

'Put my brain back in! Hahahaaa! Cheeky sod!'

'Just sit down and don't touch anything, woman. Calm yourself and get your head together. The last thing I need on our afternoon out is you running off into the forest in search of Rudolph and the Elves!'

She burst into fits.

'Why don't you go and bubble in the tub for a bit?'

'Great plan, Batman!'

'Go on. Off you pop, there's a good happy, lil fairy!'

She walked of guffawing and went for a soak, where she languished for a good forty-five minutes.

Stewart came in. 'Have you managed to put the basket case switch back in the OFF position yet, young lady?'

'I won't know until I get out and try to 'adult'!'

'Let's test the chaos machine then. Out you get!'

She climbed out and dried herself while Stewart went back to the kitchenette.

When she joined him, she had her sweater on backwards, her thermal leggings on inside out, her knickers on her head and her socks on her hands and she just stood there, waiting for him to turn around.

He did and he looked mightily shocked. 'What the fuck! Scarlet, what have you done?'

She couldn't keep up the pretence any longer and burst into cackles.

'Oh you're 'avin' me on, you cheeky bloody mare! Go and sort yourself out, you nutcase!!'

She did, still cackling. His face and reaction were just what she'd hoped for. Brilliant!

They needed to meet the sleigh driver at the hotels main entrance in half an hour so Stewart nagged Scarlet to get her skates on. They made it just in time with Johannes the driver introducing them to his Reindeer. There were four of them and he gave Scarlet and Stewart carrots to feed them which they loved. They were the sweetest animals and let Scarlet get up close for cuddles which delighted her. Stewart just stood back and watched as she nuzzled up to them, talking to them like they were human babies. It was an adorable sight to behold! They got into the sleigh, Johannes tucked them up with his fluffy blanket, geed on his Reindeer and they were off, sleigh bells jingling. Because it was dark, lantern lights were attached to the sleigh to light the way ahead. It was the most magical experience!

Here she was, sat snuggled with the love of her life living her romantic dream in the snow. She wanted to pinch herself to make sure it was real!

As they jingled through the forest, it started to snow lightly and the snowflakes sparkled as they fluttered down past the lanterns. Scarlet pointed her chilly face skywards and stuck out her tongue, trying to catch snowflakes. Stewart copied!

'What do they taste like, these snowflakes?'

She just stared at him. 'Really? You're really asking me that?'

'Yeah. Why?' he frowned.

'WATER, Stewart. They taste like water, you numpty!'

It was his turn to put his head in his hands and he laughed into them too.

'I'm such a twat!'

'Yes! Yes you are. And now we're even!'

Luckily, the snowfall hadn't got any heavier so their ride wasn't thwarted. They carried on and as the snow kept gently falling, the Northern Lights appeared above them. 'Oh looooook darlin'!'

'Wow. That's beautiful. What a sight!'

The entire sky was lit up with a myriad of colours and they were entranced, their heads looking upwards constantly.

Johannes stopped so he could take a photo of them both with the Northern Lights above them, the Reindeer and sleigh behind them. That's gonna be one to blow up and put on canvas!

Before they set off again, he also got out a flask and two stainless steel mugs with handles and poured them some boozy hot chocolate which they drank. 'Bloody hell, that's strong!' Stewart bellowed, coughing slightly.

Johannes laughed. 'It keep you warm. Make you very strong!'

'I'll say. Blimey!'

Scarlet was sipping hers, savouring it slowly. 'It's bloody YUM is what it is. I hope there's more.'

Johannes piped up. 'You want more, Mrs? I have more!'

'Ooooo yes please, Johannes!'

He filled her mug and she settled back, the hot brandy starting to warm her insides and make her feel fuzzy.

Then the snow started to come thicker.

Johannes looked slightly concerned. 'Emm, I think maybe we go back now. Maybe it will get worse. Safer to go back now, yes!'

'Yes, of course! Best to be safe,' Scarlet replied.

They'd been out for a good forty-five minutes so far and it would take another forty-five to get back, maybe more in the thicker snow so they headed back, both herself and Stewart snuggled up close under the cosy blanket, sipping their heavenly hot drinks.

Back at the hotel and after having witnessed more of the Aurora Borealis, they thanked Johannes profusely, Scarlet said goodbye to each Reindeer with a cuddle and they went back to their cabin; deliriously happy, relaxed, satisfied and very tipsy.

No sooner had they stumbled through the door, they were pawing at each other, items of clothing being tossed here and there until they were naked.

'Make a mess of me, Mr Sloane, and use every damned surface you can find!'

'Certainly, my lady!'

He grabbed her and flung her onto the dining table, making a mess of her there before he dragged her off and bent her over the back of the sofa, making an even bigger mess of her there. Next, he chose to sit on a dining chair so she could make a mess of him and then he picked her up and tossed her on the bed where he finished them both off!

And boy, were they finished. Somehow, they'd managed to keep going for nigh on two hours and thirty minutes and they were both wrecked, flopped on the bed in a dripping heap, panting, shaking and mumbling.

'Well fuck me, Mr Sloane! Honestly, where do you get your stamina? My poor vagina doesn't know what's hit it!'

'It must have been that hot chocolate we drank. He said it makes you strong!'

They both laughed but not for long as they were breathless.

'You'll be lucky if you can walk tomorrow!'

'You'll just have to carry me if I can't, seeing as it'll be all your fault!'

'Ah no. See, you told me to make a mess of you. I was just obliging a lady!'

'I have a question!'

'Mmmm, what?'

'Do you think we have too much sex?'

'Sex is important. Well, it is to me anyway. For me, it's gotta be a regular occurrence or I get bored. That's why some of my previous relationships didn't work out as they couldn't keep up. It was too much for 'em. But with you, we're perfectly matched! We both have very healthy sexual appetites and you're willing to explore with me and let me teach you. I'll never be bored with you. Never! So in answer to your question: No! We don't have too much sex. In fact, I could handle more!'

'MORE? Fuck me, I'm gonna need that wheelchair you mentioned months ago!'

'Haha. Probably! But seriously though, would you be happy with more?'

'Darlin', apart from loving every part of your heart, mind and soul, I happen to think you're the sexiest man on the planet. You're a magnificently virile, masculine creature and I get horny just looking at you. So, if you want more sex, you got it, babe!'

He moved on top of her 'Oooo good!'

She shoved him off. 'Not NOW, you lunatic! Get off!'

They had a shower, hopped into bed and Stewart grabbed her. 'I'm afraid, young lady, that this old geezer needs more!'

'I think I've recovered enough but no hi-jinx. My legs are still weak!'

'I'll do all the work, my love!'

And he did, making love to her for most of the night, making a complete mess of her over and over again!

*

Saturday – New Year's Eve.

She'd not been able to move much yesterday and quite notably, neither had Stewart. He was positive the highly alcoholic drink they'd had on the sleigh had given him a sexual boost because he'd gone on all night long, having a good few orgasms and giving her a few too! They were knackered! Needless to say, they'd not even gone out for their regular, daily walk in the daylight hours. They'd just vegetated. It was all they were capable off.

New Year's Eve had arrived with them both rather excited! The hotel was hosting their annual New Year's party in the main building with dinner, music and fireworks at midnight. The perfect way to end their magical holiday!

It promised to be a high-class, fancy affair with 'evening attire' being obligatory so they'd brought the same outfits they'd worn on Scarlet's birthday; her red and silver gown and his black suit. She wouldn't be cold as it was to be held inside with the fireworks being watched through the floor-to-ceiling windows.

They dressed and Stewart draped a long, black coat over her shoulders to keep her warm on the short walk to the main building.

Once inside, they found their table and the festivities began.

It was a set five course menu and choices had been made in advance.

As this was a convivial affair, nobody sat separately. They were seated at large, round tables with eight place settings so everyone could natter and be friendly.

They had a cracking bunch at theirs. They all got along famously and there was much hilarity and loudness. As the wine flowed and the courses came and empty plates went, their raucousness got worse but nobody minded. It was supposed to be a fun-filled evening!

Desserts arrived; dark chocolate dome bombs with hot salted caramel sauce that melted the bomb when poured, revealing the gooey dark chocolate and ice cream centre. It was bloody divine and Scarlet, turning into Mrs Filth after way *WAY* too much wine, started being rather vulgar with her spoon. Stewart joined in and the rest of the table followed. Utter filth all around – to Scarlet, this was bloody priceless!

Coffees came next, putting an end to all the vulgarity and everyone was asked to make their way to the windows for the countdown to midnight!

Stewart slid his arm around Scarlet's waist and pulled her close. 'Are you ready to start a new year with this old man, Scarlet?'

'I've been ready my entire life, Stewart!'

10
9
8
7
6
5
4
3
2

1
HAPPY NEW YEAR!

As the fireworks kicked off, Stewart whipped her around, held her face in his hands and kissed her for as long as he could. Not a snog, no tongues; just a long, loving, soft kiss on perfectly puckered lips. They inhaled each other's essences as the kiss went on with Scarlet reaching up behind his head to stroke his neck. The love and romance in the air was tangible and other guests were watching them, commenting on what a beautiful couple they were.

The kiss came to an end with Stewart professing to Scarlet, still clasping her face in his hands. 'I don't know what this new year will bring us, Scarlet Adams, but I can promise you this: my heart, my body and my soul now belong to you just as I hope yours belong to me and they will do until I take my final breath! I LOVE you. You've changed my life and have made me the happiest man alive.' And he dropped to one knee. 'Will you do me the honour of becoming my wife?' and he flourished a tiny, vintage jewellery box, flipped the lid and inside was the daintiest, most exquisitely designed white gold, vintage Art Deco engagement ring with a cushion cut ruby in the centre, wrapped in a luxurious vintage-frame, which glistened with round diamonds adorned with milgrain detailing. Along the milgrain-edge, two rows of shimmering diamonds were paved onto it, adding extra sparkle to the ring and Scarlet was completely floored! Flabbergasted! She had not, in a million years, seen this coming!

Her jaw dropped as the reality of what was happening hit her like a bullet train and her hands went up instinctively to cover her wide-open mouth. Tears filled her eyes as she looked at Stewart, on one knee at her feet, his own beautiful eyes now glistening with his own tears. She reached out, grabbed a gentle hold of his face, bent forward and nodded. 'Yes. With all of my heart, YES!'

He allowed his tears to fall as he took the ring from its box, placed it on her finger and kissed it softly. He got up, picked her up in his arms and swung her about while she hugged him, her silver stilettoed feet kicking up behind her! As he put her down, she asked him, 'Is this a dream?'

'No, baby. This is very real!'

They hugged again then she realised the whole room was applauding, cheering and clapping!

'I can't believe this, Stewart. You told me you'd never marry again!'

'I know but you've changed everything. Literally everything. I only wish we'd met sooner. But now, we can't waste any more time! I want... no... I NEED you by my side!'

'And you shall have that. I'm all yours and always have been!'

A tray holding glasses of champagne was passed around, especially to toast them. Scarlet didn't like champagne but decided to drink one anyway. This moment was way too important to fuss over her drink. A toast was raised, they clinked their glasses and they both necked their champagne. Gone in two gulps!

Scarlet lifted up her hand to the light to have a proper look at her new ring which was glinting and sparkling as the fireworks let off pretty coloured sparks into the air. She was mesmerised by it. She'd never seen anything quite so beautiful in her life, especially not on one of her fingers!

She glanced at her new fiancé. 'It's the most stunning ring I've ever seen. I'm speechless!'

He stroked back a wisp of her hair. 'You deserve the world!'

'I have the world, Stewart, because I have YOU!'

He kissed her forehead and there they stood, watching the rest of the fireworks that danced like fireflies in their bemused eyes, holding onto each other, relishing this moment and their unshakeable, undying love, not realising just what was around the dark corner and also not realising that the coming year was going to test that love and their bond to its absolute limits!

*

Scarlet Adams and Stewart Sloane will return in *The Red Wine Diaries, Volume 2: Darkness Descends.*

Their infinite love and Scarlet's profound dedication will be tested beyond limits as Stewart's mental health sinks further into the dark abyss, wreaking havoc on their lives! His only relief and therapy will come from Scarlet's determined willingness to help her beautifully broken man heal with an abundance of soulful love, steadfast loyalty, unequivocal devotion and lashings of desirous submission in the bedroom where his savagery will know no bounds, taking Scarlet on a dripping, pulsating journey of painful yet erotically delightful pleasure.

Stewart's heart may be shattered and his mind fractured but Scarlet's devoted, determined, submissive love will be the glue he desperately needs as she begins to repair his brokenness, finally leading him out of his darkness and into her blinding light!

Packed full of hilariously creative scenarios, profanely inappropriate humour, darkly erotic nights, profoundly emotional moments and magically mesmerising love, *Volume 2* promises to take its reader on a heart fluttering, insanely provocative and rather shocking ride!